ROOKIE PRIVATEER

JAMIE MCFARLANE

Cover Artwork: Sviatoslav Gerasymchuk

DEDICATION

For my mother. A promise fulfilled.

CONTENTS

Acknowledgments   i
Tag   1
Mars Competency Test   13
Sled Repairs   16
A Bright Future   21
Big Pete's Big Haul   27
Pirates Attack   33
Aftermath   48
Goodbyes   57
Trial   64
Privateer   81
Sterra's Gift   86
Dinner with the Commander   97
Ready to Sail   104
East Bound and Down   121
Passage to Baru Manush   143
Pirates of Baru Manush   175
Wuzzies   190
Fortune Favors the Bold   199
Escape from Baru Manush   214
Incursion   230
Revenge is Never Sweet   251
Epilogue   258
About the Author   265

ACKNOWLEDGMENTS

Diane Greenwood Muir, for enduring patience, encouragement, and expert editing. My wife, Janet, for heroic continuity checks. Jeff Rothermel, for amazing insight related to technical details and preventing the flying guillotine. Sheri Harper Gann, for the generous gift of her time. Carol Greenwood, for excellent help with phrasing. Finally, my youngest son, Jacob, for converting my pencil scratches into a rendering of the interior layout of *Sterra's Gift*.

TAG

Dock Control, I said to the ship's always listening Artificial Intelligence (AI). A virtual, t-handled lever emerged from the translucent blue panel next to my left hand and I gave it a forward flick. A small chirp indicated the lever had reached its destination. Subtle vibrations reinforced the assumption that station clamps had released my ore sled, but a pulsing red triangle showed on the panel.

"Frak." I swiped my hand impatiently and waited. The panel continued to pulse red even after I felt the clamps re-engage.

Show failure, I instructed tersely.

One of the two large vid screens in front of me displayed a single spindly leg of the ore sled. A slight bow in the leg pulsed with a red outline indicating the point of failure. It was bent just enough to prevent the station's clamp from either releasing or re-engaging.

Vent atmo. Open cockpit. The smudge of my irritated breath rapidly disappeared from the clear faceplate as the AI puffed dry air across it. I dismissed the display of the ore sled's leg with a sweep of my hand and the screens darkened.

Small plumes of expanding vapor billowed out of numerous ports below the cockpit. Once the plumes lost their intensity, a well hidden door levered up like a bat wing from the canopy. The minimal gravity of the station beckoned me slowly downward. I fired the suit's arc-jets, and rushed toward the bent leg ten meters back. I communicated navigation commands to my AI through a nearly infinite series of micro-gestures. The AI, in turn, caused the bright blue cones of arc-jet propulsion to fire appropriately. My movements came easily, since I had been navigating an arc-jet suit

1

since I could eat solid food. I took the skill for granted.

I pushed away from the sled to get a clean view of the problem leg. My AI projected a pulsing red outline directly onto the retina of my eye, highlighting the bend in the sled's leg. A quick inspection showed that the leg and the station's clamp had engaged in such a way that the simple linear movement of the clamp couldn't overcome.

The legs of the sled had an incredible amount of vertical strength but were spindly and prone to a bit of bowing when too much horizontal force occurred. My landing had probably been a little sloppy. It wasn't difficult to fix, so I strategically placed the top of my boot against the leg of the ore sled and fired the arc-jet in short, strong bursts from the heel. I felt a shudder through my gloves as the metallic alloys in the sled's leg slipped back into the correct position.

I pushed back a couple meters and called out, *Dock Control*. A familiar display lit up and I flicked a lever to release the clamps. This time the panel pulsed a pleasant green and I noticed with satisfaction that the clamps had indeed receded beneath the floor. The sled wasn't connected to anything now, but at least the low gravity of the station was sufficient to keep it in place.

From the corner of my eye, I caught the movement of a small runabout lifting off from the station about three hundred meters away. The craft belonged to Tabitha Masters and I chortled quietly at my good luck. There was no time to waste and I leaned over and engaged the arc-jets, quickly slithering to the front of the sled and into the cockpit.

Close cockpit. Engines online. Throttle control, I spat, while scrambling to pull the restraining harness over my suit and get it buckled between my legs. Once the cockpit finished closing, atmosphere flooded the small cabin. My clear face plate retracted upward into the helmet when the pressure equalized and I worked my jaw, causing my ears to pop.

Craft tracking. A new display popped up with flight controls and subtle icons next to the many different moving objects. It took me a moment to orient on Tabby. I jabbed my finger through her craft's floating icon and a green ring encircled the runabout. A reverse pinch motion caused the icon to enlarge many times, showing her craft's attitude and bearing. Virtual arrows indicated velocity and acceleration relative to my own.

Without looking, I grabbed the flight joystick with my right hand and then with my left, I jammed throttle controls forward. It didn't take much for the ore sled to break free of the refining station. Tabitha Master's runabout had a strong lead on me, so I pushed the sled's thrusters into the red.

Since I had a good idea where Tabby was headed, I knew better than to fly directly at her. She was much too crafty for that and her AI would warn her if it picked up on my approach.

I directed my sled toward the back side of one of the large asteroids between me and the colony's habitation complex. It was a little out of the way, but I would be out of Tabby's visual range and could accelerate hard without gaining unwanted attention. Rounding the asteroid, a new, small green oval appeared on the cockpit's canopy. I knew immediately whose small craft it was.

Open comm channel, Nick James, I instructed.

Before I could say anything, the quick, high-pitched cadence of my best friend interrupted. "Burning it pretty hard, aren't you?"

"I'm on Tabby's six and I don't think she has me yet. I'm going for a point."

Nick's only response was a sigh. I noticed with satisfaction, however, that he had adjusted to fall in behind me. He might not approve, but would ride along just the same.

I rocked the sled back and forth, dodging rock outcroppings as I hugged the asteroid, hiding me from my quarry. The thrusters of the sled weren't overly sensitive, so in order to achieve the complex maneuvers, I had to change the orientation of the arc-jets along the length of the sled by rotating the entire sled and firing the right jets at the right time. It was tremendously complicated, but I was born for this.

My sled cleared the asteroid and my heart hammered loudly in my ears when Tabby's sled slid into view. She was still on the same vector as when I lost visual on the other side of the asteroid.

I pushed the sled even harder on an intercept course with the runabout. Warning chirps sounded in my ears as my AI anticipated a collision.

"Frak! Hoffen! Seriously?" Tabby's startled face appeared in the upper left corner of my display.

"Tag! Point Hoffen!" I yelled in victory.

My sled bumped the side of Tabby's runabout hard enough to jolt both of us, but I fired the bottom thrusters, causing me to roll away gently.

"Dumb ass!" Tabby exclaimed, struggling to level out her own flight. Then her craft rotated abruptly, pointing directly at me.

I chuckled into the comm and aimed my sled toward another large asteroid, roughly twenty seconds away on a hard burn. Tabby's runabout was quicker and she was a good pilot, but I had chosen this particular course because I knew the asteroid had a large hole running through its center. If I could keep her from tagging until we got there, I would lose her. It was risky, but it would be epic if I could pull it off.

Tabby's approach was hotter than I anticipated and her ship closed the distance quickly. Upon reaching the asteroid, I dropped in to hug the surface. Tabby closed to twenty-five meters, but I had made it to the asteroid and didn't think she would see this move coming.

At less than five meters away, she was triumphant. "I own you, punk!"

"Too late," I said.

I pushed the joystick and throttle forward at the same time and then pulled the joystick back a second later, leaving the throttle wide open. The shoulder straps dug in as the pressure of my own momentum tried to eject me from the cockpit. The nose of the ore sled pitched about seventy-five degrees down, pointing into an opening in the asteroid. I was forcing the top thrusters wide open and they whined while pushing against the big rock opening. Without the rock wall to thrust against, I couldn't possibly have made the turn and I basked in the moment of my brilliant maneuver. My forward momentum bled off quickly and I shot into the tunnel. Even with the jets at 120% on the top, I was going to end up closer to the wall of the tunnel than I would like, but it was working just as I had pictured it in my mind.

A microsecond later I was jarred from my reverie by a three dimensional display of my ore sled jumping to the forefront of my display, bright flashing red on the bottom aft section of the hull. The intensity of the red indicated an imminent collision underneath the craft. It didn't make sense. I had made it, what was the AI seeing?

The AI's prediction was spot on as the sled indeed crashed into the wall of the cavern. "Frak me!" was all I could grunt. The air pushed out of my lungs and I felt and heard the screeching crash of metal on metal behind me. The top side of the sled lit up in my visor's display as a dark crimson, yet nowhere near as bright as the aft collision.

Then I caught a glimpse of the aft camera's view. Another sled flew past the opening of the tunnel with its own nose starting to cartwheel away as it reacted to a collision. Tabby had run into the bottom of my sled, and in turn, caused my sled to careen into the cavern's wall. The all-seeing AI had put it together, but not in time to do anything but warn me.

"Jerkbait! Point Masters," Tabby yelled.

I didn't have time to respond. A split second later the top side of my sled slammed into the tunnel wall, bringing my relative speed directly into line with the asteroid. The sled slid along for about two hundred meters while I worked frantically to stop its forward progress. If there was critical damage, I didn't want to shoot out the other side of the asteroid.

"Frak Tab, you could have killed him. What the frak!" Nick demanded.

I considered it a good sign that I could hear Nick's voice. I checked the visor's display for signs of atmo leaks in both the cockpit and my vac-suit. The cockpit's integrity was definitely blown. There was no remaining atmosphere in the sled, but my faceplate had slid down upon impact and my suit's readouts were all green.

"Frak off, Nick! How was I supposed to know he was gonna pull a jerkbait move." Tabitha's voice was husky with adrenaline.

My sled slid slowly along the wall and rolled onto one side. Sliding my finger along an interior panel, I found the button to manually release the cockpit. The remaining puffs of compressed nitrogen and oxygen escaped through small ports below the transparent shield of the cockpit's canopy and expanded into the vacuum of space. I was grateful the cockpit door opened successfully.

"Liam, you okay?" Nick's voice cut through my concentration.

"Yeah. I think so, but I really messed up the sled. Dad's gonna be pissed."

The asteroid wasn't large enough to have noticeable gravity, so I didn't have any trouble pulling myself out of the cockpit. I oriented myself to inspect the topside of the sled. The cockpit was connected to a seven meter square hull that extended twenty meters back. Directional thrusters were just behind the cockpit, ten meters back and at the stern. A large matter reactor engine, located a few meters behind me, provided the massive thrust required to move the many tons of ore the sled was designed to haul.

Bright lights swept across the wrecked sled as Nick's smaller vehicle approached.

"How bad?" Nick's voice was noticeably less intense. He eased his craft into a position about twenty meters above the wreck, providing maximum light.

"Can't be good, it was a hard hit. The cockpit isn't holding atmo."

Small puffs of vapor escaped as Nick depressurized the cabin of his passenger vehicle. Before he could exit, however, Tabitha's runabout pulled up to the crash site with lights blazing.

"K. Lemme look." Thrusters on Nick's suit fired small blue cones and he zipped over to the wreck. A second, much taller shape, exited Nick's vehicle and the bright red hair of his younger brother, Jack, showed through his visor.

Nick bumped my shoulder slightly with his own as he joined

me in surveying the worst damage on top of the sled.

"You pretty much obliterated the top thrusters," he said. Nick leaned in and pulled a couple of twisted panels off, laying them to the side. A couple of moments later he turned back to me, "I hate to say it, but you were doomed either way. These guys are burned through, how much matter did you run through them?"

"One sixty at the end," I said, as straight as I could manage.

"Whaa? That's crazy. You know that's a percent, right? As in one hundred is the max ... not just a number?" Nick's voice was calm and unperturbed. This wasn't our first time through this conversation. "How did you get them to one sixty? I thought they cut out at one ten or so?"

Another figure stepped in front of the lights. Even after everything that had just happened, it was hard not to be distracted by the shape of my other best friend, Tabitha Masters. Over the last couple of years, she had gone from being just another one of us to causing me a great deal of confusion.

She approached with a wide grin on her face. "I guess that's my point then," punctuating her words by slapping the top of my helmet, her body slowly rotating to vertically orient with my own.

The slap pulled me from the stupor she sometimes caused in me and the excitement of the moment returned, "Frak, you didn't have to wreck me."

"Learn to fly, dumb ass. You hit the brakes when I was only two meters back. You're lucky all I did was tag you." Tabitha gave me a hard look and thrust her hands onto her hips. I tried to return the look, but found it impossible to muster and started laughing. Soon, all four of us were laughing like hyenas.

"Well crap. I guess this thing isn't going anywhere." I swept my hand grandly over my now ruined ship.

"Let's get it after school. I have a couple of drop-offs and we can swing by and bring it back to the shop. Hop in," Nick said.

"Yeah, I don't need Mom being mad at me for not showing up for school. Dad is already going to be all over my case," I agreed.

Jack climbed into the vehicle first, grabbing one of the two front seats in the six-person cabin.

"Don't even think about it." Nick stared his brother down, floating across the outside top of the canopy in a slow, cartwheeling arc.

Jack sighed and shuffled back to the middle row of seats. Moments later, Nick and I both loaded into the powder blue passenger vehicle.

I didn't want Jack to feel too bad about being punted to the back seats. "Thanks, man. I appreciate the lift." Jack nodded amiably and stretched out across the bench seat.

Tabitha was first to take off and Nick followed her sled out of the asteroid. We burned hard, arcing to a new trajectory toward Perth Zero, or P-Zero, if you were a local.

P-Zero was built out of a watermelon-shaped asteroid that stood on its long end and was roughly ten kilometers tall and five kilometers at its equator. It had semi-spherical domes littering its surface, as if some giant soapy brush had left behind bubbles after a vigorous scrubbing. Splotches of the rock surface were visible at several locations, but the station's fifty-three hundred inhabitants had sprawled across much of the surface. After nearly a century of habitation, the rock was as much a space station as an asteroid.

Tabby lined up on a large docking pad located at the equator. It was the pad with the shortest distance to the station's one and only school. I imagined the proximity alarm was beeping, since she was well over the allowed velocity. She was the second best pilot I knew and I watched with a certain amount of pride as she burned off her excess speed at the last moment and landed.

I was only mildly annoyed that Tabby arrived a solid thirty seconds before us. Nick was considerably more careful than either Tabby or me. As soon as his vehicle landed, he popped the canopy and the three of us jumped out onto the pitted metal landing pad of the station.

I felt the vibration through my boots as the docking clamps engaged. An asteroid as small as P-Zero wouldn't normally generate much pull, but the gravity system of the station generated roughly 0.6 gravity.

We used our suit's arc-jets to augment a bounding dash across the pad to the first set of locks into the station. Jack arrived before Nick or me, which I expected. I knew firsthand he was even better in a suit than I was - a fact we often exploited in our sports league. The three of us, Tabby, Jack and I, were the heart of our school's pod-ball team and were pretty much unbeatable.

"Looks like Tabby's through," Jack said. I was surprised when we entered the lock and saw her bright blue suit waiting next to the control.

"What took you guys so long?" Tabby needled without malice. *Cycle lock,* she instructed her AI. The door we had entered closed behind us. The entire room rotated so we would be oriented correctly with the inside of the station. The room filled with atmospheric gasses. The entire process took less than twenty seconds.

The inner door opened to a narrow, pale-yellow hallway. The letters L-1 were stenciled in black at eye level, indicating we were in a lock zone only one door from space. It was generally accepted (and even mandated on the Perth mining colony) that suits were to be worn in L-1 space. It was acceptable to have your face shield open, but in the case of depressurization, the suit needed to be able to seal quickly.

There were several well-marked locks on our right side as we ran down the hallway. The locks had L-0 in bright red letters on their door frames. They led to an open interior bay for the launch pad. After jogging for 250 meters, we came to a door with a green L-2 stenciled on the frame. The lock opened for us as we approached and we all filed into a large square room. Since there was no pressure difference between L-1 and L-2, the opposite door opened as we entered. Years of traversing these locks allowed us to flow through without ever breaking stride.

We released our helmets so they draped around our necks. Electrical stimulation of thin fibers kept the suit's helmet rigid when it was being worn, but once released, the fabric lost its shape and draped limply.

The corridors we jogged through were generally ten meters wide and six meters tall. The size was a matter of convenience since the mining drill had a ten meter diameter. The remaining four meter tall arc beneath the floors were used to run electrical, sewage and atmosphere conduits. P-Zero's asteroid had a lot of iron deposits making it suitable for hollowing out and a ready source of materials for habitat construction.

We had a couple of kilometers to travel to get to the school complex in the center of the asteroid. The final long hallway had a small overhead rail on each side with gondolas hanging from it. We were in luck and found a car waiting for us. The gondolas didn't normally take long to arrive but we were already a little late. Once everyone was in, I instructed, *We're all in, let's go.* The gondola doors closed, then it lurched forward and up. The track was lower where we jumped in, but within a few meters it raised up to follow along the ceiling, allowing for pedestrian traffic to pass easily below.

When we neared the school complex, the gondola slowed, and lowered back to the floor. I was relieved to see there were still a number of other kids arriving at the last minute. There were over two hundred kids between six and eighteen years of age attending school at the complex for three hours each day. This education was mandated in order to work a claim or be allowed employment on the Perth colony.

For Nick, Tabby, myself, and nine others, this would be our last day of school if everything went well. This afternoon we were entered into a colony pod-ball tournament and tomorrow was the big test. I'd made plans to stay overnight on the station with Nick, so I pushed off worrying about my sled for at least one more day.

A quick stop in the locker room and we peeled off our vac-suits, then exited straight into the chamber where we played pod-ball and gathered for events. The stands were already packed with students, but we found a place to sit, even though it required a bit of shuffling from younger students.

The speaker at the podium was already into his speech. I had hoped to enter unnoticed, but my mom, Silver Hoffen, caught my eye and gave me a slightly disapproving nod. I had to look away so she wouldn't see my grin.

"Claim 40000.001 was originally sold to a cooperative group of miners and settlers as the Perth Mining Colony. The original twenty million shares of Class A stock were sold to one hundred and thirty five parties. Eighty-three years ago a convoy consisting of over a hundred ships carried the intrepid beginnings of this humble ..."

I thought I might go crazy if I had to hear Superintendent Harry Flark's 'Humble Beginnings' speech one more time. I caught myself and chuckled, realizing this would be my last time.

The assembly lasted nearly an hour, a third of the entire school day. The school had been built for several hundred students but enrollment had steadily declined over the last couple of decades following the decline of the colony's general population. Many of the richest claims were played out or bought up by speculators who weren't working them. The highly profitable claims on the biggest rocks were owned by large corporate interests and worked by hired hands.

It was ironic that the objective of the Colony's original inhabitants was to escape to the wide open frontier and be free from the corporate interests. Now, most found themselves working for a corporation, barely making enough to slide along. My dad, Big Pete Hoffen, didn't work for a corporation, but he wasn't doing any better than anyone else. Each year it seemed things just got worse for us. The equipment got a bit older and we had to lay off more employees. At this point we were down to just Big Pete, Mom and me. Worse yet, I really despised asteroid mining.

We filed out of the pod-ball court with the rest of the students. Nick and I left together, with Jack following close on our heels. Neither of us minded Jack's quiet company. He didn't have many friends of his own and enjoyed following along in his much smaller, but older brother's wake.

"Hoffen, are you guys entered into the tournament today?" Beagil Chen, one of my senior classmates, asked from behind us. Beagil was the captain of one of the school's other pod-ball teams, Paradox Blue.

Before I could answer, Tabby's angular shape sliced through the small knot of people eddying around Beagil and me. "We'll be there, Mutt," punctuated with a push to Beagil's shoulder. Beagil's nickname was Mutt due to the similarity of his first name to a breed of Earth animal that were kept as pets. Pets were extremely rare on a colony, although Old Millie had recently received a kitten named Spaz from the last M-Cor visit. It was a stowaway and the captain of the freighter had threatened to space it. I had never seen a dog in anything other than a vid, much less a beagle. But like most nicknames, this one stuck easily.

"What gives?" Beagil asked.

"Ah, don't be such a baby. Make sure you are suited up and ready for practice at 1200, Hoffen," Tabby said.

I was distracted by her change of clothing, although it was pretty standard for her. She was dressed in tight blue jeans, a pressed but loosely-fitted white blouse. Her long straight coppery hair was neatly braided to one side and pulled forward over her shoulder. Everything in place and in order.

My gaze lingered momentarily. Tabby was tall and thin like most spacers. Over the last couple of years, while she hadn't lost her tomboy attitude, somehow her body hadn't gotten the message. Her always-tight jeans showed new curves and her loose blouse ... well, I didn't like to admit how much I thought about all of that. It was one thing when she was in her ore sled playing tag or on the pod-ball court navigating through low-g. There she was just Tabby. But here in the hallway I felt off balance. I saw Tabby's fingers snapping in front of me and I realized with some amount of shame that I had been caught staring.

"Eyes front and center, Hoffen." Tabby simply didn't mince words. It was one of my favorite things about her, although in this case it proved to be embarrassing.

MARS COMPETENCY TEST

The pod-ball tournament went pretty much as expected. Beagil and his two older brothers were strong, agile, and worked well together. They provided our only real competition. We obliterated the other two teams quickly. Our team, Loose Nuts, gave up strength for endurance and raw speed. Tabby was by far the most aggressive, and my role was to keep her reigned in until the right moment. Once unleashed, she was devastatingly fast and had very little concern for anything other than scoring.

The tournament ended well past 2300 and I slept on the couch in Nick's mom's apartment. Wendy was used to me staying over, since my family lived in a habitation dome thirty minutes away on an asteroid near the claim Big Pete and I were working.

The next morning we made our way over to school for our last official act of secondary education.

"Are you set for the MCT today?" Nick asked on the way to the classroom.

"I didn't think we were supposed to study for that one." I said, feigning indifference.

"Well, they have practice tests. I hear Tabby went over to Fundus 12 for a prep course over break."

Tabby caught up and pushed her way between us, tossing an arm around both of our necks. Man, did she smell good.

"Talking about me again boys? Don't be jealous, not everyone can have looks and brains." She squeezed my shoulder. Maybe she squeezed Nick's too, but I chose to believe it was all for me. "Good game yesterday, by the way. Sorry, I had to bolt out of there so quickly. Had to get some last minute studying in." She squeezed my shoulder again. "Speaking of studying, let me guess. You

13

haven't thought about it until just now, Hoffen."

I managed to squeak out, "Uh, well, I guess I've been too busy. On break dad had me over on O-92 working to clear off that shelf. The mag-scans are showing strong pos' for precious."

"Well, precious metals or not, I want offa this sand-pile. I'm gonna get accepted to the Naval Academy," she replied briskly.

"Good luck with that." My words came out more bitter than expected.

We entered the testing room and I sat down in a daze and logged into the terminal panel embedded in the desk's surface. I hadn't forgotten about the MCTs (Mars Competency Tests) and had run through a couple of practice tests. School came easily for me, but I wasn't even sure that it mattered. I came from a long line of miners and would probably die in this sand pile.

An hour and a half into the three hour test, I reached the final question. I had always been quick on tests and while I considered reviewing the questions, I was still convinced it couldn't possibly matter. I would grow old out here making little rocks out of big ones. The future was nothing I could get excited about.

Just outside the classroom, I looked up and down the familiar hallway and felt a strange sense of no longer belonging. My last official act here had been to take the MCT. With my back to the wall, I slunk down into a seated position and stared at the floor.

Thirty minutes later Nick exited the room. "So, how do you think you did?" he asked.

"Eh, oh, not too bad, you know, not that it makes a difference to anyone. Hey, you guys have time to help me tow my sled in? I thought maybe we could get it running before dad has an embolism or something."

"Yeah, let me find Jack. We have a couple of deliveries, but if you help, we can finish faster and then use the hauler to bring your sled back to the shop."

As if on cue, Jack came loping around the corner, grinning widely. I acknowledged him by lifting an eyebrow and giving a quick head nod. Jack already had his suit on and had energized his helmet.

Instead of heading for the powder blue cruiser, we grabbed the first upward elevator we could find. Since the school was in the centermost complex, it was the safest structure in the entire colony. Such was the protective nature of miners with their children.

Station security against asteroid collision was a continual investment and one of its largest budgetary expenditures. Scattered around in nearby space, several thousand small detectors were linked into a distributed computer processing array that measured all strikes and warned of anything big enough to threaten the station. In some cases, asteroids were allowed to strike if they were determined to be sufficiently small and slow moving. Other times, the station's massive engines fired up and nudged it out of the way. And once in a while, other asteroids were flung into the path of the approaching disaster.

Even so, every few years something would make it through and cause a breach. A small miscalculation would allow a perfectly aimed rock anywhere between the size of your big toe and a large melon, to strike a poorly seated window, causing a section of the station to instantly decompress. Station building codes had limits on how large any open space was allowed to be. If you were perfectly unlucky, you could be standing close enough to the event to be sucked out into space without a suit. A slightly less unlucky person might be struck by that same object, killing them instantly. This happened every once in a while and had the effect of convincing the station's inhabitants that wearing a vac-suit in an L-1 section was important. It was one of several hazards of living in a mining colony.

SLED REPAIRS

After what seemed like an E-year (Earth year), the elevator's air-lock opened automatically, depositing us on the Mercantile. Initially, just a deep crater in the top of the station's asteroid, the Mercantile was the first and oldest settled area.

The original inhabitants had set up refining operations on the lip of the two hundred meter diameter hole. It had taken them less than two months to establish positive pressure by building the first of several transparent domes across the opening. Storefronts and apartments soared up from the base of the circular courtyard to the giant transparent dome.

The storefront we approached was filled with all sorts of different pieces of equipment. An old sign hung over the main doors and read "James On-Time Rentals." A quaint old bell rang as we pushed through the store's airlock doors.

Nick walked behind the counter and snagged a pouch of soda from the cooler and tossed it to my waiting hand. He then grabbed an oversized reading pad and swiped his gloved hand across the top. "Looks like Mom added two deliveries. One is on the way, the other is in the station." Nick said at his normal rapid fire pace, then said to his brother, "Jack, grab the blue vac-bot and run it over to Bab's Carpet Emporium."

Jack stared at Nick, looking lost.

"Here, give me your arm." Nick made a pinching gesture at his clipboard as if picking up a tissue from the display. He dropped the imaginary tissue onto a small display panel on the forearm of Jack's vac-suit and a map of the station appeared, with a well identified path between the rental shop and Bab's. Jack grinned and loped off to the back room, only to return a moment later with a blue robot the size of a twenty liter bucket. Once he cleared the front door, he set off at a jog.

"He's a good kid." Nick said.

"I can't believe he can run with that thing." I replied with amazement, watching Jack through the transparent doors. When Nick didn't reply I turned to watch him disappear through a door in the back.

I jogged to catch up. A large cavern behind the store housed bulky mining machines that required much more space. A warning chime sounded and the display on my arm pulsed with an orange glow. I punched an escape sequence acknowledging my arrival in an L-1 section. I had thirty seconds before I would have to acknowledge the warning again, but I wasn't ready to put the helmet on. I did, however, set it to rigid so I could quickly activate the face shield.

"Grab one of those big grav-carts. I think we can get it all in one trip," Nick directed. He donned his own helmet and darted down an aisle, out of sight.

I grabbed the handle of a large hovering cart. A couple of aisles over, I heard the sounds of heavy objects being moved around and pulled the cart in the direction of the noise. The sight of Nick's small frame wrestling with a grinding machine that easily out-massed both of us was hilarious, but I stepped in to help. Together, it took us nearly thirty minutes to get the cart loaded with the various machines on Nick's list.

Just as we finished loading, Jack returned through the back door with an amiable grin.

"We need to get this onto the big hauler and then we can go rescue your sled," Nick said.

He led the way through another set of doors, while Jack and I followed, pulling the loaded grav-cart onto an old beat-up lift. Once the doors closed behind us, Nick started giving directions. *Lift Control Nick James. Verify seals, Jack James, Nick James, Liam Hoffen. Vent Atmo. Surface.*

The seal around each of our helmets pulsed green and I heard a quick whoosh as the station attempted to reclaim the atmosphere before it opened the surface seal. We were on a very old industrial elevator Nick's mom had been lucky enough to purchase from a salvaged freighter. It was slow and banged up, but was rated to carry items well beyond anything they would ever have in the shop. I often wondered what sort of things this old elevator had seen in its lifetime.

Once it came to a stop, we found ourselves on top of the station overlooking James' Rental's exterior yard. Drilling lasers, dusters, combiners, oxy-shovels, screeners and all manner of large equipment lay on the deck of the yard.

"Jack, you guys take the sled to container eight. I think it is empty. But grab two more of the big sleds and put them in first."

Jack pointed toward a standard ore container they used to haul larger equipment. It only took a couple of minutes to load the container with the equipment and empty carts. Just as Jack and I were finishing, a sled hovered down to our position.

"Clear out guys," Nick's disembodied voice directed as he landed the James' Rental sled. "Oh, and grab a couple of come-alongs too, Jack."

The design of the hauler wasn't significantly different than that of an ore sled. The cabin sat on top of a long spine with long, spindly legs. Nick deftly rested the spine down on the container. Automated systems made fine adjustments, allowing docking pins to neatly attach and then lock, drawing the container snugly up to the ship.

With Jack not far behind, I scrambled up into the cabin of the container hauler. It was close quarters for three of us, but wasn't the first time we had squeezed in. Physically spent from lugging around the equipment, we made the delivery rounds in silence, except for Nick's spat-out commands at each stop. It was interesting to see how easily he took charge. He was small enough that he wouldn't play pod-ball with us, but out here he was large and in charge.

With the deliveries complete, Nick made his way to the asteroid that held my ore-sled hostage. We piled out to inspect the damage and then pulled three large mechanical winches out of the back of the hauler. We attached them strategically to the hauler on the side closest to my ore sled. I moved between the units and touched a button on each of them in sequence instructing the AI: *Synchronize come-alongs, A, B, C.*

A small chirp indicated acknowledgment.

Come-along tension to ten newts. Ten newtons would provide a small amount of resistance so I wouldn't have a rat's nest of cable unspool while I pulled on it.

Three small chirps of acknowledgment sounded as the units responded.

I grabbed the end of one of the cables and pulled, playing it out behind me as I jetted to the opposite side of the sled, then called to Nick and Jack, "Hey guys, grab the other two cables and drag them over."

After attaching the cables to the roof of the ore sled, I drove meter-long spikes into the floor of the cavern next to the sled's legs. I then ran a small length of cable through both the spike and each leg using a quick cable tie off. Ultimately, I wanted to keep the sled's legs from moving, while causing the sled to roll over and rest on its legs.

With cables attached, I instructed, *Come-alongs to twenty-five newtons.* The cables retracted and pulled on the sled. It started to lift and then rotate around the anchored legs.

The three of us scrambled to the top of the sled and inspected the damaged thrusters. Nick had already pronounced them ruined, but that was when we were in a hurry.

After twenty minutes of flitting between the two top thrusters, I stopped and squared up with Nick. "Okay, I agree. Back thruster is shot, but I think I can get the front one running. They just aren't that complex. How about you grab some new b-ports and nickel linkage. I'll salvage out the back thruster."

We worked for a couple of hours, salvaging parts from the ruined aft thruster. We banged and bent the frame around the salvageable fore thruster and in the end, it looked pretty good.

"Whew, it ain't pretty, but it might just work." Nick stood back to admire our work.

"Jack, jump in the cabin and give us 5% through the top fore thruster," I requested after making some final adjustments.

The sled, without so much as a clunk, fired up and a telltale blue pyramid glowed in the thruster.

Nick slapped the back of my suit with his open hand. "Hoffen, you have to be the luckiest guy in these rocks. I wouldn't have bet anything we would get one of these going. It's gonna run like crap and you can't seal the cockpit, but at least you can limp home."

"Great. Dad said he wanted to talk tonight. I completely forgot." I caught myself in a moment of self-pity and then straightened up, "Hey, you guys are great, sorry to be a downer. I couldn't have gotten it back up without you. Talk tomorrow?"

Clearing the asteroid, I turned toward our family's claim. It would take longer than normal, but at least I had a ride. I watched the James' hauler slowly accelerate in nearly the opposite direction back to P-Zero and my mind turned to the conversation I did not want to have with my father.

A BRIGHT FUTURE

Mom and Dad were in the main room of our habitat when I arrived. It had been constructed on the largest asteroid in my dad's claim. Now in reality, it wasn't his claim. Dad was leasing it from the Geoffrey Bros Corporation. The claim had never been particularly high producing, but paid out enough for us to survive. Dad was an eternal optimist, always believing we would strike it rich with the next dig.

Our reality was much different. We made just enough to eke out a fairly meager living. I think Big Pete was glad to be able to work for himself. I didn't hate every moment of it, but as far as I could see, it was a life without a future.

It bothered me that Big Pete refused to see that even though we had a nice pile of iron out here, the expense to get it hauled to a supplier wasn't worth the effort. If forty-five metric tonnes of iron were sitting on Earth or Mars, it would be worth a small fortune, but out here, fees, taxes and transportation ate up 90% of that fortune. He worked six days a week, ten hours a day and expected me to do the same. In return for that, we had a four room habitat, food and atmosphere. I didn't think it was much of a life.

Mom looked up from her reading panel. "Take off your suit, dear and grab a meal bar." Even though we were technically in L-1 space we generally didn't wear our suits. The habitat was inside a cavern and we had moved a large asteroid fifty meters off the opening so there was no direct line from space. It wasn't completely foolproof, but the risk was reasonable.

I went into my room, which wasn't much bigger than the bed that occupied it, and allowed my suit to relax off of me. It had been a busy day so I chucked it and my suit-liner into the suit-freshener and pulled on my alternate liner.

Before I could sit down with the meal bar I'd taken out of the cabinet on the wall, Dad opened with, "Now that you are done with school, we need to talk about getting after that new claim."

I fell into a chair and expelled my breath in a sigh. Instead of responding, I extracted the meal bar from its recyclable wrapping.

"Pete. Give him a chance to eat." Mom knew this wasn't a great conversation and even though I appreciated her saying something, it wouldn't do any good. Big Pete Hoffen didn't give up easily on anything. It was a great trait to have as a miner, but was also a reason why miners were generally loners.

Before Dad could get going, Mom interjected again, "Liam, how did you do on your MCT today? I saw the report that said you passed. Have you seen your results?"

Nick and I had been so busy, I'd completely forgotten about the test. Passing was essential since most jobs required at least that. Passing also meant I was now an EMC (Earth/Mars Citizen). I could legally enter into contracts, get sued, get married or anything else that indicated I was an adult. Since I was done with daily trips to school, Big Pete was ready for me get on with my life, beating rocks into submission.

I stayed quiet, tossed the meal wrapper into the recycle bin and grabbed a clear tablet. The tablet recognized my swipe signature and other biometrics it read through my finger's touch. I had several outstanding comms from Nick, Tabby and other friends. Tabby had started a v-party (virtual party) and it looked like all of my classmates were online.

"I'm gonna eat this in my room." I knew that not answering either of them would cause problems, but I didn't care at the moment.

"Sit down Liam. You aren't going anywhere. We agreed to talk," Dad said, his voice raised.

"Yeah, no shite, Dad. I'm not going anywhere." It just slipped out. I had never cussed at my Dad before. I didn't know if it was out of respect or fear, but probably both. His wording had struck such a raw nerve that I lashed out. I took the short steps into my room and closed the privacy screen. If there had been something to slam, I would have done that, too.

I heard their voices – Dad was angry and Mom was trying to calm him down, but I just didn't care. I considered it a good sign that he didn't break my privacy screen. I wouldn't have been surprised and I was prepared to escalate.

I put on a reading lens and flopped on the bed. Hot, angry tears trickled down my face. This had been building for a while. I could see myself living in this same tiny room twenty years from now, eating meal bars and hoping for a big strike. Feeling sorry for myself seemed to be an appropriate response.

I brought up a list of comms. Several from Nick, an invite from Tabby to her v-party, and there, prominently at the top of the list was the M-Cor logo glowing brightly.

No reason to wait, not like it mattered. Like Big Pete said, I wasn't going anywhere. I opened the MCT comm. A bald head appeared on my vid screen. I couldn't tell if the head belonged to a male or a female. Whoever it was, they were generally nice looking, if not a little disturbing in their lack of identifiable features. I had heard about this from other students. Apparently MCT didn't want to offend anyone, so they had a computer generated mix of races and both genders so everyone would find something to identify with. The face of MCT was everyone and no one.

"Good evening, Mr. Hoffen. Congratulations on successfully completing the Mars Competency Test. Are you prepared to receive your scores?" The avatar's face was inscrutable. Although I understood I was talking to a higher level AI, I hadn't seen one that presented itself as a person.

"Yes." I decided to keep it short. I was a little intimidated to be talking to a representative of such a large corporation, even if it was an AI.

The AI's lips turned up into a small smile. "Very well, Liam. Do you mind if I call you Liam?"

What a weird conversation with an AI, but then this had been a great day for weird. "Sure, why not?" I replied a bit warily.

"Thank you, Liam. My name is Astra and I represent the Mars Colony Corporation. I would like to share your test results with you. We are pleased to inform you that you achieved a composite score of 93%. Would you like to review your subject matter scores?"

"Uh, no, that's great. Err, well, could you send them to me?"

"Yes Liam. These tests are part of your permanent record and are accessible via your Mars Colony Corporation account. You have the right to view them at any time. Are there any institutions you would like to send these results to? There is a special if you send to ten or more educational or vocational institutions."

"No. End comm." I couldn't afford tuition at any of those places, much less the cost of the trip from Colony 40.

I flipped over to Tabby's v-party and found the majority of my classmates chatting. My AI superimposed avatars representing each person in the party onto my reading lens. It did a nice job of representing individual postures and locations.

I had never taken the time to customize my avatar like some of my friends, but across the virtual room I could see Nick dressed in a black tuxedo with a flamboyant red, black, and orange bow tie.

He approached with a champagne glass in his hand. He must have been working on his avatar for some time to have so many customizations. His obvious good mood provided me with instant relief from my personal pity party.

"Now we get on with our lives!" Nick exclaimed as he walked up to me.

I smiled and nodded in acknowledgment. Nick knew exactly what he wanted to do with his life. He would take over his mom's rental business and expand it. His skill as a mechanic and access to the necessary tools and equipment had set him up for a nice life. He wouldn't be rich but he would do well.

I scanned the room for Tabby and caught her eye. Her voice was in my ear before the AI could transition her to walk up to us. That created an eerie effect as it seemed like she was communicating telepathically, when in reality she was most likely sitting in her room on P-Zero, talking into her own reading lens.

"Are you happy with your test, Liam?" she asked softly. Tabby knew this was a touchy subject for me but coming from her, I didn't mind. She wasn't wearing her normal brown jumpsuit but was dressed in a dark blue uniform. Her gorgeous long hair had been reduced to a buzz cut and she had a beret on her head.

"Uh, yeah, fine I guess. What the frak are you wearing?" I was completely distracted by her avatar's changes.

"I've been accepted to the Naval Academy." The pride in her voice caused a lump in my throat.

"Wow, that's great Tab." I had to work hard not to choke on the words. This meant a lot to her and I realized how much I didn't want her to leave. The three of us talked well into the night.

I must have fallen asleep because the next thing I knew Mom was gently shaking me awake. "Time to get up, Liam. Your Dad wants to get out to O-92 early."

I groaned sleepily, but my previous day's anger was gone. I had been mining most of my life and it wasn't lost on me that if we wanted to eat and breathe, the work had to be done.

I changed into a fresh liner and pulled my vac-suit up. Ultimately, a suit was composed of a few different parts. A liner wasn't particularly required but it was the best way to keep things from getting stinky. The material was engineered to neutralize most things the human body produced other than actual waste. A person could live months with a liner and still not smell too bad. Mom insisted we clean our liners weekly. Whenever I would let mine go a second week, she had a sub-routine running that caught me and then she would gently remind me to deal with it.

The main part of the suit was something like a baby's pajama that enclosed both the feet and hands with a hood hanging off the back. Small electrical currents stimulated nano-fibers in the material, making it extremely strong. When pulled up, the hoodie formed an air-tight seal with a transparent shield over the face. This level of suit was sufficient for traveling around in a space station and was designed for constant exposure to zero pressure environments. Underneath the vac-suit we wore a suit-liner that was cleaned regularly.

The biggest issue we faced was running out of atmosphere. The reserves in the suit lasted about three hours, even though the suit was very good at reclaiming atmosphere. The oxygen found in body waste was easily converted to usable elements and the suits constantly checked for contact with oxygen sources which were plentiful on most ships and stations. Unfortunately, the cost of oxygen was well monitored and one of the major expenses of living.

For a miner, the other parts of a suit were hardened boots and gloves, called AGBs or arc-jet boots and gloves. Stepping into the AGB boots caused them to join up with the suit. The AGB gloves slid over the vac-suit's integrated gloves. Fuel cartridges for the AGBs were relatively inexpensive. There was even a spot for the oxygen crystal material that added several hours of reserve atmo.

Small computer processors were salted throughout the material of the suit. A small chip had been implanted into the back of my neck allowing my AI to transfer to whatever suit I was wearing. The chip didn't interface with my body other than to upload itself into nearby processors so my AI could interact with the environment. Long gone were the days of individual computer chips being used for one single purpose. Computer processors shared information and the processing load so much that we simply didn't think about them as being interesting.

A suit with boots and gloves could keep a miner warm, safe, and breathing for nearly a day. It wasn't uncommon to get knocked off an asteroid while mining, but arc-jets made it a simple matter to return to your original position.

BIG PETE'S BIG HAUL

"So after you told your Dad off, you guys just went back to work and didn't talk about it at all?" Tabby stared at me over the top of her untouched beer.

"I didn't think anybody talked back to Big Pete and lived to tell the tale," Nick added dramatically.

"I was pretty fired up. I think Mom probably said something to calm him down. I doubt we are done talking about it, though."

I looked around Old Millie's tavern. It was nothing more than another room a dozen meters away from the James' rental business. No one knew how old Millie was, but for as long as I could remember she had owned this place and she was old.

The tavern was the highest spot in the station and sat next to the dome so patrons could look out into space and think deep thoughts. It was considered L-1, even though it was technically two locks from space. An unimpeded view of space meant an object could crash through both the dome and Millie's front window. If you weren't wearing a suit, you would receive a fine from M-Cor, but it was okay to have your hood off and vac-suit gloves retracted. In a depressurization event, the suit's sleeves would seal and you'd have sufficient time to pull up your helmet and gloves.

Nick shrugged. "Bad timing on his part to spring that on you the night you finished the MCT." He pushed my arm. "You never did answer me on how you did. Since they served you beer, apparently you passed, but how did you really do?"

"Meh, it doesn't matter. I did okay but I am going to be a miner. Right?" I stared down at the metal table. "So when do you take off, Tabs?"

"Just a little less than three weeks. And that was a bullshit answer." She stared at me hard.

"What would you have me do? Hitchhike my way off of here?" I asked hotly.

We stared at each other for better than a minute.

Nick finally broke the silence, "So, does that mean you're getting a ride back on the M-Cor transport, Tabby?"

The schedule of the Mars Colony Corporation, or M-Cor, freighters was well known and highly anticipated. We all waited for several months for supplies to be delivered. M-Cor freighters would pick up all of the refined ore in the form of ingots, which were destined for sale. It had been almost four months since the last freighter, and there were large piles of ingots at P-1.

Conversation at the table stopped and the three of us listened to the music and experimented with our mugs of beer. While I didn't specifically dislike the drink, I wasn't sure what the big deal was. I did find myself becoming more relaxed as I quickly drained the mug. Within a few minutes of my empty mug hitting the table, our waitress asked if I needed a refill. I wasn't sure why I said yes, but it felt like the right thing to do.

"You know Liam, the thing I don't get is why you let him push you around." In a million years I wouldn't have expected that from Tabby. We were friends, but she generally steered clear of family conflicts.

"Say again?" I looked at her incredulously.

"Okay, so maybe it's the beer speaking," she started out, although she was still only about a third into her mug. "But I bet anything you scored better than I did. You've always been ahead of all of us in math and spatial systems. You are a natural pilot, yet when you're faced with your future you just frakking roll over and play dead!"

"Holy crap, Tabs. Tell us what you really think," Nick replied defensively for me.

Tabby leaned back in her chair and took a sip of her beer. "Sorry, but it had to be said."

I was completely caught off guard. Tabby and I verbally

sparred all of the time - it was pretty much our thing. In a single sentence she had defended, attacked, complimented and challenged me. I was excited and upset and had no idea how to respond.

So I said the only thing that made any sense to me, "I'm sure gonna miss you, Tabs." And I meant it.

Nick and I spent Sunday working on my sled. One advantage to being a miner is that you work with a lot of equipment and used parts are easy to come by. James' Rental had a considerable workshop where equipment was repaired. We had everything we needed and, with the help of our AIs, it was just a matter of work to get my sled back to better than it had been. Generally speaking, repairs never look like new, but then just about no piece of equipment in a colony does.

To pay Nick back for his time, I agreed to drop off some equipment on the way back to my family's habitat. On the ride, I couldn't stop thinking about what Tabby had said the previous night. Was that why I was so upset with my parents and refused to talk about how much I didn't want to be a miner? What other stupid option was available?

Monday morning and the week started back on O-92. For the last several months, we had been clearing off a shelf of material that had extremely low yield. It was junk rock we commonly referred to as gravel.

Work on a Hoffen claim ran for five - ten hour days in a row. We preferred to line up our workweek with the standard Mars/Earth calendar and Saturday mornings were reserved for transporting ore back to the P-1 refinery.

We rent space at the refinery where we make giant piles of our collected ore. The refinery sorts the piles and refines the materials into intermediate products called ingots. These ingots are sold to M-Cor and that money pays for equipment repairs, salaries for crew, fuel, habitat atmo, claim fees, etc. As it turns out, the list of expenses is very long and everything else is paid before the miner makes any money.

The mining process is pretty straightforward. First we have to figure out where we want to mine. Knowing where is what separates miners who make money from those who don't. It doesn't do us any good to mine gravel - we want high mineral content and around here the most common mineral is iron.

Test holes are drilled with high-powered mining lasers that can punch a hole twenty meters through solid iron, vaporizing everything in its path. It takes about fifteen minutes to drill a twenty meter hole. Once the test hole is drilled, a robot called a groundhog is sent down the shaft. On the way down, the groundhog analyzes the minerals it passes in the hole.

Regardless of the mineral content, the process of removal is the same. Large augers grind and break the surface material and gather it into a container. Most of the work I do on the claim is ferrying these containers around. Estimation algorithms let us know if a load is valuable enough to haul back to P-1 or if it should be dumped. In some cases, we run it through a pre-sift machine to separate minerals from gravel. It's a lengthy process and we tend to reserve that for when we just can't get anything useful from the claim.

Last week we had gathered two good containers with a decent iron yield, but this week we had high hopes for a small pocket promising copper and maybe even some platinum. It only takes four or five containers of copper to pay the bills for an operation like ours for a year and a single container of high yield platinum would set a miner for life.

Our finances were tight enough that Big Pete had released all of our help. It was just the two of us out here, but the fact was, we were good at it. We had worked together for so long that we rarely had to speak, even though we were maneuvering hundred tonne machines within several meters of each other. We had a comfortable rhythm.

One of our superstitions was that we didn't check the yields on our keeper containers until the end of the week. If the AI indicated a junk container, I ran it out to the giant junk pile at the end of the day. If it was a keeper, we stacked it up for transport back to the P-1 refinery.

By midweek we started to share a level of excitement. The stack of containers to ship was already at five and the AI recommended a pre-sift on a sixth. At the end of the week, we finished with nine complete containers and a tenth we had pre-sifted from three others.

"I had a good feeling about this spot." Big Pete broke the silence, causing me to jump. He walked up next to me and placed his hand on my shoulder. I looked over at him and saw a large grin on his face.

"Did you run the numbers yet?" I didn't think he had since it was customary for us to run them with the entire crew. There were few exciting moments on a claim and tallying the week's work was one of them.

"No, but we haven't pulled ten containers in the last six months. If it is all iron, it will still be worth it."

Dad was right. With ten containers of iron we could hire a couple more crew and run the rest of the claim more quickly. Moreover, the timing was excellent, with the M-Cor transport showing up in less than two weeks. Payout would come relatively quickly.

Report yield Hoffen Channel One, Dad instructed his AI.

I was a little surprised he had chosen Channel One. We used that when we wanted to include Mom in the conversation. I heard a small chirp indicating she had accepted the linkup and was listening in real time. The report was by no means a final tally, but gave a percentage breakdown on what the AI had detected. It could be off significantly, but at this point in the week it would be our best indication of the result of our efforts.

Iron forty-one point two percent, the AI started out. I heard a gasp from Mom and could see the eyebrows rise on Big Pete's face. The numbers had to add up to 100%, so a low iron number was significant. I had never heard an iron report this low before.

Copper thirty-four point seven percent.

In the background I heard Mom whisper, "Oh Pete ..."

Just as I was shocked to hear the low iron number, such a high copper number was equally shocking. Of the ten containers, that meant roughly three of them had copper. This was the biggest week I had ever seen.

Silver eight point two percent.

We all listened in shocked silence.

Nickel six point eight percent, tungsten six percent and platinum three point one percent.

My mind spun with numbers. The tungsten and platinum alone were worth a fortune. A portion of it would go to the claim owner, but the lion's share would end up with Big Pete.

"Be home late tonight. Don't want to leave this sitting until tomorrow. Hoffen out."

I grinned and shook my head on the way over to my ore sled. Loading and transporting ten containers would take both of us the better part of the next three hours. Though we had been going solid for twelve hours already, I felt energized by the good news.

It was past 2300 when we got back to the habitat. It felt good to get it all delivered. Tomorrow would be easy. All I had to do was grab the empty containers sometime after 1200. The ore processing would happen automatically and the ingots would then be delivered to our secure storage. Once M-Cor picked them up, the money would be transferred into Big Pete's account.

PIRATES ATTACK

I finished at the refinery by midafternoon and headed over to see Nick at the rental shop. The James' shop was at its busiest on the weekend as miners were either dropping off or picking up equipment. Big Pete had asked me to keep our good fortune quiet until M-Cor made the pickup in ten days or so. Technically, we hadn't made any money until the ingots were picked up by the buyer, who was always M-Cor.

We loaded a couple of laser drills and an auger into the first container on my sled so I could deliver it on Sunday morning. I had arranged with Nick to spend the night at his shop so we could head over to Old Millie's and meet up with Tabby. Tabby only had ten days left so we wanted to spend as much time with her as possible.

"Hey Liam," Tabby began, a little sheepishly, "I'm sorry about needling you about your dad last week. Still friends?"

"No worries, Tabs," I returned easily. "You've always got my back. I just wish I knew what I wanted to do differently."

"Okay, just as long as we are still cool. That's all I want."

Nick shook his head in feigned disgust. "You guys want to get a room or something?"

Tabby jumped up, landed on Nick and rubbed her knuckles into the top of his head.

"Give. I give," Nick giggled, out of breath.

"So ... Tabs. Any idea what you are going to do at the Academy?" I asked, not knowing what to expect.

Tabby sat down after letting Nick go. "Well, really, it's just like every other college out there, but I want to be a captain."

About mid-sentence my suit's warning system started shaking

and pulsing red around the neckline and I felt the sleeves around my wrist contract. My AI was responding to a rapid depressurization event I hadn't yet recognized. Instinctively, I reached back for my hood and pulled it up. Nick and Tabby were doing the same thing. I had just reached to pull on my left glove when everything went to hell.

Depressurization warning klaxons blared from every surface. The front window of Old Millie's blew straight out through a now non-existent dome. The three of us, and the half dozen or so other inhabitants, were sucked toward open space, tumbling haphazardly with the loose chairs.

Explosive decompression isn't something that happens over a long period of time, especially in a large area. One second everything is stable, the next couple of seconds are complete chaos, and then it's all done.

The three of us had taken up a position at the back of the bar next to a wall and we had been sucked toward the window, but not pulled through. My first thought was to make sure Tabby and Nick had their suits sealed. I couldn't immediately locate them since the lights were flashing red in sequence with the klaxons. The sound of the klaxons had diminished almost completely due to the very low atmospheric pressure we were currently experiencing.

Mute background. Channel Loose Nuts One. Even though we were no longer competing in the pod-ball league at school, we had left the channel configured for the three of us.

"Tabby, Nick, check in. Are you sealed?" I asked. I located Nick and saw a reassuring green glow around his wrists. All of our suits were of the same general make and for the first few minutes of pressurization they glowed green at the extremities - wrist, ankle and neck - to indicate a safe seal had been established.

Nick, who was always quick on the draw replied, "Good, Liam. Tabby?"

"Frak. Yeah, good. I jammed my leg into the frakking table. I think it might be busted." Tabby's voice carried pain. I was finally able to locate her under the table where we had been sitting. All of the tables in Old Millie's were bolted to the floor and made of steel. Nobody picked a fight with a table on a mining colony and won.

Nick got to her first, but she had already rolled over to a seated position.

"Do you really think it's busted?" Nick was inspecting her leg.

Glancing around the room, I could see a few more suited people helping others. A quick look out to the dome and I realized a foam barrier had attempted to deploy, but failed. The Mercantile was completely open to space. The severity of the problem started to sink in, but something in my peripheral vision was wrong and I hadn't yet processed it.

Locate casualties. A red glow showed on the side of my helmet directing me to turn my head to the left. As I panned left, an outline formed around a shape behind the bar. I processed the image and turned away in horror as I saw part of Millie's broken body pinned to the back wall by a large object. Panicked, I looked around further and identified several other partial bodies that had been ripped apart. I fought to push back the gorge from my stomach. In a suit, it would be hard to live with the smell. The suit would take care of the vomit, but for whatever reason, it was unable to remove the smell. As a kid, I had once thrown up in my suit and had to endure a very long ride back to our habitat.

I heard Tabby gasp and Nick, who was still looking at her leg said, "Sorry, does that hurt?"

"No, Nick. Millie got hit," Tabby filled in and started to stand up.

A terrible thought went through my mind, "Back in a sec." *Hoffen Channel One Emergency.* A small chirp was followed by some ragged breathing.

"Dad. Mom. Millie's just took a kinetic hit." I was concerned by the ragged breathing but figured they would want to know about this right away.

Mom replied immediately. "Liam, are you safe?" Without waiting for me to say anything more she pushed on. "Hole up and stay out of sight. The colony is under attack."

"What? What do you mean?" I asked, confused.

Big Pete jumped on, "Pirates, Liam. They are hitting the refinery. Do as your Mom says. Stay out of sight and stay off the comms. Perimeter defense is compromised and they have a group of us pinned down on P-1." *Channel One close.*

A lump rose in my throat as everything got real in a hurry. It was one thing to have Millie dead from a rogue asteroid. It was another thing entirely to have it be on purpose. My Dad had used the phrase 'pinned down.' He had been a Marine at one point in his life and had even seen combat. He hadn't sounded scared. He sounded deadly serious. Big Pete had never backed down from anything and now I was terrified he was going to get himself killed.

I slid over to Tabby and pushed my faceplate up next to hers. I pulled Nick in so that we were all uncomfortably close, "Nick, can you get us comm without it going through Central?"

His reply sounded a million miles away, "Sure. Easy"

Line of Sight. Secure. Loose Nuts Channel One. Initiate.

Nick pulled back and I could see him talking behind his face screen. My AI announced, *Secure link initiated; Nicholas James, Tabitha Masters. Local Communication only. Do you authorize?*

Authorized, I replied tersely.

Nick's previous attempt at communication replayed, "What's going on, Liam?" As with all secure communication there was an odd, tinny sound to his voice.

"You on, Tabs?" I asked.

"Yes," she answered.

"Okay. I talked to Big Pete. Apparently, the colony is under attack. This wasn't a rogue asteroid."

"What happened to perimeter defense? That should have stopped anything." Nick was already analyzing the issue.

"He said perimeter defense has been compromised and a bunch of them are pinned down on P-1."

It was Tabby's turn, "How is that even possible? They would have to have taken over the control tower."

"Frak, that's right on top of us!" I realized out loud.

The thought of the large plasma guns shooting at Dad was hard to take. Those could easily vaporize a small ship, much less a man sized target. The perimeter defense guns fired periodically at small runaway rocks that breached a well-defined sphere around P-Zero and in extreme circumstances they could be manned to repel pirate attacks. Colony 40 hadn't seen pirate activity for at least sixty years and even that attack was easily defeated, precisely because of the perimeter defense guns.

"We gotta do something," Tabby said with determination.

"Dad said to get out of sight." Even as I said it, I knew I wouldn't be able to live with that.

"The Liam Hoffen I know never once rolled over. Don't start now, you pissant." Tabby was spitting mad. I recognized that tone of voice, having caused it a few times in my life.

Nick spoke up. "Look Tabby, this is real. Big Pete has military experience and he knows what to do."

"No Nick, she's right." I grabbed his shoulder to communicate my resolve. "I can't let my Dad down, even if it kills me."

"Frakking aye." Tabby grabbed the table and struggled up to a standing position.

"I thought that was broken." I pointed at her leg.

"Nope, just hurts like a mother. Had worse in that game against those navy brats."

I feared for the naval academy when Tabby showed up. The first cadet who slapped her on the ass would end up with a surgical team attempting to extricate that same hand from his own ass. It made me cringe just to imagine the pain she would deliver.

"What's the plan?" Nick joined in.

"Okay. The control tower is only a couple hundred meters from where your lift exits on top. We have to get up there and see what's going on. I'm thinking they did a fly-by and dropped the kinetic mass through the dome to keep people in the station. Every airlock is locked down by safety protocol for the next hour or longer. This was a tactical strike." I didn't know anything for sure, but it was the best I could work out.

I took a moment to think. "Let's find some AGBs. We might be the only ones on the station who can get up to the control tower since the foam didn't completely seal us in." Nick and Tabby didn't have AGBs because they had come from on-station to Millie's. Nick's were twenty meters away in the James' Rental shop, on the other side of airlocks which weren't opening anytime soon. Tabby's were probably in her apartment, even deeper in the station.

I looked around at my friends and felt the responsibility of our actions. We were willingly heading toward danger. I could tell by the rapidity of my speech that adrenaline was surging through my body.

My boots and gloves had been sitting behind the table and the decompression slid them forward only a small distance. Hard boots and arc-jets immediately made me feel more confident, even though they certainly wouldn't help stop any sort of bullet.

Just then the gravity on the station turned off. It wasn't quite as devastating as it sounds. The gravity generator has to be serviced and we learn to deal without it for short bursts of time, but it made our external maneuvers considerably more dangerous for Nick and Tabby.

"Crap." Realization of the problem hit Tabby.

"One step at a time," I said, as much to Tabby as to myself.

We linked hands and I used my arc-jets on very low power to nudge us around the debris in Millie's. In horror, I realized some of the debris was body parts. Minutes ago, they belonged to people who were hanging out, just like the three of us. Panic coursed through my body and I started to rethink heading top-side.

"Hold it together, Hoffen." Tabby must have sensed my hesitation.

"They're dead, Tabs," I replied quietly.

"And if we don't do something, your dad could be next," she said.

"Point Masters," I thought wryly, but she was dead right.

I nudged my jets again and we wriggled through the blasted out windows of the bar. It was almost a hundred meters straight down to the floor of the Mercantile. If the gravity generator kicked in, we would have precious little time to find safety.

Looking up to the ruined dome, I could see safety foam had nearly sealed the entire opening, but had failed at a couple of locations. Undeployed canisters were evident in the opening. I wasn't surprised, considering the opening was almost two hundred meters in diameter and the foam was a difficult system to test. A maintenance crew would need to patch up the gaps before atmosphere could be restored.

I nudged us in the direction of an opening closest to James' Rental. We pulled up next to the ore sled I had parked there the day before. From the yard, we had a clear view of the security control tower.

The control center was a small tower that floated a kilometer above the station and was located less than a hundred meters from the edge of the rental yard. The center was tethered with a cable a few meters wide at the base, tapering off slowly to about a meter when it connected to the control room. An open elevator ferried inhabitants up and down the tether. Security staff had a direct view of most of the nearby station assets and most importantly, the P-1 refinery.

The control center was only large enough to hold three or four people and was often only manned by one person on a four hour shift. The staff's responsibilities were to watch the monitors, respond to emergencies and control the perimeter defense guns. An AI backed up the security staff and did a better job of watching for problems than the humans did. Firing of the perimeter defense guns, however, was something the AI wasn't allowed to do without direct commands from authorized personnel. Now, those guns were firing at my dad and others down at the refinery and it meant someone in the control center was deliberately helping the pirates.

"Tabby, grab my spare AGBs from the sled. Nick, do you have any on the platform?" I had to come up with a plan, but needed more information. "Go dark and don't use your jets. I'm going to get eyes on the tether base."

I approached the side of Nick's yard, pulled myself up to the top of a three-stack of containers, and peered over in the direction of the control tower's base.

My heart sunk as I made out the long shape of a fast attack craft. It was thirty meters long and rectangular in shape and I could make out a slug-throwing turret mounted on top and at least one missile rack. It wasn't much to look at, but I had watched vids showing how devastating one of these medium range ships could be. The only ships I'd ever seen like this were naval escorts. This particular ship showed carbon scoring, dents and hastily repaired tears in the steel hull. The ship screamed pirate to anyone who saw it.

I sat for a moment and surveyed the area to see if there was any movement on the outside of the ship. I knew a ship of this size could have up to a crew of eight. Only two were required to fly it, but there was easily space for at least six and if you weren't excited about comfort, then you could bring on more. For short distances, a ship this size could hold a couple of dozen people, but I didn't think that was likely since there was no launch point close to Colony 40.

My patience was rewarded and I saw two figures outside the ship. They appeared alert, albeit bored.

Colony 40 had a sheriff's department, but they wouldn't be a match for the turret on top of that ship. Even worse, Sheriff Blaen Xid or one of his deputies had probably been in the control tower when the attack occurred.

A plan formed and I knew what we needed to do next. We couldn't possibly approach the ship with those two guys hanging around. Plus, there had to be at least one more in the ship to man the slug-throwing turret. The turret was top mounted and it was unlikely that it would be able to target anything closer than thirty meters, which was why the guard had been posted. If someone breached that perimeter, the guards needed to deal with them.

There was little chance of any sort of organized resistance occurring anytime soon. Breaching the main dome had effectively shut off everyone in the main station. The station had gone into lockdown because of the large breach. The failure of the foam sealant was lucky for us, otherwise we would have been locked down in the station, too. I have heard it said that fortune favors the bold and it certainly seemed like the pirates had proven the truth of that.

As I thought out the process, it seemed they had made one critical error. It remained to be proven whether we could take advantage of that mistake. I met back up with Tabby and Nick, who had both found AGBs and were hunkered down by my sled.

"Good news and bad news," I started off, sounding like we were on the pod-ball court and not preparing to assault heavily armed pirates who were already responsible for the deaths of many today. "Bad news first. They have an armed ship sitting at the base of the security station tether." I went on to describe the turret and missile launchers. "Also, there are two goons hanging around the entry hatch. I didn't see guns but I think it's a fair assumption they're armed."

"The good news is, I have a plan." I grinned, feeling excited and a bit terrified. As I explained my plan, Tabby's face took on the same grin I had. Nick was expressing nothing but dread. To his credit, he didn't once suggest we should back down, but I could see he understood how serious this was about to get. They both offered adjustments to the plan and within a few minutes we were settled. We spent the next twenty minutes moving equipment around and then we were ready to execute.

I crept to the side of the James' rental yard so nothing was between me and the ship. Nothing had changed. The two pirates were sitting next to the entry hatch and no one else was in view. I thought I could make out movement in the cockpit, but I was at the wrong angle to be sure. I had brought several tools, each massing a kilogram, from the rental yard. I braced my back leg against a container and started tossing tools at the pirates as hard as I could. At a hundred meters if they didn't move, I would likely hit at least one of them. I had three heavy tools flying directly at each pirate and was ready for phase two. Much of our plan relied on this next sequence working correctly. Although every step in the plan was pretty brittle, I hoped luck would favor us. Once the lead tool was within ten meters, the pirate's suit must have alerted him to an imminent collision, because he jerked backwards to get out of the way. His partner wasn't nearly so lucky, because he dodged one tool only to jump into the path of another. I had thrown them hard. I'd been hit plenty of times in pod-ball and knew the feeling well. The suit would prevent permanent damage but he was going to have a nice shiny bruise to show to his other pirate friends. It was my only hit and I hoped it would be enough. Point Hoffen.

I fired up my arc-jets and scooted around the end of the stack of containers behind me. Just before I made it, I felt a burning in my thigh. I'd been shot. Panic coursed through me. I hoped I hadn't doomed us. "What were we thinking?" I refused to give in to doubt. Millie and others were dead, Dad was being shot at.

It turns out the shot to my thigh was a simple graze. The tear to the vac-suit was minor and it was able to repair itself almost immediately. The wound hurt like a bitch but I would live.

I ducked my head back around the container and saw the two pirates were halfway to my position. They were on a hard burn with their arc-jets, so I ducked behind the containers, not wanting to provide them another easy target. My training kicked in and then I started jetting between the containers. For a while both of them were completely stymied, trying to follow me through the maze. Then they got smart and jetted up above the surface for a clean look down.

"Birds are up!" Tabby called from her hidden position.

It was the signal I was waiting for. I dove between two closely placed containers, and slid down, careful to not touch the sides. I looked up to see the pirates glide over the top, five meters up.

"Give up, dumb ass," one of the pirates broadcast on a close-range channel. He was pointing his gun directly at me.

"Just shoot him. Who cares?"

The first pirate nodded his head and there was neither hate nor joy in his eyes as he took aim. I was looking into the eyes of a cold-blooded killer. Instinct compelled me to raise my hands.

Without warning, the two containers on either side of me shot straight up at high velocity. The pirates had just enough time to start turning away when the container they were directly over, rammed into them. Even as amazing as suits were, they couldn't absorb anywhere near that much kinetic energy.

Since there was no gravity on the station, the pirates and containers tumbled away on their new trajectories. I hoped they wouldn't hit anyone or any structure. Growing up in a mining colony constantly reinforced that launching something at a high velocity was dangerous and should be avoided. Today it had proved unavoidable.

"Man, I didn't think the gas bags would launch those containers so hard." Nick was breathing heavily from the excitement. Tubular gas bags were lined up neatly in two rows where the containers had been sitting just moments ago. When mining, we drill holes three meters deep, spaced a half meter apart. Then we drop gas bags into the holes and simultaneously blow the bags. The rapid expansion has roughly the same force as if we dropped in a couple of sticks of dynamite. We had unclamped the containers from the station, placed flattened bags under the containers and connected them to a gas supply. Nick hid, waiting for the pirates to get above the containers before he triggered the bags. I was the rabbit who drew them in and nearly paid the ultimate price.

"Take cover." Tabby's voice was as panicked as I had ever heard it. I tracked her movement and dove behind the containers. The attack ship's turret was tearing up the surface around us. The message was loud and clear. The three of us snuck back toward the station to gather equipment for the next phase of my plan.

Fifteen minutes later, the turret was still pointing at the yard, but no longer firing. I wondered how much damage the James' equipment had taken but didn't have time to dwell on it. People were dying and equipment could be replaced. It was a lesson my dad drilled into me. People were more important than equipment, period. No questions. It was a poor miner who forgot this lesson.

Tabby and I would be exposed for ten seconds on this next

round. There was no defense if that gunner picked up on us, the turret would rip us to shreds. On the plus side, we were nearly invisible with our dark suits and much smaller than anything an attack ship would be configured to track. It occurred to me too late that a pirate ship might be configured differently.

"Go," I whispered, for no reason other than stress.

Tabby and I jetted from opposite sides of a new stack of three containers on the edge of the yard. The goal was to manually free the bottom container's locking clamps so that they would be able to float in zero-g.

"Frak, it's jammed," Tabby swore.

Mine had detached easily but it wasn't uncommon for them to become stuck and Tabby had never spent much time working with clamps. I joined her and pulled out a pry bar I had strapped to my shin. We worked on the clamp and it finally gave way. We pulled back behind the containers, completely out of breath from excitement and exertion. We repeated the same exercise on two more container stacks without issue. I checked my HUD (Heads Up Display) and realized the attack had been going on for at least forty minutes. Not good. How long could Dad hold out?

"Remember. Three seconds apart. We have seventy meters to go before we are out of sight of that turret. We will hit open space at full speed, two seconds after the first shot," I reminded Nick. It wasn't necessary but it made me feel good. Nick was all about details. He didn't say anything and simply nodded back.

Tabby and I cautiously pulled ourselves back to our calculated starting position. We had done the math and knew where to start our attack on the ship. We were both carrying mining lasers and the extra burden made it hard to estimate, but then we had a lot of unknowns. I nodded to Tabby and we jetted along a path toward the ship. We were dodging containers so we had difficulty reaching our intended speed. "Nick, first salvo in three, two, one. Hit it!"

The three-stack of containers jumped forward, tumbling toward the attack ship on what I was afraid would be a near miss. Two seconds later, Tabby and I emerged from the cover of the rental yard and entered the open space between the yard and the attack ship at the base of the tethered control tower.

One second later, another smaller stack of containers broke loose and started tumbling toward the ship on a different trajectory. This one would miss by quite a significant margin. The gunner within the ship decided to be safe rather than sorry. He shredded the first containers with an awesome display of the turret's firepower and we were thirty meters from being inside the turret's minimum range. The third container fired off in yet another direction, but the gunner wasn't fooled. He quickly whipped the turret around, and the station floor was shredded by slugs as they ripped a line toward us. I heard Tabby yowl in pain as we crossed the boundary where the turret could no longer reach us.

"Tabby, talk to me," I shouted.

"Shrapnel. I got this. Stay on target!" she commanded.

I flipped over and burned hard to come to a stop directly under the ship's turret. Tabby was beneath the cockpit and we both had our feet on the skin of the ship. It was one of the advantages of being a spacer. Up and down didn't mean a thing to us unless there was gravity.

I attached my mining laser against the hull of the ship on the underneath side opposite the turret. I was able to set up much faster than Tabby, since I worked with mining lasers just about every day. I pulled a steel spike and null-hammered it into the plating of the ship. In less than fifteen seconds I had five spikes securing the laser tube. I pulled the power pack off my back and allowed it to float, set the laser to a depth of twenty meters, and flipped the switch. I figured the armor would be hard to penetrate, but we drilled through solid iron in the mines all the time. It might take a couple of minutes, but it would be going through.

I jetted over to Tabby, who was struggling to hold the mining laser straight while working the spikes in. I steadied the tube while she drove her first spike. With one already planted, she made quick work of the remaining spikes. She pulled off the laser's power pack and I dialed it to ten meters. She had chosen a spot beneath the ship's cockpit which wasn't as thick as the rest of the ship.

I looked back to the ship and saw with satisfaction that Nick had begun welding long strips along the door frame. He continued to add structure to his welds and I doubted the door would ever be useable again.

A bright light burst from the top of the gun turret as my laser broke through. Molten metal froze in puddles on the chamber of the now completely useless gun. Satisfied with his work on the door, Nick jumped down and welded the station clamps to the attack ship, turned brick.

"Nice job!"

"No celebrating at half-time," Tabby admonished, but her grin said it all. She was loving this as much as I was.

We looked up the length of the tether. The elevator was docked next to the control tower, but with the station gravity out, we wouldn't need the elevator to get up there. Disabling the perimeter defense guns was our last and most important objective.

"Grab the plasma cutter, Nick. Let's do this thing," I said.

Tabby and I both carried pressurized canisters that were about a meter tall and Nick had his welding rig that doubled as a plasma cutter. We glided up the tether toward the security control office. Down below, I saw the warm reds and oranges of the slagged metal.

The elevator was docked at the only door to the security control center. We would have to go through the elevator to get to the control room. Nick switched his portable welder to cutting mode and broke through the locked outside door. It didn't take much time, but it meant we had lost whatever element of surprise we might have otherwise had.

The door to the control room led to an airlock we could see through. The problem was, those inside could also see us. There were three people inside who were completely suited up. Two of the inhabitants were pointing long guns at the door. From the corner of my eye I caught the tell-tale signs of atmosphere being vented from the control room.

"They are venting," I informed Tabby and Nick, who both understood the implications. Once the atmosphere was vented, the pirates would be able to simultaneously open both doors of the airlock. There was no place to hide.

"Nick, get out." This was about to get real sketchy. I placed my pressurized canister directly in front of me, blocking the pirate's view.

Nick started to argue, but Tabby simply grabbed him and shoved him out the door.

"I got it," Nick shot back excitedly. "Get your canisters in the airlock when it opens. Trust me!"

There wasn't time to argue and the Loose Nuts pod-ball team thrived on running the play that was called. I had always told myself that I trusted Nick and Tabby with my life. Today I would prove it. The door opened and Tabby and I stuffed the meter tall canisters we carried into the lock. We pulled back just as slugs started hitting the elevator's walls and floor. My left leg exploded with pain just above my foot. It was like no pain I had ever felt and I had to fight to stay conscious.

Through the glass of the airlock, I saw a bright beam of light strike the back canister. Almost immediately, Tabby and I were violently thrown back into the windows by the force of an explosion. I felt Tabby's vice-like grip on my arm dragging me through the outside door. I was unable to focus, the pain in my leg was overwhelming, and I welcomed the blackness that invaded my diminishing vision. This must be what dying felt like.

AFTERMATH

Well, I clearly hadn't died. I woke up to faint nondescript music. My mind wandered, recalling that I had once heard this referred to as elevator music, which made no sense at all considering elevators were for moving materials, and lifts were for moving people.

I gagged when I tried to swallow. There was something in my throat and I desperately needed something to drink.

"Relax son. You are safe and you have a breathing tube. We'll get someone to take it out." It was my dad's voice.

I felt a squeeze from my right side. I was pretty foggy but I could tell that it wasn't Dad's hand since it was smaller than mine. It must be Mom.

The next time I woke up, tubes were being pulled out of my throat and through my nose. Unlike before, I was able to force my eyes open. I felt a squeeze from a warm hand on my right side. I rolled my head expecting to see Mom and instead saw Tabby. Her eyes were red and puffy and a tear rolled down her cheek.

Tabby doesn't cry. Period. Sure, maybe when she was three or four years old, but I guarantee never since then. I cried more than Tabby, not that I would ever admit it to her.

My mouth was so dry that I couldn't squeak out a question. I felt sore everywhere and had a giant throbbing pain just below my left knee. I reached toward it with my free hand but a stronger hand held my shoulder back. I had absolutely no capability to resist so I swiveled to look over at Big Pete Hoffen. He had a strained *I don't want to break him* look on his face. I don't know if Tabby's tears or my dad's face freaked me out more, but if I hadn't been so drugged up I would have probably figured things out right then. As it was, I just faded back into the pillow.

48

I felt gentle stroking on my right hand and opened my eyes. I was considerably less foggy than the last time. The throbbing in my leg was a significantly sharper and localized to just above my foot.

"My leg is killing me," I said, turning to Tabby. She squeezed my hand tightly and fresh tears all but squirted from her eyes.

"Liam ..." she started and then stopped, looking across the room.

Peripherally, I saw a figure stand up and my mom's soft cool hand grabbed my left hand. I turned to her, Big Pete sat on the edge of the his chair. Mom's nose was bright red and her eyes were also puffy.

"You guys are freaking me out," I said, but right then I had a moment of perfect clarity. Big Pete wouldn't be here if it wasn't something big.

"Liam ..." Mom started and then paused, her eyes searching my face for how to break it to me.

I put a hand up to stop her and turned to Big Pete. "How bad is it?" I was going to be strong for my family, they were suffering. It would be easier for Dad to deliver bad news and he wouldn't mince words.

"Liam, you lost your left foot just above the ankle. The damage was too much and there was no saving the foot. If not for Tabitha and Nick, you would have bled out in vacuum." His voice was strained.

I pulled up to almost sitting in the bed. I flashed back to the moment just before the explosion where I felt a slug tear into my leg. I turned to Tabby, concern lined her face. "Are you okay, Tabs?"

"I am so sorry, Liam."

"Tell me. Are you hurt?" I pushed. Tabby would lose her chance at the Naval Academy if she was hurt and couldn't leave on the M-Cor freighter.

"I'm fine," she said.

"Hardly." Nick joined in, unable to let her tough it out.

"The Academy?" I looked at Nick. He nodded positively.

I lay back, loss and relief spinning through my mind. The assault was my plan and if I had ruined Tabby's future, it would have crushed me. But what would my future be like without full use of my leg?

I was on some heavy pain killers, so leaning back, I dozed off again. When I came to the next time. Tabby was dozing in the chair next to me and Nick was sleeping on another chair. Mom saw me come awake and gave my hand a squeeze.

"Pete had to get back to the claim. The pirates took all of the platinum and most of the copper. M-Cor will be here in a week." It was another crushing blow. I had never seen my dad as happy as he had been when we hit that pocket of minerals. M-Cor wouldn't be back for months and we needed that big haul.

Big Pete would work himself around the clock until M-Cor showed up, to attempt to recover his loss. It was a testament to how critically I was injured that he had been here when I woke up last time.

"How much time do we have?" I asked.

"Five days," she replied.

"You should go Mom. He needs you."

We argued about it but she knew I was right. Our family was on the financial edge already. I was stable but couldn't help. She finally agreed and I fell asleep again. When next I awoke, Nick and Tabby were chatting quietly next to my bed.

"Hey, it's sleeping beauty." Tabby's face was no longer splotchy red.

A nurse came in to work on my leg.

"I want to see it." I pulled myself upright. Sure enough, just above where my foot used to be was a molded white cup with tubes and wires running into it. The throbbing had reduced considerably. With modern medicine, I was surprised that they were still drugging me. The nano-bots do a pretty good job of healing things quickly.

The nurse addressed me. "The doctor will be in this afternoon to talk to you. We have been overwhelmed since the attack."

"When can I get up?" I asked.

"Soon. We have been pumping you with sleepy drugs and those will stop today. This afternoon the doctor will fit your permanent cuff. You have some helpers here, so I expect you to be up on crutches this afternoon before the doc stops in. I wish I could stay and help more, but we are slammed. Tell your AI if you need anything." He didn't wait for my response, spun on his heel, pushed open a seam in the fabric wall and was gone.

I looked at Tabby and Nick with a bewildered look and we all started laughing.

"Fill me in on what I missed. I'm guessing our gambit worked."

Nick gave it the first shot. "After Tabby tossed me out of the door, I realized that I could open the bottles with the cutter by just hitting them through the control room wall. Once I hit it, the foam exploded into the room and trapped the three of them. You'll never believe it, but one of them was a deputy. It took an entire day to cut them out of the foam, but they all lived through it. Tabby pulled you out of the gondola and your foot was already gone and you were spewing blood like a fountain. It was disgusting, but she didn't waste a second and plastered it with suit sealer and then tied it off with a tourniquet."

"What about the refinery?" I asked.

"Well, once you were stable, we pinged Big Pete. Without their attack ship and the perimeter defenses, the pirates had to take off in the freighter quick. Most of them were able to get away, though Big Pete actually brought one down with his bare hands. They only got away with half of what they could have. They had loaded all of the platinum, gold, rhodium and were working on the copper when they decided to leave. They had to leave all of the iron and nickel behind."

"How bad was your yard shot up?" I was worried about the damage we had seen.

"Not completely sure, but Jack did a survey. We definitely had some losses, but we'll recover."

"I am sorry for dragging you guys into that. If I had lost either of you I would never have been able to forgive myself."

"Sack up Hoffen," Tabby said, clearly not wanting to go down any more emotional conversational paths.

"Roger that. Last we'll speak of it."

"So I've been doing some research and I have a crazy idea." Nick started.

Tabby and I turned to him, wondering what he could be on about.

Nick continued, "I did a serial search on that attack ship. You know, to see if it was stolen. There is no record of the ship one way or another. It's never been registered."

Nick looked at us meaningfully, but Tabby and I returned blank stares.

"Well, if it was stolen then it would go back to the original owner. If it belonged to a police force or the Navy, then it would go back to them. A ship that has no registered owner could be considered salvage. If the inhabitants don't claim it, we can make a rightful salvage claim under the Mars Privateer Act, which says that a ship forfeited during an illegal act of aggression could be salvaged by the defending force."

"Wouldn't that be the colony?" Tabby asked skeptically.

"Well, maybe. But I have been talking with Mr. Ordena, the lawyer we use for the shop and he thinks we have real shot at this. He will take it on for 30% contingency if you guys agree. What do you think?"

"Why not?" I looked at Tabby.

"Sure, I'm in," she said.

That afternoon the doctor stopped by and talked to me briefly about my injury. It wasn't an unusual injury on a mining colony and while a basic prosthetic foot was a bit expensive they weren't hard to come by. The cap already on the stump was nearly finished knitting my flesh back together, but I wouldn't be able to fit a prosthetic for at least a week. The rapid healing brought on by the cuff would allow me to be released in a couple of days. All I needed to do was learn to walk with crutches. Just like the nurse, he was gone in less than ten minutes.

I spent the next couple of days working with a physical therapist AI. I had thought it would be a person, but it turned out that people were in high demand. I arranged to stay with Nick on the station so I could make daily visits with the hospital staff. It was frustrating, spending hours at the hospital waiting for a five minute visit only to be told that things were progressing well.

On the day that M-Cor was scheduled to arrive, I got into my ore sled and headed out to O-92 where Big Pete and Mom were working to get everything loaded. Working around the clock for the last five days, they had loaded five containers. The yield was almost entirely iron with just a bit of nickel and copper. Nothing close to the big payload we'd lost to the pirates. With the ingots at the refinery already and this load of iron, Big Pete would be able to keep the operation going, pay for repairs, and retire some of his debt. Any chance of getting ahead had disappeared with that pirate freighter.

"It means a lot you coming out here, Liam." Now I knew Big Pete was tired. It was his second sentimental comment in as many weeks.

"I came out so I could run loads back to P-1. M-Cor is twelve hours out," I informed them.

"Liam, I need to be able to trust your answer. Shoot me straight on this. Can you make a run or would it be touch and go?" Big Pete wanted a look into my soul. He wasn't interested in me playing games of bravery, he wanted straight talk.

"Fact is, flying an ore sled is about the only thing I can do and I gotta do something. Let me do this." I knew I had to lay it out plain, nothing extra.

"Silver hasn't slept for over thirty hours," he replied. He didn't often use Mom's first name. It was all he was going to say on the matter, but he would accept my help.

We attached the containers to my sled and I filled them in on my recovery. Mom had a lot of questions, but wasn't tracking my answers very well. She repeated several of them to the point that I was certain of her exhaustion. I arranged to have Jack meet me at P-1 to help unload the containers.

I saw with satisfaction that as I took off for the refinery they had loaded into the other sled and were headed back to our habitat. It felt great to know that they trusted me with this responsibility.

Jack and I finished off-loading the containers an hour before M-Cor's arrival. The refinery would turn our raw ore into ingots over the next twelve hours, which was in plenty of time to be sold to M-Cor. Pride welled up in my chest thinking about how my parents had risen to this challenge. I checked in with the habitat to assure myself that they were safe and snoozing at home. It was also a relief to have not been thinking about my leg and doing something else for a bit.

Nick chirped my comm. "Heya, Liam, want to come over and check out the Control Center? It's crazy."

I met him next to the attack ship we had taken out. My mind flashed back to the stress of that evening and my leg throbbed sympathetically. I noticed with satisfaction that the ship's entry door had to be cut off and Nick's welds were still very evident. Nick told me that sheriff deputies cut the door off to extract the pirates who were trapped. They had given up pretty easily, having lived in their ship suits in vacuum for better than a day before anyone got to them.

My eyes followed the tether up. A new platform was lashed to the gondola and control room. Workers were working on the security control center at the top of the tether.

"Want to go up?" Nick offered.

"Think they will let us?" I asked skeptically.

"Hah. You haven't been out and about much. Liam, people are treating us like heroes. We're being given credit for stopping the attack, because who knows what they would have done once they finished with the refinery."

"Huh. Guess I didn't think about it that way."

The gondola met us at the bottom of the tether. Deputy Stella Bound stepped off and offered her hand. Fortunately I was balanced on my left crutch and I wobbled a bit when I reached to shake it. I mentally noted that I would need to be more careful about that.

Deputy Bound said, "Sorry 'bout your leg there. It's just, well, it's a real honor and I wanted to shake your hand. You kids did good work here, although you might not hear that from the guys upstairs. I don't think they're real happy about cleaning the station foam out of all of the equipment."

I didn't know what to say, so I just nodded.

"Load up. Let's get you a first class tour." She seemed to be in a good mood. "Never saw it coming ..." She let it hang there without specifying what it might be.

Nick finally gave in. "Saw what?"

"Sheriff Xid and Andy just didn't seem like bad guys. You know they were the inside guys, right? Andy shut down the perimeter defense and Xid held down the refinery staff with an automatic, ended up killing ten people. I wouldn't have thought either of them was capable of that, never in a million years." Deputy Stella Bound shook her head remorsefully. "Even worse is that Xid got away."

"How's that?" I turned to her.

"He was one of them all this time. Once you all shut down the guns from the perimeter defense, he loaded up into the freighter with the rest of them and took off."

"Any ideas on where they went?" I couldn't believe he had gotten away.

"Nah. They say it was Red Houzi, so I bet they ran off to some hideout. That ship is long gone," she replied.

The gondola arrived at its destination and Deputy Bound jumped off. A temporary work platform had been constructed next to the gondola and was filled with parts from the security control tower's one room. Two workers in suits were pulling the last pieces out. They couldn't pressurize the room until they removed all of the equipment. They were confident they could get things fixed in a couple of days and actually bore neither Nick or me any ill will. They even wanted to shake our hands.

A chirp notified me that a priority message was waiting. The M-Cor freighter had arrived. It would be docking mid station. *Track M-Cor*, I instructed and followed my heads up display. At thirty kilometers away it was still pretty small. It would take them the better part of two hours to dock up with the refinery.

For the next three days the activity around Colony 40 would go into overdrive. We were the second to last stop on the way back to Mars for the M-Cor ship and as a result it had grown to well over a kilometer in length. The freighter's design was similar to my ore sled. The front of the ship was dedicated to the flight deck and passenger quarters. The segments that trailed the passenger section were individual bundles of tightly packed containers. Each segment was joined with a coupling and could extend indefinitely.

The ship I was looking at was stacked using a 12 by 12 by 6 container cube format coming out to 864 containers per segment. I counted 14 segments with a small container trailing along. Between each segment was a tractor unit that provided thrust for nearly 120 degrees vertically and could rotate freely for 360 degrees horizontally. It was definitely a big one. The tractor jets burned brightly in deceleration mode. I couldn't imagine how much the cost of the fuel was.

There were two ways to ship with M-Cor. You could pay for the trip by mass or simply sell directly to the corporation. If you had good contacts at both ends, it was possible to come out ahead by shipping the materials and selling them to the market, but Colony 40 had a deal with M-Cor and we weren't allowed that option. We were free to ship other materials that way, just not ore or ingots. Dad explained that it would be hard to get M-Cor to make regular stops if they couldn't count on a good cut. As it was with the recent pirate action, M-Cor would not be at all pleased to have lost so much material. If they hadn't been so close already, they might have skipped us entirely.

GOODBYES

I was thankful for all of the activity that took my mind off my missing foot. I didn't feel any pain at all and had even inspected the stump without the medical cap on it. It looked like any other part of my leg. The doctor showed me a replacement prosthetic I would be able to wear. The least expensive technology could be manufactured on one of the station's replicators. It spent a considerable portion of my savings to buy the pattern. I knew my folks would want to pay for it but with their recent losses, I couldn't let that happen. I was a free EMC and didn't want to lean on my parents. Yup, I did just say that.

The break-in period for a prosthetic takes several weeks. This basic unit would interface with my AI and had the ability to mimic fairly realistic ankle and foot movement. I would never dance with it, but I would eventually be able to walk without crutches. Trying it on for the first time took me nearly two hours. It probably would have been easier if I had taken the doctor's advice and waited for a human physical therapist to help me learn how, but I was done with all that. My AI and I could get through this on our own.

Nick and Jack were at the shop with their mom, Wendy. Between M-Cor's arrival, new equipment coming in, and miners scrambling to make their final load, they were run ragged. Nick offered to let me use his apartment for the maiden voyage with my new leg.

I wasn't supposed to wear the prosthetic for three more days, but I wanted to see Tabby off to the Academy standing on my own two feet. The idea of her thinking of me as a cripple drove me like nothing else could.

I soon discovered the feedback you receive from an inexpensive prosthetic leg is extremely limited. For the first couple of seconds, I thought I had it down cold, only to discover I was leaning past the point of no return. At .6 gravity, the apartment floor showed me pretty quickly who was boss. Gravity was a bitch.

By the end of the afternoon my leg was unbelievably sore. It chafed where the cuff attached and hurt like crazy where the stub rested on the prosthetic foot. I hoped it wouldn't always be like this. I thought about taking some of the pain meds the doctor had prescribed, but I didn't like doing that. I would rather be sore than foggy. I removed the prosthetic (I couldn't refer to it as my foot yet) and headed over to the Gravel Pit, another diner/bar much like Millie's, using crutches.

It was hard to get through the crowd at the Pit. People stopped me to ask how I was doing, shake my hand and whack me on the back. All of these things play havoc with my balance and I was getting annoyed. Fortunately, Tabby saw me and knifed her way through the crowd. I was surprised by her new haircut. Her long copper hair had been cut off. She now boasted a flat-top with shaved sides. I wasn't sure what to think about that.

After a couple of "frak off" and "stow it dickhead" responses from Tabby, the crowd around us thinned out. Tabby had decided celebrity wasn't something she was interested in. I gave a couple of apologetic shrugs to some of the more offended, but I really didn't care.

Tabby grabbed my arm to help me through the crowd, but a short bark from me stopped her in her tracks. She settled for clearing a path back to the table where Nick and Mutt were sitting. It took us nearly ten minutes to get beer ordered.

"How did team Paradox Blue do? Didn't you play M-Cor One today?" Mutt had been pretty quiet since I arrived.

Mutt shifted his gaze uncomfortably from Nick to me. He knew our team, Loose Nuts, had been originally slated to play M-Cor One. Since we had to forfeit, Mutt's team took our place.

"They creamed us forty two ta twelve." Mutt hung his head.

"I watched. You guys hung in there solid in the beginning. It was the second half where you got beat down," Tabby offered analytically.

"Yeah, it was like they knew everything we were going to do before we did it. Solid team to be sure. I bet they play in the Central Core League back on Mars," Mutt said. The Central Core was a league that included the best teams from Mars, Earth's Moon and Earth.

"Yup, they do. Play under the name Red Monkeys," Nick said. "They are ranked pretty low, but that is in the semi-pro division of the Central Core league."

"Man, I would like to have had a shot at them," Tabby said without thinking, immediately regretting it. "Shite. Sorry Liam."

Both Nick and Mutt looked away uncomfortably.

"Knock it off Tabby. It is what it is. I would have loved taking a shot at them, too, but don't go getting all soft on me."

Nobody said anything for a few minutes. We didn't know what to do with awkward. I couldn't stand the silence, so I forged ahead.

"Look guys. I get enough of that sorry crap from everyone else. Does it suck that I lost my foot? Yes. Do I feel bad? Yes. Do I want to break down and give up sometimes? Yes. You know what I can't handle the most? Pity. So deal with it and move on. That's what I gotta do. You too."

Yeah, that was me, bringing the awkward. I let it sit there for a few and then decided to try a different tack.

"Tabs, when do you report to the ship?"

She seemed relieved to find familiar ground and looked down at a small display on the back of her forearm before replying. "2200 hours. I report an hour before burn."

"How much mass are you taking?" I was curious about how this worked.

"All in, I am allowed seventy kilos, which leaves me thirteen kilos after counting this svelte form. It's pretty much me, a case of clothing and some trade goods. Every kilo counts, so I will end up buying just about everything when I get there. I won't even be able to take my AGBs along, they're too heavy."

Nick piped up, "How long before the first semester starts?"

"Actually, I'll be two weeks late if M-Cor is on schedule. The Academy at Coolidge makes exceptions for spacers," Tabby explained.

"Any idea what Coolidge is like?" Mutt asked. It was a question we all had. None of us had ever experienced a real city.

"Beats the hell out of me. All I know is they have atmosphere over the entire planet. That's something I want to see." Tabby said. I agreed, it was such an odd idea that a person could walk outside and still have atmosphere.

"What's the gravity like?" I asked.

Nick piped up. "It is naturally .38, but most of the cities run generators to bump that up to .75."

We all knew about the problems people had with long term exposure to low gravity. In fact, none of us would find Earth to be comfortable given the normal .6 gravity we had grown up with. Apparently, a spacer could adjust over time, but that period was painful.

"They say you can't really tell the difference between .6 and .75 gravity," Mutt said.

It was well into morning when the crowd in the Gravel Pit finally thinned down to a handful. Tabby and I were sitting next to each other on a bench against the wall and Nick was draped over a chair. Mutt had long since given up on us, citing that he had a long day of work ahead of him.

At some point I'd reached over and taken Tabby's hand. I didn't want to make anything weird, but I was sad to think of her leaving and it felt natural. Instead of pulling away and making a sharp comment, she slid down a bit into the bench and laid her head against me. I knew it was short-lived, but I welcomed the warm feeling.

The Gravel Pit was a twenty-four hour operation and the manager didn't mind us taking up residence as long as we weren't sleeping. At 0200, we switched to stim drinks and water.

"How about we meet up at 1800 at the refinery to see you off.

I'm exhausted and can get four hours of sleep in if I head out now." Nick was barely holding his head up.

"Yeah, works for me. Want to walk him back, Tabs?" I said.

Tabby kept hold of my hand and I used her to maintain my balance as I maneuvered around a few tables. If she noticed, she sure didn't let on. We walked back to Nick's apartment, then Tabby and I watched the door close behind him. Without any warning at all, Tabby grabbed the sides of my face and pulled me in. It caused me to stumble a little, but she wasn't to be dissuaded. If it was awkward, I wasn't going to say anything. Her lips met my own and I closed my eyes, focusing on her warmth. Her lips parted ever so slightly. I pulled her in closely. With one hand behind her head, I allowed my other hand to slide down, resting just above her hip. I expected to feel her tense up, but she simply pulled me in even closer.

I found myself shifting, trying to deal with my body's response to her. Apparently, Tabby felt my growing excitement because she pulled back a bit and took a breath.

"Glad to see the bullet didn't get anything important," she said in a rough whisper.

"Sorry." I was a little embarrassed.

"Look. So... that isn't on the table tonight, but I'm leaving in fourteen hours and I want us to spend it together."

Classic Tabby. Don't worry about guessing what she is thinking because you will know it shortly. We made our way back to the apartment she shared with her dad. He was a member of the CO-OP board and was probably at the refinery overseeing the loading of cargo.

"You sure this is okay?" I asked, not wanting to incur her dad's wrath.

"Look, my problem. Not yours."

I didn't push it.

We lay down in her bed after she removed her station suit. She pulled the top shirt of her two piece suit liner off exposing a bra.

"Okay, that's as far as we go. Got it?"

I smirked. Oh, how I would miss this girl. I pulled her down on top of me and we started where we had left off. I spent the better part of an hour holding her and exploring her body with my hands and she did the same with me. We mostly avoided sensitive areas, although she was pretty curious. She did have a good idea of how far she was willing to go and finally we backed off and simply held each other, awaiting her pending departure.

At 1300, we woke to an alarm she had set. I sat on the edge of the bed while she readied herself for a shower. I was thrilled that she allowed me a small peek when she changed, but I knew better than to push it any further.

When she had finally changed into a fresh suit liner and pulled her suit back on we grabbed a small snack. I planned to spend every second I could with her until she took off. Why the frak hadn't we figured this out before yesterday? I mentally kicked myself, then laughed. I had lost my foot and this was my big regret. I felt so alive!

Her gear was already stowed in the freighter's passenger cargo area and she had a small bag that would stay with her on the trip. We walked back to Nick's apartment so I could shower and refresh my suit liner. I would have been willing to let her have a peek of me getting in the shower, but she didn't seem interested.

"Hey! Close your eyes. I want to show you something." It wasn't as important as it had been, but it was still something I wanted her to see. I strapped my prosthetic foot on and straightened my suit liner over the top. If I stood very still you couldn't notice a difference between my legs. My foot was another thing entirely, but this is what I had to work with. I positioned myself in front of where she sat with her hands over her eyes.

"Okay. Open up," I said triumphantly.

She looked me up and down for a moment and gave me a small grin. "Hah, look at you. I didn't think you would get to that for a few days."

It wasn't exactly the reaction I was hoping for, although in retrospect I wasn't sure what I was looking for.

"Don't you like it?" I asked, trying to keep the disappointment out of my voice.

"Sure I do," she answered.

I was confused and maybe a little hurt. She seemed completely unimpressed. I knew better than to whine at her but it just came out.

"Crap Tabby. I look normal, don't I?"

"Don't get your panties in a wad, Hoffen. Maybe you don't get it. Foot. No foot. Doesn't matter to me. If you weren't so darn dense, I wouldn't have had to throw myself at you last night. Imagine what we could have been doing if you would have figured that out a couple of years ago." Tabby looked at me, her eyebrows raised with a sort of school teacher disapproving look.

"Oh, geez, I want to space myself." I muttered.

"No kidding, right?" she replied.

Five hours couldn't have gone faster. We finally ended up at James' Rental and picked up Nick, who along with his mom, was suitably impressed with my prosthetic foot. The three of us loaded into my ore sled and made our way to the refinery.

I stood next to the gangway that Tabby would be walking up in a couple of minutes and felt an overwhelming sense of regret. We were down to kissing, at which point Nick definitely felt like a third wheel. He decided to head back to the sled. A chime warned the passengers that it was time for final loading.

We released each other and Tabby looked at me and delivered a knockout punch I would never forget, "Liam, I will always love you but get this straight. If you don't find yourself you will be no good to anyone. Live a good life my friend. I hope to see you again."

I was stunned and didn't even know how to respond. She gave me a peck on the cheek and a swat on the bum, then walked up into the freighter without so much as turning around. Wow, did she know how to make an exit.

TRIAL

Colony 40 falls within the jurisdiction of the Mars Protectorate. Roughly a tenth of the asteroid belt that occupies the space between Mars and Jupiter is under this Protectorate. The North American Federation has claim to fifteen percent, India claims another ten percent and China claims twenty. Other nations make claims, but have no capability of defending or enforcing their will in those areas.

The claims on these vast regions of space are generally a little ridiculous. The number of cubic kilometers in one percent of the belt is orders of magnitude larger than any individual nation. To most, however, claims of ownership appear to be an agreement between these nations more than some sort of patrol area.

The Mars Protectorate is much different. Mars was founded as a nation by representatives from each of Earth's countries. The history of the Mars Protectorate isn't much different than that of how the United States (predecessor to the North American Federation) was founded many centuries ago. Governments on Earth were making decisions for and about the citizens of Mars. The citizens rebelled. It was mostly a bloodless revolt, simply because Earth's nations didn't have the military capability to enforce their will over such a great distance.

Over the next several centuries, the citizens of Mars, under a single government, focused on building defenses and transforming the planet. It now had a breathable atmosphere and served as a busy base for the miners venturing into the asteroid belt.

With no other nations abutting, the threat of war was only possible across the vast expanse of space. The Protectorate was able to concentrate all of its security forces into a single entity which became known as the Mars Protectorate Navy. The Navy had two main missions. The first was defense and the second was as the peace keeping arm of the Judiciary.

A throbbing red light in my peripheral vision indicated I had received a priority communication. I nodded slightly, telling my AI to retrieve the message. The comm I received was in vid format from a Commander L.L. Sterra of the Naval Corvette *Kuznetsov*. The camera focused on a well groomed, middle aged woman in a dark blue flight suit. Her suit was adorned with a passant, also known as an epaulette, or shoulder strap, resting on the top of each shoulder. The passants were the same dark blue material as the flight suit and boasted gold stitching in the shape of a comet, complete with tail on the inside, next to the neck. Her rank was indicated by four bars stitched between the comet and her shoulder.

Commander Sterra's face was narrow. She boasted a thin nose and her hair was close cut, with the beginning streaks of gray. She seemed to be a very serious woman, but her voice was pleasant. I imagined that could change quickly.

"Greetings, Liam Peter Hoffen. Please listen to this recording in its entirety. You will be given an opportunity to respond to each of the charges at your formal hearing. First, you have the right not to respond directly to this message. Second, the responses you provide to this recording can be used as evidence in any matter before the Mars Judiciary. In order to listen to the contents of this message, you must first acknowledge these two rights by repeating them." She delivered these words as if she had said them many times before.

My AI prompted me, *I have the right of no response.* I repeated the words and heard a confirmation chime.

Any response I provide can be used in any matter before the Mars Judiciary, it prompted again. It took me a couple of shots to get it right and I wondered if my stumbling responses would be reviewed by Commander Sterra.

The image began speaking again, "Very good. There are three

issues concerning you for which I have been given judicial oversight." She looked down at a reading panel in front of her, "First, the matter of the deaths of Earth-Mars Citizens Gaben Fuse, Ajun Benda, and Liet 'Bobby' Zui."

She looked back to her pad, "The second matter is the destruction of property on Colony 40, specifically the removal of foam-sealing safety containers and the release of their contents in the security control tower."

I gasped and pushed the hold key, not wanting to inadvertently provide a reply. I was furious. This was a pile of crap. I stewed for a few minutes, but decided I needed to get through it, so I pressed play again.

"The third is the matter of privateer's claim of salvage filed on your behalf." Commander Sterra looked up from her tablet and her face softened slightly. "Liam, I urge you to obtain counsel on the first two matters. If you are unable to afford competent legal counsel, it will be provided to you at no cost. I have already been in contact with your counsel, Mr. Ordena, with respect to the privateer claim. I will arrive at Colony 40 within seventy-two hours to convene a court hearing. Sterra out." The video faded to black and cut off.

To say I was stunned was an understatement. I was accused of killing pirates and destruction of the station.

I pinged Nick, who was quick to pick up.

"Did you get a message from Mars Judiciary?" I asked.

"Yup, she must have sent mine first. I just got off the comm with Mr. Ordena," Nick replied.

"So what did he have to say?"

"He said we should ask for legal counsel from the Mars Judiciary. Commander Sterra was clearly giving us her opinion and we would be wise to take the hint. None of the lawyers on the colony have any experience with this type of thing. Ordena said he sure didn't."

I pondered this for a minute, "Do you suppose Commander Sterra brings a defense lawyer with her?"

"She'd almost have to. Look, we didn't do anything to the Navy so they don't have a reason to mess with us. I've already made the request. Oh, and you need to sign that thing Ordena sent you. Basically, we created a corporation between you, me and Tabby. Company name is Loose Nuts. Ordena said it gives us an edge in our claim. Just sign it, though. We need to have it before the Navy shows up."

I decided to take Nick's advice and requested a public defender. I also signed the document that had been successfully ignored in my in-box and sent it on to Mr. Ordena. "Have to admit I was surprised Sterra brought it up," I said.

"Mr. Ordena says it's a good sign. Commander Sterra had the authority to deny our claim of salvage without hearing arguments, but she didn't. That means she is considering it," Nick explained and then changed gears. "When will you be able to talk to Tabby?"

"They are still in hard burn. Radio transmissions are blocked for a couple of weeks yet."

Nick and I met up the next day to watch as the *Kuznetsov* was nudged into place by a seemingly never ending series of micro adjustments. At one hundred and twenty meters long, the Kuznetsov was shaped something like an arrow with six long tapered tubes strapped to the back third. A good portion of the surface of the ship was covered with turrets and missile launchers.

Spindly arms unfolded from the station and attached magnetically to several key points along the length of the hull. Docking collars from two different docking bays were extended and mated up to the docking rings of the *Kuznetsov*. The whole process took the better part of a couple of hours. Nick and I sat and watched from an observation dome a couple hundred meters above the equator of the station.

I finally broke the silence, "Frak, that thing is death on a stick."

I had never seen a ship that sleek. Most crafts on a mining colony were meant for moving large amounts of material from one place to another. A high premium was given to moving large volume and mass and virtually no consideration for the aesthetic. The lines of the *Kuznetsov* were sleek, the paint was a satiny black.

"It's all about sensor signatures." Nick broke my reverie.

"What do you mean?"

"It has clean lines so enemy sensors can't easily pick it up. Imagine if it was sailing directly at you. It would be nearly impossible to see. Its skin is all about absorbing and confusing sensors."

"Look at all those slug-throwers tucked into the side of the ship. I'd hate to get into a fight with that thing. Hard to imagine it's one of the smallest ships of the line."

Nick nodded in agreement and then changed the subject, "Did you get an invite to meet with a Lieutenant Commander Telish?"

"1800? Yeah. I think he is our public defender."

"Agreed. Let's head down there. I don't want to be late. We only have thirty minutes."

We rode a lift down to the same level as the docking bays. The station's docking bays were used every couple of months when family trading company ships would dock up. The trading companies created a lot of excitement on the station, filling the bay with trade goods.

The docking bay had the familiar black L-1 stamped on the wall. It struck me as odd to see it quite so empty. When a family trading company showed up, they spread goods across tables and many people moved between the tables looking at the trader's offerings. Everything from exotic food to ship parts and anything in between could be expected and the place took on a festive atmosphere.

Today the bay was almost completely empty. The *Kuznetsov* utilized two separate bays and all of the refueling and ship maintenance tasks were taking place in the lower bay. Two figures were standing by a docking ring on the space-side edge, otherwise there were no others in the bay. Nick and I crossed over and approached the occupants. Both wore armored suits and stood relatively motionless with their feet slightly less than a shoulder width apart.

The armored suits on our local sheriff deputies were nothing more than a bulky vest over a flight suit. The armor worn by these two was closely fitted and followed their body's every contour. It was thicker than a normal space suit, but rippled with the slight movements they made while waiting for us to approach. The armor had a similar satin textured finish as the ship and was the bright royal blue of the Navy. I correctly assumed they were Marines, as opposed to regular Navy.

The Marine on the left held a long-barreled weapon comfortably across her chest. One hand was on the stock with easy access to the trigger. The other hand gripped under the barrel. I was a little embarrassed to notice how well the suit conformed to her body. What must have been a well-muscled body was nicely highlighted by the slight extra bulk of the suit. Above her right breast was the text: Marine, above her left was the name: Gunders. She didn't have any rank insignia, which meant she was a private. She also wore a holster on her right thigh holding a pistol. Physically, she was very intimidating.

The Marine on the right had a rank insignia on his upper arm below the shoulder. It was two upside down Vs with the familiar Mars Protectorate Navy comet beneath them (I later learned this indicated the rank of corporal). I wasn't interested at all in how his suit fit, although he looked very tough as well. He also wore a pistol holster, but instead of a long gun, he held a reading pad. His name patch read Dahwan.

"State your name and business." Corporal Dahwan looked up from his reading pad.

"Nick James, Liam Hoffen to see Lieutenant Commander Telish."

The corporal held his reading tablet up, facing us, "Retinal scan."

Nick and I bumped shoulders, inadvertently both trying to comply at the same time. To the corporal's credit he didn't even crack a grin at our bumbling.

"Follow me." Corporal Dahwan turned and rotated the wheel-shaped chrome handle that disengaged the mechanism of the docking bay's airlock. The heavy door swung inward and we followed him down the telescoping hallway connecting the bay to the ship. The airlock door on the ship side required the corporal to push on a slightly inset panel within the door. The panel pulsed green a couple of times at the presence of his hand and then the door seal released, swinging into the ship.

"Gravity point nine five," the corporal informed us as he walked through the door. The additional gravity pressed my body down onto my new prosthetic ankle and foot. So far the nano-tech had done a great job of healing up and toughening my leg. I grunted into the pain. To take some weight off of my stub, I pushed down on my left crutch.

Once both Nick and I were through, the door closed automatically behind us. The hallway we entered was two meters wide and painted pearly white.

Stairs were something I didn't often encounter in the station. Fortunately, we must have entered mid-deck because the steps didn't go far. They only went two meters in both directions, although at a fairly sharp angle. In addition to the hand rails on the stairs, there were also handholds along the ceilings. It didn't take much imagination to think that sometimes they would be operating in zero gravity and the stairs would be just a pitched corridor. For me it was a new experience with my crutches.

Corporal Dahwan turned right and headed down the staircase. When he got to the bottom, he waited patiently for us to catch up.

"Take this, would you?" I handed my arm crutch to Nick and grabbed the two hand rails going down. I lifted my legs up and slid to the bottom. I pushed up with my arms and swung back to the ground neatly with a hop. The corporal raised a single eyebrow and gave me an approving nod. I appreciated it much more than the pity I expected.

It was hard to see these soldiers, most of them only a little older than myself, in a job I would never be able to have now. Not that I wanted a military career exactly, but it still hurt to think of how this injury had changed my options. I had promised myself that I wouldn't feel sorry for myself, but three lawsuits, a missing foot, and being almost entirely broke was taking a toll. Except for a few fantastic hours spent with Tabby, my spirits could not have been lower. Even those last great hours with Tabby came with the regret of knowing that I'd blown years of opportunity.

Corporal Dahwan stopped at a door marked L-10. He rapped on the door twice and stepped back. The door swung open, pulled by a tall, thin, middle-aged man.

"Nick James, Liam Hoffen. Lieutenant Commander Brandon Telish." It was an efficient introduction.

Lieutenant Commander Telish nodded to the corporal. "Dismissed." He turned and offered his hand to each of us in turn. "Pleased to meet you. Come in and have a seat."

He led us into a sparsely appointed rectangular room. On the far end, the ceiling curved down to meet the wall. We were obviously next to the hull. Lieutenant Commander Telish was my height and had to duck as he slid behind the metallic table attached at one end to the left wall. He gestured with an open hand toward a bench along the opposite wall. The commander took his seat behind the table. It was slightly cushioned and had arm rests, but no legs - it just sort of hung from the wall. It appeared that everything was meant to fold back up into the walls when not in use. Other than two reading pads on the table there was nothing else in the room.

Initiate Communication Bridge, Telish directed.

The wall to left of the table instantly popped to life with a crystal clear video image of Tabby, who looked a little startled. I probably looked just as startled as our eyes locked. Navy communications had to be quite sophisticated and powerful to pull off this link while Tabby's freighter was still in hard burn. Man, did she look great. It was crazy how I had gone from thinking of her as my buddy, to not being able breathe when I saw her. I wanted to bang my head into the wall. How I regretted not figuring out our relationship earlier.

"Greetings, Miss Tabitha Masters. I am Lieutenant Commander Brandon Telish of the Mars Protectorate Public Defender's Office. I assume you are alone in the room?"

"Yes, sir."

"Very good. As you can see, I have Mr. Nicholas James and Mr.

Liam Hoffen with me. If any of you would like to separate your defense you must tell me now. It is still possible to split your cases during the hearing, but these things can go pretty quickly and it would be expedient to know this right away." Telish folded his hands on the table in front of him and looked at each of us in turn.

After twenty seconds, he continued. "Very well. We have two matters to prepare for. The first is the deaths of three citizens: Gaben Fuse, Ajun Benda and Liet 'Bobby' Zui. The Colony's administration has filed a wrongful death suit on their behalf. The second is the willful destruction of Mars Protectorate property, along with a secondary charge of disabling safety equipment. I understand you have also made a privateer claim on the captured ship, but that is not something I will be able help you with at this time. I am defending the three of you, so whatever you tell me is protected by privilege. I cannot share anything you say with the Navy or the station administrator without your previous consent."

"The Colony Administrator had charges filed against us for defending ourselves against pirates and stopping an attack against our own station?" I wanted a good answer to this. It was ridiculous!

Lieutenant Commander Telish raised his hand to cut off my rant. "I appreciate and share your outrage on this, Mr. Hoffen, but we must deal with what has been done."

I knew these were serious charges and couldn't understand how this was even happening. We had defended the station, risked our lives, and I had lost my left leg. I knew corporations were without honor, but this was insane.

"There will be a discovery hearing first, at which time the Colony Administration, represented by one Harold Flark, will present their charges and evidence. There is significant evidence that shows your participation in both events, so I am certain we will go forward with a trial. Fortunately, this will be an expedited trial with Commander Sterra presiding. If we are not successful in our defense, you will have a chance to appeal."

Telish continued explaining the process, but I found myself fading in and out as my attention drifted to Tabby. She looked so real sitting there I just wanted to ...

"Mr. Hoffen?" I had missed something important since Nick jabbed my ribs to get my attention.

"Sorry. What?"

"I need you to fill out a statement detailing the events of that day. Be as detailed as possible. You can refuse to do this, but it is my opinion you have nothing to hide. Moreover, I believe that getting your perspective of the events into evidence will allow us considerable latitude. Discovery will be at 2200 this evening. It is 1830 now. Please complete your statements by no later than 1930. Miss Masters, I have arranged to have a ship's steward collect your statement."

"Okay. Could I talk to Liam and Nick privately before we close comm?" Tabby asked.

"No can do. Sorry. However at 1930, we can reopen comms for ten minutes."

Tabby nodded.

"Telish Out." Tabby's image disappeared from the wall in the room. The room felt stark and lonely without her.

"Please don't talk to each other while filling out your statements. I will post a Marine in the room while you complete them and they will be required to report if you share details." Telish handed us each one of the tablets. They were in writing mode.

Private Gunders, please report to L-10, he addressed his AI. Immediately, there were two sharp knocks on the door.

"Enter."

Nick and I turned to see Private Gunders enter the room in her armored suit, but no longer holding a long gun. She saluted Lieutenant Commander Telish, who returned it and left the room. Private Gunders stood a bit stiffly just inside the door and looked over our heads at the far wall. Nick and I turned back and started writing. An hour later we were both finished and Private Gunders collected the tablets without saying a word.

Tabby's face popped back up on the wall. The image was crystal clear. The Navy must have some incredible equipment to overcome the distance and interference from the freighter's engines.

"I think the corporation is after Dad's money," Tabby said.

"Are you kidding me? Does he have that much?" I asked.

"Seriously, Hoffen? My grandfather was an original claim holder."

"Then why didn't he get you a lawyer?"

"Apparently if convicted, we can immediately appeal it. He said it would be better to start with the Navy's public defender. Dad says Flark is playing with fire and doesn't know it. It is better if Flark gets burned this time."

"Flark? Like Harry Flark, school superintendent?"

"Did you forget about Colony Administrator? He is both. Remember?"

"Oh, right."

"One of the many things I love about you; you are completely clueless. I hope it doesn't get in the way of the Academy."

"And that is what I love about you, Tabs. Nothing breaks your focus."

"Frak, Liam, I am so sorry, I didn't mean it that way. It's just ..."

I cut her off, not really upset. "Don't you have to be broke to request a public defender?"

"I have two thousand m-creds to my name. I couldn't afford to buy coffee for one of my grandpa's lawyers. Dad says to trust the Navy on this, they have no love for corporations going after citizens for profit."

After the conversation with Tabby, Nick and I had a couple of hours to burn so we left the *Kuznetsov* to hang out at the Gravel Pit. I couldn't afford to buy anything more than a fizzy drink and a meal bar. I wasn't going to ask my folks for money especially since they had lost so much as a result of the pirate attack. I was down to my last couple hundred m-creds and I had medical bills that needed paying.

Somewhere along the line I had finally decided I wasn't going to be a miner. I might work for Big Pete for a while, but I would get off this sand pile one way or another. Today, I hoped it wouldn't be in the brig of the Corvette *Kuznetsov*.

At 2200, we were back on the *Kuznetsov*, but in a slightly larger room. I recognized Commander Sterra from her initial video communication. She was already seated at the end of a large table centered in the room. Lieutenant Commander Telish sat us at one side of the table and, this time, instead of a video projected on the wall, Tabby was projected in three dimensions. We could see the front of her as if she was there, but the image was only true to 220 degrees. On the other side of the table was Colony Administrator and School Superintendent Harry Flark.

Private Gunders stood to the right of Commander Sterra and was in the position I was beginning to associate with her; legs slightly less than shoulder width apart and hands clasped in front. I was startled when she spoke, since I had always seen her standing at attention.

"All rise." She waited for everyone in the room, with the exception of Commander Sterra, to stand up. I struggled a bit to gain my balance in the higher gravity. "Mars Protectorate Judiciary Court is in session. The Honorable Commander L. L. Sterra presiding."

In the video, Commander Sterra had taken up the entire screen, so I hadn't gotten a good reference for her size. In person, even though she was seated, it was easy to tell she was fairly short with the narrow build that was common for spacers.

The Commander's voice was a hoarse alto but not at all unpleasant. "Please be seated. Gentlemen, Lady." She paused while we took our seats, and then said, "This hearing is to determine if there is enough evidence to move forward with an expedited trial. I have video logs and affidavits that have been presented by the Station Administration Office and the defendant's statements. Is there any other evidence to be presented? Defense?"

Telish answered quietly, "No, your honor."

"Mr. Flark?"

"I thought we would have a prosecutor on this. Why don't I have a prosecutor?"

"Mr. Flark, this is just a hearing. If we get to trial we will bring in a prosecutor. In your current position, you have the responsibility of presenting the evidence. I understand you also have the required degree in law. Are you requesting to recuse yourself from this hearing?"

"If I did, what would be the outcome?"

Commander Sterra's lips pursed slightly, "I would rule on the evidence presented."

"No, I don't recuse myself. You may proceed."

Commander Sterra's head pulled back a centimeter with a slightly shocked look. "Very well. Defense proceed on the charge of wrongful death."

Lieutenant Commander Telish answered, "There are three deaths the defendants have been charged with. These occurred as part of two distinct actions. A careful review of the evidence shows Tabitha Master, Nicholas James and Liam Hoffen acted well within their rights to defend themselves and their family from an unlawful act of aggression and piracy. If you will allow, I would highlight an exchange between Liam and Pete Hoffen."

"Proceed."

Speakers in the room played back the conversation between myself and Big Pete.

"We are pinned down ..." my dad's voice said and Lieutenant Commander Telish paused the playback. A video played on the wall behind us of the pirates shooting at me while I was navigating between the containers. It then showed them rise up above the containers and take aim. Lieutenant Commander Telish stopped the video before the containers struck the two men. The video started up again and showed the slug-thrower from the small attack craft tearing up the station trying to find us within the field of containers. The Lieutenant allowed the video to continue until we launched the first stack of containers. The slug-thrower impressively tore it to pieces and then tracked along the surface of the station when the gunner discovered our ruse. Our narrow escape from the turret's reach was recorded with perfect clarity. The video continued, but at twice the normal speed. We watched as the three of us attacked the ship, lancing the cockpit and slug-thrower turret with mining lasers while Nick welded the door shut.

"In a trial we will show these highlighted events as both defense of their person and defense of their family. On the matter of wrongful death, the defense rests."

"Mr. Flark do you have any evidence you believe to be significant?" Commander Sterra asked neutrally.

"Yes. No. The point is that if these kids had stayed put, the deaths could have been averted."

I started to rise up, my temper going from quiet to boiling in the space of a second.

Commander Sterra caught me with her eye, "Not now, Mr. Hoffen." Her voice was like steel and I sat back heavily. She continued, "Mr. Flark, I will forgive your unfamiliarity with our proceedings, but this is a hearing where evidence is presented. In layman's terms you have the opportunity to provide a quick sketch of the evidence and how it builds your case. It is not the time for arguments. There is some latitude, but your comments are summary statements and not appropriate for this type of hearing. Do you have any evidence you would like to highlight or present on the matter of the wrongful death charges?"

Harry Flark looked down, slightly deflated. "Nothing further."

"Very well. On the matter of willful destruction of Mars Protectorate property and the secondary charge of tampering with safety systems of a public space? Defense?"

"Defense rests."

I glanced sharply at the Lieutenant who simply looked forward with his hands resting on the table.

"Mr. Flark?"

"Oh, yes. Please show the video sequence of the kids removing the foam containers from the dome breach."

Commander Sterra looked over to Lieutenant Commander Telish, who navigated to a video sequence showing us taking the canisters of station foam from around the opening where they had failed to deploy.

"Good. Thank you. Also show where the little one punched a hole in the bottles with a welding torch and damaged the security control room."

"Objection, your honor. Would you instruct Mr. Flark to refer to the defendants respectfully? 'Kids' and 'Little One' are both prejudicial references."

"Sustained. Mr. Flark, you will refer to the defendants as either the defendants or by their individual names. It is also acceptable to shorten this with a title such as mister or miss while using a surname. Do you understand?"

"Fine." Harry Flark appeared aggravated. "Show the video already."

A view from within the control room showed the door of the control room open and a pirate lower a long gun and fire the round that ripped my leg off just above my foot. I grew hot and grabbed the table in front of me, barely feeling the cold metal. Sweat broke out on my forehead and I fought to contain my stomach's contents. Nick placed his hand on my shoulder to stabilize me. It barely worked. I had woken up several times with this nightmare running through my mind.

The video started from inside the security control room with a view of Tabby and I standing outside the air-lock. We were holding station foam canisters. The pirates were shown firing into the air lock. A bright light lanced through the side of the air-lock and the canisters exploded, filling the room with station foam. Almost instantly the camera picture went white. I laid my head down on the table, wishing to be anywhere but here. The all too familiar throbbing in my leg threatened to overwhelm me.

"Mr. Hoffen. Ten minute break?" Commander Sterra's voice had lost its edge.

I looked up, immediately aware of everyone's eyes on me. I wiped the tears that burned from under my eyes and sat up straight. "No, ma'am. I am fine." I would not give Harry Flark any further satisfaction. What an ass-clown.

"Any further evidence to highlight on either charge from the defense?"

"Yes your honor. I would like to show one final video sequence." The video was of one of the perimeter defense gun turrets actively shooting at a position on the P-1 refinery. After less than a minute the turret rotated away from the refinery and powered down.

Commander Sterra reconvened the hearing at 2400. Nick and I were pretty wrung out. I hadn't expected this to be so exhausting.

"I am dismissing the charges of wrongful death. Tabitha Masters, Nicholas James and Liam Hoffen acted without concern for their own wellbeing and it is the opinion of this court that they saved numerous lives. A report will be filed prejudicially against Station Administrator Harry Flark for his handling of this issue."

"Why, you bitch!" Harry Flark jumped from his chair and started toward Commander Sterra. Private Gunders' reaction was quick and efficient. She stepped between her Commander and Flark, jabbing a palm into Flark's solar plexus. He stumbled back and doubled over, dropping to his knees.

"Private Gunders, would you escort Mr. Flark into the hall so he can compose himself?"

When Gunders returned with Flark, he was quiet.

"Let's continue. This court also dismisses the second charge of willful destruction of Mars Protectorate property and the subordinate charge of tampering with a public safety apparatus. It is clear from the presented evidence that the security control tower was no longer under the control of station authority. Moreover, it again shows extraordinary bravery and selfless action on the part of Tabitha Masters, Nicholas James and Liam Hoffen. Mr. Flark, I would have expected a person in your position to have been lining up to pin medals on these new citizens. Instead, you chose to bring suit against them. If it were in the jurisdiction of this court, I would find that you are a despicable human being. Sadly, it is not within my purview. I do, however, thank you for providing an opportunity to Private Gunders to enforce the strict discipline of this court."

"Finally, I find you, Mr. Flark, to be in contempt of this court and sentence you to a night in the *Kuznetsov's* brig. If by 0800 tomorrow you are able to supply this court with an apology, you will be released. Private Gunders, please escort the prisoner to the brig and make sure he is comfortable. Court dismissed."

Once Flark had been removed from the room, Commander Sterra stood up. I struggled to a standing position, the .95 gravity of the ship still throwing me off. The commander stepped toward me and stuck her hand out. I shook it.

"I have seen bravery and loyalty in my career. It is what fuels my faith in my comrades and provides me solace when faced with the likes of Mr. Flark. The three of you demonstrated what I find to be the best of humankind and it is my honor to have made your acquaintance and to have witnessed your heroism." She turned to Nick and offered her hand. When she turned to Tabby's image she saluted. "Miss Masters, I look forward to following your career in my Navy."

"Lieutenant Commander Telish, when did you schedule the Loose Nuts privateer claim?" Commander Sterra asked.

"1300 tomorrow, Commander."

"Looking forward to it."

I thought I might collapse from the roller coaster of emotions of the day and then remembered that Tabby was on video.

"Miss you."

"Damn right you do." The video blinked off.

PRIVATEER

It was 0930 and my alarm was ringing. I had sacked out on Nick's couch again, since we had a meeting with Mr. Ordena this morning about our privateer claim. If the last couple of days were any indication, I wouldn't be looking for a career as a lawyer.

Mr. Ordena was a pudgy man with unruly, wavy brown hair. He was the same height as Nick, half a head shorter than Tabby and me. On a space station one thing is certain, vac-suits are not flattering to the pudgy. He wisely wore a short coat over his. We had arranged to meet at the Gravel Pit at 1000.

"To the best of my reading, the privateer act allows citizens to attack enemy combatants during wartime. Captured ships are declared as prizes and citizens can take ownership of those prizes. The good news is that Mars Protectorate enacted a Privateer Act over a century ago. The bad news is that you have to apply for a Privateer License. It's called a Letter of Marque."

"Does that mean we don't have a chance?" Nick asked.

"Not necessarily, but there is an additional problem. The ship in question isn't specifically identified as an enemy combatant ship. If you had a Letter of Marque and the ship was clearly identifiable as an enemy combatant you wouldn't need me at all. Last week we formally submitted an application to the Mars Protectorate for that Letter of Marque."

"Can you do that after the fact?"

"It isn't clear, but nothing specifically forbids it. I found examples of a letter being issued no more than a couple of days before a prize was claimed. It's an older law that isn't often exercised. If not for young Mr. James here, I wouldn't have even known such a thing existed."

81

I was disappointed that Private Gunders wasn't standing watch on the door to the *Kuznetsov* when we arrived. A Marine private by the name of Betendorf escorted us through the Corvette's hallways. We ended up back in the large courtroom we'd occupied the night before. The room was empty other than the table and chairs, but we were a few minutes early at Mr. Ordena's prompting.

At 1300 on the dot, the door opened and Commander Sterra entered the room. I had read about command presence before, but this small woman defined it. It was impossible not to stand when she entered the room.

"Gentlemen, good to see you again. Mr. Ordena, I don't believe I have had the pleasure." She offered her hand. The contrast between her impeccably neat suit and hard narrow features and Mr. Ordena's sloppy hair and chubby build was hard to miss.

"Please have a seat." We all waited until she had made her way to the head of the table and sat down.

"There are two issues in front of us today. The first is an application for a Letter of Marque under the Mars Protectorate Privateer Act by the trading company Loose Nuts. The second is a claim of prize on an unnamed cutter class attack vehicle.

"Mr. Ordena, I appreciate the references you have forwarded to me. Would you like to make a formal statement before I rule on this issue?"

"Ah. Yes, ma'am. As you know, the Privateer Act was put in place to allow citizens to protect themselves against outlaws and foreign governments. It was created during a time when the Mars Protectorate Navy was unable to provide adequate protection due to the vastness of space."

Commander Sterra steepled her fingers thoughtfully and nodded her head for Mr. Ordena to continue.

"Corporations have always been allowed to protect their trading and industrial ships from attack. What the Privateer Act added was an active incentive for these corporations to capture enemy ships and bring them back as prizes. The act specifically states that the prizes are to both reimburse the corporations for losses and be considered a source of profit. It is one of the few points of Mars Protectorate law where the profit motive is referenced or encouraged. Finally, the Act allows for a corporation to be formed specifically for this purpose."

"Is there no requirement for military experience or some sort of competence?" Commander Sterra asked, though it seemed she already knew the answer.

"No ma'am. The corporation is still bound by all laws of the Protectorate. If they fire on a non-enemy ship, it is a crime just as it would be if they did it without a Letter. The Protectorate does not assume any new liability."

"That is how I read it also, Mr. Ordena."

After an additional thirty minutes, Mr. Ordena finally completed his presentation.

"Thank you, Mr. Ordena. That was both informative and well considered. The Navy provides me with a tremendous amount of latitude when granting a Letter of Marque. I am not blind to recent events, but I am also not willing to encourage an atmosphere of vigilantism. These are the issues I have struggled with. That said, I am pleased to grant your petition for a Letter of Marque to the corporation Loose Nuts. It is the opinion of this court that the Privateer Act was created to foster exactly the actions of corporations such as Loose Nuts."

"As to the second issue, the claim of salvage, I assume you would like to register this as a prize claim?"

"Yes, Commander," Ordena said.

"How do you reconcile the timing difference between the Letter of Marque issuance and the actions that caused the capture?"

"Could I present evidence?"

Commander Sterra grinned. "Certainly."

Mr. Ordena typed on his arm band and we all heard Nick's voice, "Sure, easy, line of sight. Secure Loose Nuts Channel One, Initiate." It was a recording of when Nick, Tabby and I had started discussing our plans to defend the station.

"The time code on this is just after Liam heard from his dad that they were being attacked by pirates. Nick James clearly identified a corporate action by establishing a secure tactical channel."

"Impressive, Mr. Ordena." When Commander Sterra smiled it seemed like the entire world lit up. "The Mars Protectorate Navy awards the prize of the unnamed cutter class vehicle currently welded to the top of the Colony 40 station. As it stands, the Navy has no interest in purchasing the vehicle but will award a sum of one hundred, eighty thousand Mars Credits to the corporation Loose Nuts for the missiles already seized from that ship for safekeeping. The ship and its contents are now property of Loose Nuts Corporation. With that, this hearing is adjourned.

Point Ordena.

Commander Sterra stood and we followed suit.

"Mr. Hoffen, Mr. James. The *Kuznetsov* will be docked for at least two more days. I would very much like a chance to meet with you both in a more relaxed setting. Would you consider an invitation to dinner aboard the *Kuznetsov*?"

Nick and I exchanged a quick glance. "Uh, yes ma'am. That would be great," I said.

"I will have the steward contact you with arrangements." She smiled, turned and exited the room.

"Anyone for a steak? My treat," Mr. Ordena offered.

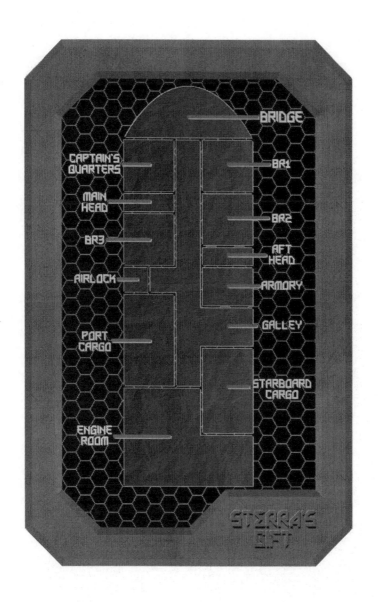

CAPTAIN'S
QUARTERS

MAIN
HEAD

BR3

AIRLOCK

PORT
CARGO

ENGINE
ROOM

BRIDGE

BR1

BR2

AFT
HEAD

ARMORY

GALLEY

STARBOARD
CARGO

SIERRA'S
GIFT

85

STERRA'S GIFT

"I want to sleep on the ship," I told Nick on the way back from dinner with Mr. Ordena. We were in high spirits, having had our fill of rich food and wine. I was having a lot of difficulty navigating with my new foot, (probably because of the wine) but I felt absolutely great. We had our very own ship.

"I don't think it can hold atmo," Nick replied.

"Oh, right. I guess I should have remembered that. Then maybe we should lock it up."

"Navy already took care of that. They welded a lock on the door."

"Man, I still want to go take a look at it. How do you think we can get the combo?"

"Sterra already fixed that. The locks are I-dent scanners. She added us."

"When did all of that happen?"

"Pinged her while we were at the Gravel Pit. I wanted to get an inventory put together. By the way, did Tabby mention that she declined to be part of Loose Nuts?"

"What? I can't believe she didn't tell me."

"Yeah, she didn't want me to say anything. Didn't want the distraction."

"Weird."

We had taken a lift up to the Mercantile. I looked straight up the eighty-five meters to where the Atrium's transparent dome used to be. The foam had been replaced with thick steel panels and the atrium was holding pressure, but I wondered if anyone would ever have the courage to replace the steel with transparent panels again.

"What should we call it?" I asked, as we made our way over to an elevator that would take us up to the level where James' Rental was.

"The Navy names smaller ships after naval heroes. Private ships can be named just about anything." Nick said.

We stepped onto the elevator, *Level one*, I instructed.

"How about *Old Millie*?" I asked.

"Nice. How about *Sterra's Gift*?" Nick countered.

"Perfect."

We walked through the front door of James' Rental and Wendy looked up from behind the counter.

"That took longer than I thought. Must be good news." Wendy was a middle-aged woman, solidly built and even shorter than Commander Sterra. Her hair, originally jet black, was streaked with gray and she had the same quick cadence to her speech as her son. Nick and I had been friends since our first day at school and she was like a second mom to me.

"We're in business, Mom. Liam and I own that ship we captured. We were headed up there now. Anything critical you need?"

"No. You boys do your thing. Liam, you have a shift in you tomorrow? I have some deliveries and I can send Jack along to load."

It wasn't the first thing on my mind but it was hard to turn her down. "Sure, Wendy." Years ago, when Nick's dad had passed away, Wendy had gone through a rough spot. She took over the rental business and raised Nick and Jack on her own. From that point forward, she made me call her Wendy. It had taken time for me to get past the whole Mrs. James thing.

Nick and I headed through the store and found Jack in the back, moving equipment around.

"Hey bud, wanna go check out that ship with us?"

Jack looked up with a smile and came over to meet us.

"Think that's okay?" I looked at Nick.

"I'll ping Mom, but he can come back in a few."

The three of us jumped on the big lift leading to the top of the station. Nick engaged the safety protocols and our masks closed, causing my ears to pop. When we got to the station's surface, I could see all the damage the pirates had caused.

"Crap Nick, how much damage did you guys take?"

"Seventy-five thousand. Insurance will cover sixty of that."

"What about the other fifteen?"

"They are saying that was the damage we caused and they won't cover it."

"Fifteen thousand? Really?"

"Yeah. We ruined a handful of containers and one of the mining lasers was pretty junked up. It adds up."

"Seems like we should pay that back, don't you think?"

"Probably. Mom won't ask, though. She told me not to talk about it."

"Not how I want to start a company. We pay our bills. You think fifteen thousand is fair?"

"Yup."

Sterra's Gift was thirty meters long and looked a little sad. The main entry door showed significant scarring from Nick's original welding job and its subsequent ripping off by the Sheriff's deputies. The surface of the ship bore no comparison to that of the Navy Corvette. The angles were sharp, the paint was scored, and welded patches were everywhere.

The ship had a straightforward design. Like the *Kuznetsov* it was narrower at the front. The three main engines were located aft and integrated into the hull. Two were located at the bottom of the ship on both sides and the third was on top in the middle.

The cockpit was located on the front with missile launchers mounted underneath. The nose of the ship was rounded and three meters wide. The ship widened out to ten meters after you got past the cockpit.

Just in front of the midpoint and almost directly behind the entry door, was the slug-throwing turret. I could see the melted slag where I had driven the mining laser. Now that I owned the ship, I wondered if I could have been a bit gentler with the damage.

The Navy had applied a field repair to the door and put on a sophisticated lock. Nick registered with the lock and the door swung inward unsteadily. We were in a vacuum, but I could imagine the unhappy squeal of poorly matched up metal hinges. I was surprised to see a green bar and an orange bar on the interior door frame. It was one of a few universal indicators for airlocks. The green bar with the word ATMOS in its center, indicated there was pressure on the other side of the door. The orange bar which read VACUUM indicated a lack of pressure on our side.

The airlock was designed for one or two people and the three of us were a tight fit. Nick closed the exterior door and sealed it. I was curious at how well it might hold. I pushed on the orange panel expectantly. Nothing happened.

"I think it's busted."

Nick stepped in front of me and peered at the panel. He looked around for something and apparently didn't come up with it.

"Hang on, there's junk in it."

He reopened the exterior door and hopped out. He was wearing his AGBs and bounded across the top of the station. I wondered when I would have the courage to try that again.

He returned with a tool belt strapped around his waist.

"How about you guys give me some room?"

Jack and I walked back down the ramp. Nick closed the door behind him and cycled the lock. Ten minutes later both Jack and I were getting impatient. Well, truthfully I was impatient. Jack was leaning against the ramp.

While Nick worked on the door, I hunched down and walked beneath the cockpit. I was curious about what had been used to seal the hole Tabby drilled with her mining laser. The hole was wider than I would have anticipated. During the attack, we hadn't turned the drills off, so they kept running until they eventually overheated or ran out of power. There was something similar to station foam in the holes, but it resembled thick frozen syrup.

"Got it," Nick informed us.

"What was the problem?" I staggered out from under the cockpit.

"Grime. They were caked with junk."

Jack and I cycled through the airlock. As soon as the bar changed from orange to green, the door swung outward, revealing the small airlock. Nick was standing on the other side of the door which had previously been locked.

This was exciting. I admit to being a glass-half-full kind of person. I would like to say I immediately noticed the million things that were wrong with the ship, but that wasn't even close to the truth.

There wasn't any lighting in the short hallway. Our suits provided enough glow for me to see our surroundings. We stood on a diamond-patterned steel floor, worn in the middle by hundreds of foot treads over the years.

The airlock was located mid-ship. When I stepped into the main hallway, I looked to my left and saw the opening to the cockpit so I headed toward it.

"I'm headed up to the cockpit. How are the O2 levels?" I asked.

"Not sure. I have to enter the command codes Sterra gave me on the master console and then we'll have control of the ship's AI. I'll head to the engine room." Nick turned in the opposite direction and walked away. The light in the hallway lost some of its intensity when his suit was out of range.

"How about seeing if you can get some lights on, first?" I called after him and placed my hand on Jack's shoulder, "You coming?" He responded with a grin.

Jack followed me down the hall toward the cockpit. The doors on either side of the hallway were open and random junk littered the floor. It was complete chaos. Each of the small rooms we encountered on the left and right of the hallway were littered with trash and personal effects. I might have attributed it all to messy pirates, but the mattresses looked like they had been slashed and the stuffing removed. Crap.

There were three bunk rooms that were almost identical. Each had twin bunk beds along the outer wall and next to the door was a small desk with pull-down chairs and shelves deep enough to hold a couple of foot lockers. It was a cramped space. They were labeled BR-1, BR-2 and BR-3. BR-1 was opposite the captain's quarters, BR-2 was aft of that and BR-3 was opposite BR-2, aft of the main head.

It was messy, but my sense of exploration and wonder kept my spirits high.

The room before the cockpit was the same small size, but had a single slightly larger bed. It was raised off the ground to nearly eye level and attached to the aft end of the room. A desk surface and cabinets were beneath it. The forward side of the room had a beat up couch that had also been torn apart, its stuffing littering the floor. I mourned the loss of the couch, as gnarly as it was. The room was as filthy as everything else, as if wild animals had recently been residing there.

This had to be the captain's quarters, but it wasn't my final destination. I didn't know exactly what to expect at this point and was both excited and nervous about what we might find ahead. After all, Tabby had stuck a mining laser through the cockpit only a few days ago.

When I opened the door, I realized this wasn't simply a cockpit, but rather the bridge of a real ship. At the front it was three meters wide with rounded corners and separated into two levels. The upper level had a narrow walkway leading down to where you might expect pilot chairs to be located. On either side of those spaces, instrumentation panel brackets hung from the walls where vid screens had been not too gently removed. The two large pilot chairs had been ripped out of their housing and dumped over. The top level was where Jack and I were standing. There were two seats - one on the left and another on the right facing inward, and more brackets boasted either broken or missing vid screens. The chairs, which weren't much more sophisticated than bar stools with wide bases, had been left completely untouched.

Starting at the bow of the ship, armored glass was at knee level for a seated pilot and followed the line of the hull, stopping a couple of meters from the back wall of the bridge. The glass was cut into geometric panels and joined with alloy mullions, creating webbing above the pilot's seats. The view was amazing. The pilots had an incredible view forward, overhead and to the sides. There were plenty of blind spots, but that was what the vid panels were for.

I found the hole Tabby had drilled with the mining laser. Someone had placed a hasty patch of that same syrupy-looking material I'd seen outside and allowed it to drip into the cockpit. Just like the rest of the ship there was litter everywhere.

"So, I say we sleep here tonight!" I piped up and looked at Jack's smiling mug. He was a great guy to have along if you wanted positive affirmation.

Nick's reply sounded a little hesitant, "Really? What's it look like up there? The engine room is trashed. It's like someone was looking for something and wanted to make a mess all at the same time.

"How bad?" My cheerful bubble was in real danger here.

"Pretty bad. You should come back and take a look."

I shrugged to Jack and headed aft to the engine room. I passed the hallway to the airlock on the port side and wondered about the closed mystery door to the starboard. There was an open space that had some hookups for things I couldn't initially determine and a door to the head.

Two more open doors led to empty rooms, except for the ever-present trash. The final door at the end of the hallway was open and lamps were shining up from floor level. Nick had his head jammed up under a bulkhead.

"They ripped out all of the storage and navigational equipment. And I mean ripped. They removed a few bolts, then yanked it. The wires aren't just snapped; some of them are stretched. They must have had a powered suit to put this type of force into it," Nick complained, holding up a cable.

"You think the Navy did this?"

"Doubt it. What would be the point? They have engineers and tech-bots that could take this thing apart in no time. Probably someone who didn't want the Navy to get whatever info they had on that computer equipment."

"Will it fly?"

"No way. I'm no expert, but there are more missing systems than I care to count. They did, however, leave the life systems intact. Right now this is more of an apartment than a spaceship and the hull has more patches than hull. I can see why the Navy wouldn't want it. By the way, you know Ordena owns 30% of it too, don't you?"

"Yeah, geez. It's still gotta be worth something though, right?"

"Not sure. Scrap value at least. Only real way to tell is by doing a full inspection. At a minimum, we should get it appraised."

"Hmm, no reason to clean it up before the appraisal if Ordena has a cut. Let's get him to walk through it and see what he wants to do. Want to sleep here?" I had lost most of my enthusiasm.

"Not without spraying for bugs. This place is disgusting."

I spent the night on Nick's couch again. Before sleep, Nick left a message for Ordena and Commander Sterra's steward. The steward got back to him immediately and suggested a 2200 dinner on the *Kuznetsov*. It was pretty late for dinner, but Nick and I had promised to take a shift at the rental store.

Big Pete hadn't been on me about helping at the claim recently. I suspected it was a combination of the loss of the shipment, my injury, and that there would be no payday for another four to six months. No doubt he was still out there going at it hard, but he was giving me some room for a while.

The next morning Ordena got back to us and arranged to meet us in front of the newly named *Sterra's Gift*. He was bringing a ship mechanic along with him.

"Xie Mie-su, meet my two favorite clients of all time, Nick James and Liam Hoffen."

Xie was a slight, Asian featured woman. Her straight black hair was pulled back so it was impossible to see how long it might be behind her vac-suit's helmet.

"Nice to meet you. Any friend of Jeremy's is a friend of mine, I always say. But then he's a lawyer and how many friends can you really have as a lawyer?" Xie's voice was laced with humor. Her face lit up as she spoke and she ended by punching Ordena in the arm. Jeremy? I didn't think I had ever heard Mr. Ordena's first name.

"What? Now we're not friends?"

"Aww, you know we all love you Mr. O." She turned back to me. "You see, Mr. O here got me outta some hot water a while back. Bad stuff, I tell you. I owe this big guy a lot, but it doesn't mean I can't pick on him, does it?"

I was starting to wonder if Xie had a stop button.

Nick interrupted. "It's quite a mess in there."

"Yeah. I brought Ms. Mei-su over to take a look. Not that I don't trust your assessment and all, but it's best to leave this type of thing to the professionals.

Xie spent time on the outside looking at the engines. Her earlier chattiness had all but dried up. Nick followed her around and they got pretty engrossed in all manner of detail.

"Mr. O." I liked how it sounded when Xie used it so I tried it on. "How about we check out the rest of the ship while they are looking at the guts?"

"Heck of an idea, Hoffen. I haven't the faintest idea what they are babbling about back there."

I nodded knowingly. While I felt like I had some knowledge about ships, Nick was by far the better of us with mechanical things. My answer was generally to get hold of a diagnostic algorithm and let the AI walk me through it. I know that's not as good as being trained, but I managed. Nick had trained on all sorts of machinery. He had never worked on a ship this large, but most of the systems were familiar to him.

After a tour of the front of the ship, I decided it was time to open the mystery door opposite the airlock. I knew it was near the gunnery nest and was hesitant to see the damage I had done. I had killed a man in there and was ashamed at how afraid I was to see inside. Don't get me wrong, the pirate had it coming by making it his own personal mission to kill us. Knowing that still didn't make it any easier to open that door.

"Is that where it happened?" Mr. Ordena's voice was softer.

"Yeah, I'm a little afraid to see what's on the other side."

I wasn't about to sit around and wallow in it, so I pushed the door open. The room wasn't large, just a chair sitting under a domed roof with a locking hatch separating it from the room below. I had run the mining drill right up through the chair on one side. The laser would have ripped right through the gunner.

"Wow, that's a lot of ammo."

It wasn't the very last thing I had expected to hear, but darn close. He was right. The walls of the room had deep shelves with cases and cases of ammunition. A quick inspection revealed that most of the boxes were full. There were also four empty missile racks.

Mr. Ordena continued, "I bet that's worth more than this ship to the right buyer."

"Seriously?" It didn't add up to me.

"No doubt in my mind. It's not illegal to own slug-thrower ammo. I'm surprised the bastards who tore the place up didn't steal it. Probably didn't have time. It's hard to hide a couple of tonnes of ammo crates. The ammo is probably worth a hundred-fifty thousand if we could sell it on Puskar Stellar or Bura Manush."

Bura Manush, another mining colony, was significantly closer than Puskar Stellar which was a city on Mars. "Not sure you'd cover fuel back and forth though." I was just talking out loud.

Ordena gave me an appraising look. "Be a shame to fly all the way to Puskar with just ammo to sell. You boys give me a ring when Xie gets done."

Nick and Xie Mie-su spent another hour fluttering in and out of the engine room and finally made their way up to the bridge.

"So what do you think?" I asked her.

"It's a pile of junk if you ask me." She winked. "Which you just did. The engines are better than I expected but all the nav storage systems have been removed. There isn't a single vid panel on the entire ship and some shiza drilled holes from top to bottom through a couple of spots. You are one good bump from venting atmo in a dozen places. This baby has seen a lot of action. I'd recommend it make one last trip to a junk yard."

"You saying it won't fly?"

"Didn't say that and you don't listen too well. She'll sail just fine if you get a new nav system. You don't need all of those other systems up in the bridge either. They're just for safety and tracking and all that. It's a warship and it used to do a whole lot more than sail. What I am saying is that I don't think it would be worth refitting. Its old, heavy, beat to shiza and missing a couple hundred thousand in parts."

My heart started sinking, "We'd need two hundred thousand to get her flying again?"

"Now you are listening. Yeah, and I bet that would be a low number." She considered it a little longer. "Well, it'd be pretty close. At least around here. You know the score. Ship parts cost ten times as much out here." She gave one last look around. "Well, I gotta jet. Come visit me sometime boys. I live in The Down Under by Maintenance Bay Twelve."

Everything south of the equator on P-Zero was referred to as The Down Under. It was a somewhat sketchy part of the station. Mostly, it was just people who had trouble keeping a steady job or had fallen onto hard times. I appreciated Xie's willingness to toss it out there like it wasn't any big deal. Most people would have tried to hide it.

DINNER WITH THE COMMANDER

At 2155, Nick and I had finished our work for Wendy, cleaned up and were at the docking bay. Corporal Dahwan and Private Gunders were back at their original posts. When we got closer, Private Gunders made eye contact and gave me a slight smile and an up-nod of the head. I wasn't sure how to address her so I offered a friendly "Heya."

Corporal Dahwan looked up, as if he hadn't seen us approach, and held up his tablet. "Retinal scan."

Nick and I didn't stumble over each other this time. It was small progress.

"Commander Sterra is expecting you. This way." Dahwan turned and strode down the gang plank leading to the airlock of the *Kuznetsov*.

This time, instead of taking a right toward the aft of the ship, he led us to the left and up a short flight of stairs forward into the ship. I was struck by how free of debris and clean the paint was in the hallway. The floor was covered with a plastic mat that our boots sunk into as we walked, making it a little difficult with my new foot, given the lack of proper feedback. I had to catch myself occasionally as my toe dragged on the surface and found more friction than expected. No doubt it was an advantage to people who were moving quickly in an emergency versus the harder, more slippery surface in our ship.

The stairs led to a small alcove that opened onto a hallway I considered to be quite large when compared to our new prize. The hallway went both forward and aft. Corporal Dahwan led us aft and we passed through a bulkhead's open door that could be closed in case of depressurization. We hadn't yet passed anyone in the hallway but I could hear the low tones of a few people chatting up ahead.

The corporal stopped on the opposite side of an open doorway leading to the middle of the ship. "Commander Sterra, your dinner guests have arrived."

"Our guests of honor. So good of you to join us." Commander Sterra rose and was accompanied by three other men around a free-standing table decked out with white linens and plates, glasses and silverware. I had never eaten at a table set in this way before.

"Liam Hoffen, Nicholas James, I believe you are already well acquainted with my First Officer, Lieutenant Commander Brandon Telish." He nodded at us with a smile.

Commander Sterra continued, "I am pleased to introduce you to Second Officer, Lieutenant Gregor Belcose." She paused while we shook hands with Gregor, who was one of the thickest men I had ever seen. He wasn't fat as you would expect from a military officer, but his physical mass was impressive. His muscles were evident under his non-armored vac-suit and they rippled as he moved. His hand swallowed my own as we shook and his grip was like iron, although he didn't attempt to crush my hand.

Commander Sterra continued, "And finally, our engineer, Ensign Ke Lok." Where Gregor was medium height and burly, Ke Lok was slightly shorter with a thin frame, but he also appeared to be in very good shape. Ensign Lok's handshake was quick and accompanied by a friendly smile.

"Gentlemen, please have a seat. Steward Gellar has prepared a fabulous meal for us."

As promised, the food was delicious. I wasn't sure how and when to use all of the different utensils, but I gave it my best shot. I probably didn't do it right, but no one at the table seemed any the wiser. Second Officer Belcose was very interested in the attack and how we had responded.

"What in Sol inspired you to launch those containers with the exploding mining bags and how did you know it would work?" His accent was thick, like the Russian accents I had heard in vids.

"To be honest, it worked a lot better than I thought it would. We use those bags to break apart rock shelves but we never expect the rock to move very far. It is really just to cause it to separate so we can collect it faster. It was Nick's idea to use the station foam on those guys in the security control tower. That was genius." As the words left my mouth I realized I'd never attributed that action to Nick before and he might think I blamed him for my lost foot.

Commander Sterra must have picked up on it but took a path I wouldn't have considered, "Liam, how are you adjusting to life without your foot?"

I paused. "It's weird. Since I don't have much feeling down there, sometimes I trip on things. I haven't been able to get back to mining because I can't yet use most of the equipment. Truthfully, I don't see that I will be going back to that life."

"Would you do it again, knowing the price?" she asked.

"How could we not? They were shooting at our families. Tabby's dad works in that refinery. My dad was being shot at. We couldn't know what other damage the pirates would cause after they had the freighter loaded. They had total control of the perimeter defenses. Judging by the number of missiles and slug-throwers on that ship we captured, I think they could have caused damage for days. So yeah, I would do it again."

"That's right, Liam. You three stood against lawlessness in our universe which makes what I have to say even harder. I want you to hear this Liam. Sacrifice is giving up something of value for the benefit of others. Your sacrifice has already cost you more than you might know. If you had remained whole, I could have offered you a scholarship to the Mars Protectorate Naval Academy."

Her words hit me like a tonne of gravel. I knew I'd never be able to afford to go to school, but now a naval career had slipped through my fingers as well.

"You should also know you have an extremely loyal friend in Mr. James. He turned down that same offer earlier today. I apologize for being so direct, but we have a limited amount of time and many things to discuss."

My head was reeling, but this I couldn't let go. I turned to Nick with an urgent plea, "Nick, you can't. You have to."

"No. There is nothing to discuss," he replied.

"How can you be so certain?" I knew that look. Nick was done talking about it. I couldn't understand how he could have passed on such a chance. Then, guilt set in when I realized how relieved I was that he intended to stick around.

"Let's get through this conversation and then, if you still want to know why, we can talk it through."

Frak, that got my attention. Nick was on to something. He was calling a play and I would run it. "Okay," I replied uneasily.

Commander Sterra gave Nick an appraising look and continued, "Mr. James, I believe that to underestimate you will be your adversary's greatest downfall. Which brings me to what I wanted to discuss with the two of you. You may have wondered why Mars Protectorate granted your petition for a Letter of Marque. You have no need to protect corporate assets, nor do you have the means to provide this protection. As sympathetic as I am to your physical losses, that is not a compelling reason to grant your petition. If anything, it is a dis-incentive as you might consider looking for some sort of payback.

"No, the reason to grant your petition is relatively straightforward. Mars Protectorate needs enterprising young privateers to help us. We are not fighting a war against other nations; instead we are waging a war against highly organized criminal corporations who are able to evade us at nearly every turn. These corporations are, in some cases, supported by unfriendly foreign nations and in other cases, merely allowed to operate and take refuge.

"These organizations see us coming from a million kilometers and disappear on the solar winds. Your counterattack on the station was the first productive action we have seen within the last dozen years."

"The raids are coordinated?" There were always reports of raids on smaller colonies and Colony 40 was by far the largest mining colony to have been attacked, probably due to the perimeter defense guns.

"Gregor?"

Belcose sat up a little straighter in his chair and gave a quick downward tug on his vac-suit in an attempt to remove any wrinkles. I found the gesture amusing, as if a wrinkle could find its way into the fabric so tightly stretched around his massive frame.

"Coordinated is not strictly the right word for the raids we have seen over the last nine to fourteen months, but they are certainly related. We have good reason to believe the raids on this colony, Baru Manush, Delta and Jeratorn all have ties back to the same Asian corporation called Red Houzi. What isn't clear is the objective. Certainly there is a profit motive. In each case, however, they knew exactly how and when to best strike the colony."

Commander Sterra added, "They are getting bolder and better organized on each strike."

"I feel slow in this conversation," I interrupted. "I think Nick has already figured it out, but how can we help the Navy? What can the two of us do that you can't? You're the Navy. All we have is a broken down old ship that can't even fly."

"I think there is a much more important question. Are you willing to help the Mars Protectorate? Are you patriots or simply capitalists? Liam, I saw your team in action. You didn't hesitate when the right course of action became evident. You were willing to put yourselves in harm's way to protect those you love. That is what I am asking for. The Mars Protectorate is a worthy cause, Liam. I am asking you to stand with us. Will you take that stand again?"

I have to admit I am a bit of a sucker for an impassioned speech and the Commander could obviously read me like a new headline. I looked around the table and saw pride in the faces of the other naval officers who sat straight in their chairs. When I turned to Nick, he gave an almost imperceptible nod.

"We're in Commander, but I gotta admit I still don't understand how we can help."

The tension level around the table dropped by degrees. At that moment, Steward Gellar brought out a tray loaded with plates of chocolate cake topped with chocolate frosting.

"Polly, your timing is impeccable as always. Is this the real cocoa?"

"Why yes, Commander. We just happened to have some of that left."

Commander Sterra chuckled at an apparent inside joke, "I am glad you decided on the Navy, Miss Gellar. We would all be in big trouble if you had decided on a life of crime."

"I couldn't agree more, Commander."

I know I had never had chocolate before that moment in time. I would have definitely remembered it. I also had never tasted cake that moist, sweet, and just plain delicious. It was pure heaven.

"So what would she have brought out if I had said we wanted no part?"

"Some things are best not asked, Liam." The commander delivered the last seriously enough that I considered she might not be kidding.

Steward Gellar also delivered coffee. The smell was incredible. The first sip burned my tongue and I was afraid I wouldn't be able to taste the cake anymore. Fortunately, that wasn't the case. I didn't initially love the coffee, it seemed to have an unusually bitter taste. But, when it had cooled and mixed with the flavors of the cake, I couldn't imagine anything better. It was a combination I'd never forget.

For a moment, the only sounds at the table were that of clinking forks on plates. "Have you been able to discover where the freighter went from here?" An idea started to form in my mind.

Commander Sterra put her fork down and looked at me steadily, "Ideas, yes. We have several of them, but that's not your question. You want to know if there is any chance to recover that cargo. The answer to that is no. Before we even arrived, that cargo had been offloaded and scattered. It is not the freighter you are interested in."

That pissed me off. She may have been right, but that cargo represented everything Big Pete had worked for. My next words came out hotter than I expected, "Yeah, so what am I interested in?"

"Blaen Xid."

"The Sheriff?"

"Yes. We have completed our investigation and prosecuted the pirates you captured. Their only contact was with Xid. He hired them, provided the ship, organized the raid, identified Old Millie's as a target, subverted the station's defenses and turned Deputy Zong. You want Xid."

"Revenge?" My mind whirred as I tried to process her words.

"Maybe. But revenge is not a long-term motivator. The Red Houzi will continue to prey on colonies and then run off and hide. We believe Xid had help here. The problem is, without Xid, we can't find the traitor. Liam, Red Houzi is still on this station."

"Who?"

"We don't know."

I looked at Nick again for confirmation. I could see it in his face. He was already there, but needed me to catch up.

"How can we help?" I looked back to Commander Sterra.

"What were you planning to do before you came over for dinner?"

Nick stepped in. He knew I was in over my head, "Repair the ship and set up a run."

"Do exactly that, but stay in contact. I am simply asking you to share information with the Navy. Now, let me turn the question around. How can we help you?"

I considered the question, but before I could form an answer, Nick slid a reading pad across the table.

"Help us get under sail. Nothing crazy. Repair the hull, slug-turret and nav-computer." Nick gave the pad a final push. "Also, you have a combat grade medical replicator and tank on board. Give Liam a military prosthetic."

Commander Sterra didn't hesitate, "Done. We will also install a communications system paired with the *Kuznetsov*. Now, how about a tour of my ship?"

READY TO SAIL

"So, you're telling me you're just done here? What about the claim?" Big Pete had remained relatively quiet when I explained that Nick and I were in business together. I wasn't about to mention the Letter of Marque or that we were working with the Navy. It wasn't that I thought they would talk, as much as I didn't want them to worry about me.

Mom pulled his hand over to her lap and held it, "Pete, can't you see? He's just like you. When did you leave home and join the Marines?"

"It's different." His voice was resigned.

"You don't believe that. Tell him how proud you are of him."

"It's not about that."

"Tell him." Mom was firm.

"He knows."

"Tell him."

"I am proud. He knows."

"He's sitting right here."

"I wish we had something to give you, son. Everything we have is wrapped up in this claim." Big Pete wasn't crying but his eyes were red. The pirates had taken more than I could imagine from him. I felt that they had taken away his dream.

The next morning I met Nick and Ordena for breakfast at the Gravel Pit.

"Fly it or scrap it?" Ordena was right to the point.

"Without considering the slug-thrower ammo and fuel, the scrap value of the ship is forty and maybe two hundred for the engines," I started.

"Xie Mie-su said the engines were worth a hundred each."

Ordena countered.

"Sure, but that is an off-station purchase price for engines that are transportable. You also have to consider the price of removing them, packaging and transport. Two hundred is probably high." I didn't want to tip my hand, but I had practiced that line a million times in my head and I was nervous.

Ordena sat back and a flicker of a smirk crossed his face, "Fly it then. Okay, I'll bite. Two forty and I'll throw in the fuel."

Warning bells were going off in my head. He hadn't countered, which meant I had left money on the table. Only 30% of the fuel was his to throw in, but it made him sound generous.

"Any thoughts on a buyer for the ammo?" Ordena asked.

Nick answered, "I found a buyer on Baru Manush. Two hundred for the entire inventory."

"Good price and close by. Our boat isn't setup for calcium, but the Deuterium-3 would be possible." Ordena replied.

Our boat. That was the trap. He wanted to keep a share of *Sterra's Gift*.

Time to head this off. "We accept your valuation of the ship and fuel at two forty. Nick can you send Mr. Ordena his portion of seventy two thousand with a contract? Will that work for you, Mr. O?"

He paused and appeared to reassess. His lips pursed momentarily, then changed back to a smile that didn't quite reach his eyes. "Good enough."

Nick said, "I just sent it. Mr. Ordena, if you will take a moment and sign that, we can work on arrangements for the ammo."

Ordena spread his hands in mock confusion. "What? Now? What's the rush?"

Time to put my cards on the table. He had hinted at other business and I wasn't about to be flexible regarding ownership of our one asset. I wanted to get to that other business. "Look, I don't want to be a pain in the ass, but I'm not talking any other business until we finish the ship business. We have a good deal on the table, let's get it done."

"Okay. Okay. You boys got a fire in your bellies and I can

respect that. Give me a second." Ordena pulled out a reading pad and reviewed the contract Nick had sent. At his signed response, I noted, with a little sadness, that our account balance had dwindled to thirty thousand m-creds. But Nick and I were now the sole owners of *Sterra's Gift*.

Ordena looked up from his reading pad, "Now that we have that out of the way. I have forty cubic meters for Puskar Stellar."

Nick answered, "What kind of mass?"

"Three thousand give or take."

"How much bond and what are we carrying?"

Ordena stood up, "I might have underestimated you. No bond, but it has to be off-book and no one looks in the crates. Paying fuel plus twenty-five all on delivery. No contract. Let me know."

Once we got back on *Sterra's Gift*, we split up tasks. The bridge was my problem and the engine room was Nick's. It took nearly an hour to remove all of the junk and broken parts. I marveled at how the military grade prosthetic had improved my life. I still had no feeling, but the motors and artificial sinews in the ankle and foot responded to my nervous system perfectly.

By mid-afternoon I had made it into the captain's quarters and the three bunk rooms and removed all of the litter and old clothing. My big discovery of the day was a flechette pistol and shoulder holster. The next couple of hours of cleaning duty were pretty much ruined because I was so enamored with it. A flechette pistol fires small darts at subsonic speeds using compressed gas. The gun was no good against armored troops, but the ammo was inexpensive to replicate. The other advantage of a flechette pistol was I could wear it in public. It was illegal to carry laser weapons and slug-throwers in most places, but a flechette was considered a non-lethal self-defense weapon. I adjusted the holster and strapped it on. It would take some getting used to.

"I'm going to make a run over to the transfer station." I hadn't heard from Nick in a few hours and imagined he was similarly engaged. "Any garbage you want me to haul off?"

"At least a dozen bags. We don't have a reclaimer or even a compacter."

"Put it on the list, I guess. Do you have a replicator there?" I was working my way back to the engine room, having thrown all of my garbage bags into the airlock. It would be a real trick to squeeze past them all and cycle the lock on the way out.

Nick had a pile of garbage bags blocking the hallway. I moved past them to find him sitting cross-legged with a pile of wires hanging out of a panel on the starboard side.

"Hope you know what you're doing with that." I wasn't overly concerned. Nick was pretty good at this type of thing.

"General Astral Cutter – Model CA12. Look under the folder /corporate/fleet/SterrasGift/E14. It's the gravity assist system. Give me a minute and I think I can close it back up." Nick had a tool belt on and was working with a soldering pen. True to his word, he neatly tucked the wires in and bolted the panel back in place. E14 was stenciled on the upper right hand corner of the panel.

"Where is the corporate folder?" I wasn't sure where to find it.

"Oh, sorry. Central computer was still installed, but the storage sticks were all missing. The computer is in an armored cabinet and whoever trashed the ship didn't have time to break into it. I added a couple of sticks to get us going. We'll need to buy more. Pass-key is basswood."

Link Sterra's Gift. Admin access basswood.

A new set of folders showed up, superimposed on a virtual panel floating in space. With my helmet up, the AI was able to paint imagines directly onto my retina.

Browse Sterra's Gift.

My vision filled with a translucent picture of a perfect CA12 Cutter. No banged up hull, no scorch marks, everything fresh from the factory. *View Bridge.* The model zoomed in to show what the bridge was originally meant to look like. I wondered how detailed the picture might be and decided to test it. *Schematic Pilot's Chair.* Now I was looking at a picture of the pilot's chair and could see its original design. *Inspect foot.* The diagram zoomed into the foot. Send foot to replicator queue. I wasn't interested in manufacturing the steel feet but I wanted to see if the schematic was detailed enough to manufacture replacement parts.

I received a notice that I had a part sitting in queue and it would require a Class 1 industrial replicator to complete. The good news for us was the cost of parts manufacture was always found in the intellectual property and not the materials. The replicators were expensive, but on-station replicators weren't hard to rent. You paid by the hour and material. On a mining station like Colony 40, you could replicate metallic alloy parts all day long. We had a fairly endless supply of material.

"Did the ship come with full schematics?" I asked Nick.

"No, but the Navy has them. It was on the list I gave Sterra."

"And she gave them to you? We should change our name to Brass Nuts."

"Is that a gun?" Nick asked, pointing at my left arm

I pulled it out of the holster, opened the chamber and handed it to him, "I found this in the captain's quarters. Cool, right?"

Nick turned it over in his hands a couple of times, smiled, shook his head and handed it back to me, "You gonna wear that around the station?"

"No, but watch this." I slid the chamber closed and aimed at Nick's pile of bags and squeezed off a couple of darts. The darts made a pffft sound as they left the gun and ripped into the bags, making small holes where they entered.

"Neat." That was Nick speak for 'I am not as impressed as you are, but need you to shut up because I am thinking about something else.'

I holstered the gun, then removed the holster and placed it on the counter of what I now recognized as the galley.

"Want me to pick anything up on my way back from the garbage transfer station?"

"Yes. I printed five parts on the Mercantile printer, can you bring 'em back?"

It took me the better part of half an hour to move all of the bags through the airlock. The transfer station was on the bottom of P-Zero. It wasn't a particularly busy part of the station at this time of day, so I flew my ore sled into the docking bay and parked next to the bins.

I didn't notice their approach while I was unloading. I realized something was wrong when the man I thought was a worker approached me with his face shield obscured. I decided the best answer was to continue with what I was doing. He followed me over to the drop-off bin and when I turned around he blocked the path back to my sled. Two more people were standing further back.

"Hey, I don't want any trouble." I held out my hands, attempting to be as non-threatening as possible.

"Too late for that. You shoulda left things alone, but you had to be the hero." The other two approached and the one who was talking flicked his wrist, causing a baton to extend. This didn't look good.

"What do you want? I don't know what you're talking about."

"You gonna give that ship back or we gonna mess up your family. Yeah, we know who you are, Hoffen. You got a pretty mom. Hate to see something bad happen to her."

That was over the line. I swung at him, but it was clumsy. I had no experience brawling and he did. He blocked my swing and chopped at my knee with his baton. The knee exploded with pain. Then he punched and kicked me for the better part of several minutes.

For the second time in as many weeks, I woke up in a hospital bed. I had a flashback and thought I saw Tabby sitting next to me. I was disappointed when I came to enough to realize it was just my mom and Nick. Every part of my body hurt.

"We gotta stop meeting like this." My attempt at humor got a small smile from Nick, but mom looked worried. "Anything broke?" It was impossible for me to tell.

Mom answered. "No, but what happened? They found you at the transfer station. What's going on, Liam?"

"I don't know, Mom." The guy's comment about her made my stomach turn. "Did Big Pete come in with you?"

She was suspicious. "Yes, why?"

"I think I was in the wrong place at the wrong time. Did they take the sled?"

Deputy Stella Bound said "Knock, knock," and pushed the curtains apart. "Mr. Hoffen, do you have a couple of minutes?"

Mom's protective instinct popped up. "Do you have to do this now?"

I stopped her. "It's fine."

Deputy Bound stepped in. "Do you know who did this?"

"No."

"Did you get a good look at them?"

"Basic vac-suit with darkened face masks. There were three of them."

"What did they want?"

"No idea." Okay, that wasn't true, but I wasn't feeling overly trusting at this point.

"What are you into, Mr. Hoffen? People don't just get attacked for no reason."

Mom wasn't having any of that. "Are you serious? Liam gets mugged and you blame him? How about you review the vids, track these guys down and put 'em in jail?"

"Mrs. Hoffen, I'm sorry. That came out wrong. Liam, do you have any idea what this might be about?"

"No idea." I had some idea, but I would be talking that through with Gregor Belcose.

Deputy Bound continued. "We found your sled piled into the side of the station. Someone has it in for you, Hoffen. You might want to help us figure that out." She was out of questions and excused herself.

Once I had my suit back on, I sent a ping over to Big Pete and asked if he could meet me on *Sterra's Gift*. It was an easy trip from the hospital up to the Mercantile and from there up through the James' Rental shop's back lift.

Big Pete was standing outside *Sterra's Gift* when we got there.

"Want the penny tour?" I asked.

"Sure. Glad to see you keep it locked up. Never know who you might find skulking around." Big Pete sounded almost cheerful.

I led him up to the bridge, showing him the sleeping compartments along the way. I was glad I'd removed a lot of the trash, but seeing it through Dad's eyes made me painfully aware of how long it would take to get it ship-shape.

"Let's grab a seat in the captain's quarters," I suggested.

"And I thought this was a social visit." Big Pete was definitely in a good mood. It threw me off balance. Grumpy would have made sense. I was a little surprised we were still talking.

"Dad, they threatened you and mom."

That got his attention.

"Who threatened Silver?"

"The guys who attacked me."

Big Pete stood up and hit his comm.

"Where are you, Silver?" He paused to listen. "Okay. Don't leave there, not even with someone you know." Another pause. "No. We'll talk when I get there." One last pause and I could hear her voice rise in pitch. "Finishing up with Liam in a few minutes. Don't go anywhere."

"Where is she?" He had me concerned.

"Gravel Pit. Public place at dinner time. She'll be okay there for now. Tell me what you know."

I relayed what the thugs had said to me.

"Dad, you have to keep this to yourself, but the Navy says it's a criminal corporation called Red Houzi. They think the pirates that attacked the refinery are the same ones who were responsible for attacks on Baru Manush and some of the other colonies."

"You aren't trained to deal with this, Liam. These guys are playing for keeps."

That set me back, "Do you think I should return the ship?"

"No. That won't change anything. Don't worry. I'll take care of your mom. Their mistake was giving us a warning. You know Silver and I met in the Marines, right?"

"What? Mom's a teacher."

"Sure is. A darned good one too. Point is, we'll be okay, but you need to start observing some security protocols. You have any arms?"

"Flechette pistol count?"

"Yes. I'm guessing you weren't wearing it."

"No, didn't think I needed to."

"Well, they aren't pros. It's a stupid message. Either take the ship or don't. No point in being all dramatic. You boys need to carry a weapon at all times. Always travel together. Stay aware and keep your suit up when outside the ship. I'll send you a suit subroutine that will scan a ten meter perimeter around you. If someone breaks that bubble, you start paying attention."

Big Pete continued, "Any security routines running on this tub?"

Nick, who had joined us from the engine room answered, "No, we've been trying to get basic functions up and going."

"I'll come back tomorrow and get that running. Keep it locked up."

Miner, huh? I told dad I got attacked and that they were coming after him and Mom, and he was all smiles. He said more words in the last ten minutes than I'd heard from him in the last year.

"I'm going to pick up Silver. I probably freaked her out a bit."

"We need another flechette. Any suggestions where to get one?"

"I'll bring one tomorrow. You need to get off station. You're too open here. Does she sail yet?"

"Tomorrow."

"Got it. Get some sleep and be careful."

We saw Big Pete out. Once the airlock was closed, I started to feel like we were in a prison.

"You still good with this?" I asked Nick.

"It'll work out. Glad you're okay. Would like to stop picking you up from the hospital though."

It hurt to laugh.

Nick had the bed and I stretched out on the couch. The stuffing had been pulled out of the cushions but I flipped them over and it wasn't too bad. Every time I rolled over, I could feel where the guy had tuned me up. According to the medical report, I had two cracked ribs and a minor concussion. Sleeping and breathing sucked and the pounding headache wasn't much fun, but everything else wasn't that bad. The medical patches would heal me soon enough.

I woke to a muffled banging sound. I shook the groggy out of my head and rolled off the couch. My ribs felt the same, but my headache was gone. I checked the time, it was 0530. Ensign Lok wasn't due for another hour. I walked back to the galley where I had left the flechette pistol and checked the chamber to make sure it was loaded. Good to go. I went back to the airlock window, but couldn't find the source of the noise and I wasn't about to open the door without being able to see who was out there. The banging continued. It was more of a continuous thumping and got fainter as I moved aft and grew louder forward.

I looked out the armored glass on the port side and saw Big Pete banging the side of the ship with some sort of pipe. He looked up at me and gave a wave. I wasn't sure how he knew that I had entered the bridge, but I suspected it was his own suit's security program.

Hoffen Channel One. "Dad, you could have pinged me."

He was looking through the armored glass of the bridge at me. "Yup, wanted to see how much work we had to do. Good job on the flechette. How many rounds you got in it?"

"Meet me at the airlock." No way was I admitting to not knowing how many darts were in the clip.

Big Pete had a belt holster with a pistol quite a lot bigger than my flechette gun. I hadn't ever seen it before and was surprised to see it resting so comfortably at his waist over his dark blue vac-suit.

"You don't have a single sensor strip left on the hull. Must have sailed in blind, piggy-backed on that freighter. Too bad we don't have schematics, they wouldn't be that expensive to print. The IP cost on those strips would be darn expensive. We should be able to cobble together something, though."

Grant Pete Hoffen physical, engineering access Sterra's Gift. My AI replied with an affirmative chirp.

I saw the reflection on Dad's eye while he accessed the engineering diagrams. After a couple of minutes, I gave up waiting for him and made my way to the galley. Nick had checked out the water system and declared it to be operational, so I filled a pouch of water and rummaged through the cupboards to see if there was any food. I found a box of meal bars. For most people that would be a meal of last resort, but on the Hoffen claim it was pretty standard fare. I grabbed one for Big Pete and filled another water pouch.

He finally emerged from his browsing frenzy and I handed him a meal bar.

"Find anything good?" I asked.

"Where in Sol did you find a full set of specs?"

"Neat. Right?" I wasn't ready to share everything.

"Well, it'll still cost a few thousand to print a full set of sensor strips. You could probably get by with a lot less, but they will fit a whole lot better than what I had in mind."

Nick shuffled up, trying to look alert. His wavy black hair mashed against the side of his head in an unruly 'I just got out of bed' way.

"How do people wake up this early?" he complained.

"All about caffeine, my friend." Big Pete clapped him on the shoulder.

"Hey I found some meal bars, want one? I think mine was mixed berries and nuts." It was an inside joke in the Hoffen family since all meal bars tasted basically the same. A little crunch, a little sweet and if you drank enough water with them you felt full more quickly. I pulled another water pouch out of a drawer, pushed it onto the water dispenser and then handed it and a bar over to Nick.

"What was that about the sensors?" Nick asked, after taking a couple of bites of the bar.

I got him caught up.

"Twenty-two hundred m-creds," he said after we were done.

"What's that?" Dad asked.

"Replicating cost for the sensor strips, plus delivery. They will be here by 1200. Appreciate you checking that out. I caught that yesterday. Hope you don't mind, Liam, but after yesterday I bumped up their priority. We are blind on board."

"Nope, I agree."

"That's some pretty serious cash. You sure you got this?" Dad sounded concerned.

"I think so, Dad. We got lucky being able to salvage the ship. Navy bought the missiles from us, mostly because they wouldn't let us keep them."

"Hmm." That was Big Pete's general word for letting me know he wasn't getting the full picture but wasn't going to ask. "Well, good enough. Now, let me see that pistol of yours."

I handed it over to him, after opening the chamber.

"Who taught you that?" he asked.

"What?"

"You opened the chamber before handing it over to me. If you weren't my own, I would have thought you had some weapons training."

"Oh, I looked it up. Supposed to make sure a weapon isn't loaded before you hand it to someone. Rule number one."

"You remember that. Never accept a weapon unless you know how to secure it." Dad pulled the magazine clip out from the handle and released a small row of darts onto the countertop next to the water dispenser. There were only two darts left. He then pulled the gas cartridge out and released the barrel from the stock. In less than a minute, he had the gun completely stripped down. Dad inspected each part carefully and then pulled a small box out of his duffel. The box contained some little plastic bulbs of oil, a few brushes and rags. He methodically cleaned each piece while Nick and I looked on. He finally seemed satisfied and reassembled the weapon.

"Looks to be in good condition. You should clean it at least weekly. If it's getting a lot of use, you might consider an upgrade. I brought a Colt-F12. It was your mom's but she has been looking to upgrade and I figure with everything that has been going on, this would be a good excuse. I also brought a gas charger and a couple thousand darts, same size as yours."

The airlock started to cycle and before I knew what was

happening, Big Pete had his own pistol drawn and was slightly crouched facing the corridor.

"No, Dad, that's Ke Lok. We're expecting him," I said quietly.

He lowered his pistol to his side, but didn't holster it. "Did he ping you?"

"Yeah. Just got it."

"Why does he have your security code? Don't be giving that out so freely." Fortunately, he decided to holster.

Ensign Lok turned the corner to the aft and smiled. I was surprised to see him wearing a civilian vac-suit rather than his Navy issue.

"We have a couple of pallets to unload. You guys want to help?" His eyes came to rest on the battered side of my head where my suit had failed to deflect the club. "What happened to you?"

"Trouble taking out the garbage." I didn't want to get into the entire story with Dad right there and fortunately, either the ensign didn't care or he picked up the clue.

"I see. Well, there isn't much."

"Feels like we are getting a little crowded. Ping me if 1200 isn't going to work," Big Pete said over his shoulder. As he headed to the airlock, I heard him mutter, "You'd think a guy would have free rein at six in the morning."

Nick came back down the hallway, pulling his vac-suit up over his waist.

Once Dad made it through the first door, Ensign Lok turned to me. "Anything we should know about?"

"Which. My head or my Dad?"

"Either?"

"Not really. I got some unwanted attention. Someone wants their ship back and decided to send a message. Dad is looking to install security routines."

"Marine?"

"Retired, yeah, how'd you know?"

"You can always pick 'em out."

"Hmm ..."

Ke Lok turned out to be pretty decent. When not surrounded by superior officers, he wasn't much different from Nick and myself. He had four years on us and had just graduated from Mars Protectorate Academy in engineering. Once they got started, it took Nick and Ke a couple of hours to install the nav-computer, software updates and storage systems.

While Nick and Ke worked on the navigation systems, another crewman from the *Kuznetsov* repaired the holes we had drilled into the hull. Billy was called in by Ke to remove the vac-patches. There were a couple of small decompression events aboard the ship while he filled, welded and repaired the damage. The hassle was worth it, though, because this crewman was a welding genius. The repairs looked better than the entire rest of the hull, as if those small areas were the original ship and the rest of it was a sad parody.

By 1100, Billy, the hull-welding genius, had started on the slug-thrower. No amount of welding would fix the barrel and he resorted to repair-through-replacement. Instead of repairing the single barrel I had damaged, he replaced the entire turret assembly. It was a close enough match to the small guns on the *Kuznetsov* that he was also able to replicate a collar to fit it in. I was surprised at how easily he lifted the old assembly and swapped it with his replacement. It would have been nearly impossible for Nick and me to repair it with the station's .6 gravity, but Billy had brought along a portable lift and made quick work of it.

When Dad showed back up at 1200, Mom was with him. Ensign Lok and Billy were pulling two mostly empty grav-pallets back to the station's main lift. As if on cue, a pallet with our sensor strips, pulled by a guy I recognized but couldn't put a name with, passed the two out-of-uniform navy men.

I signed for the parts, then Nick and Big Pete set about installing the sensor strips. The parts were perfectly printed to fit the ship's original design. Unfortunately several of the hull patches that had been applied over the years weren't quite as well installed as they could have been and they had to break out a welder and grinder to finish the job. I joined them after a couple of hours and it was well past 2000 when the last strip was installed. We were exhausted.

"Too bad you mucked up that turret. We could give that security routine some teeth," Big Pete complained.

"You were on the ship all afternoon and you still think that turret is messed up?" I asked.

"Yeah, I saw it this morning when I first got here, remember? I saw the holes you and Tabby drilled out with those lasers."

"Well, get your eyes checked. We had them repaired." I still didn't want to bring him in on the Navy's involvement.

Big Pete stood motionless, showing that same look of parental concern he had years ago when he found me playing with his mining lasers before he showed me how to use them. "Hmm. That was fast and must have been expensive." If he had figured it out, he wasn't saying anything. He took a minute on the pad and then said, "Okay, security routine is running. Nick, we missed a couple of connectors up front. I bet the terminals got broken off and we didn't see it. You can get 'em in the morning. You have more than enough to sail her, but be best if you fixed 'em before you do."

We re-entered the ship and I heard Mom humming where the galley was located. She looked up when I turned the corner.

"You all looking for some dinner?" she asked cheerily.

"Mixed berries?" I said, going for our family joke.

"No, and who is this Ms. Gellar? Not only did she send along a stack of sandwiches but she also packed a kilo of real coffee beans and something that looks suspiciously like chocolate cake. I thought you were sweet on Tabby."

No good answer here. I looked around the galley. It was quite a bit cleaner than it had been this morning. A silvery metallic table had been pulled down from the wall and stools had been clipped into receptacles in the floor.

"Did you do this?" I was bewildered by the amount of work she had accomplished. I also smelled a delicious scent that I vaguely recognized and associated with the chocolate cake. "And is that coffee I smell?"

Mom smiled with pride, "Yes, that's real coffee, Liam. It is excellent and this is what old people call elbow grease. I tried to do some damage control on your beds. They're trash, by the way, and son, you don't have a suit freshener. Don't you dare try to fly this somewhere without a suit freshener. Isn't it just like pirates, there's a coffee brewing station and no suit fresheners."

It is hard to explain how much better sandwiches are than meal bars. If you add chocolate cake and coffee, even cracked ribs start to feel okay. I would have to find something nice for Polly Gellar.

After dinner, dad pulled out a few boxes of dart ammo and a gas charger for the propulsion cartridges. He then handed over a flechette gun that was larger than the one I'd found.

"Never had to use it that much. Glad it's going to a good home." Mom almost sounded nostalgic. "But that was before I got this bad boy." She said with a wicked smile, pulling out a slim, matte black, laser pistol.

The next morning, my head felt much better so I found the instructions for the coffee brewer. I took a sealed mug up to the bridge and turned over one of the pilot chairs. It wobbled, but if I didn't move too much it would be fine. I wondered if we would ever get the bridge fully restored since I knew we didn't have enough money in our accounts to accomplish that. Most of that money was marked for critical systems. Even with the bridge in pieces, the quiet of the room was peaceful and I could imagine us sailing across the vast expanse of space with a load of cargo. I really wanted to get going.

Nick joined me on the bridge after an hour and I helped him turn over the other pilot chair. We sat quietly for a few minutes. Nick was completely unimpressed with the coffee and set it aside. I grabbed his cup, removed my lid and poured the contents of his cup into my own.

"Account is running a little north of twenty thousand. I probably need five of that to get the bridge back online. Won't be pretty, but it'll work." I was worried that we were going to bottom out before we set sail. "What do you think the minimum is to get us up and going other than that?"

Nick took a moment to reply, "Depends on how far we have to go. If we stick to cargo and no passengers, we're nearly there. We can't fly bonded cargo since we can't afford the bond, and we aren't registered with TradeNet, so it's pretty hard to set up orders. Things are tight."

It was the first time I had heard Nick sound anything less than optimistic.

"Okay, easy. No passengers. What does TradeNet cost?"

"Fifty thousand to register. Then we have to upgrade our communications gear, pay a minimum of two hundred thousand for the bond, which they escrow and after that each individual bond is a minimum of five thousand per load."

I whistled, "Two fifty-five upfront? That's an easy decision. How about this. You take over getting the bridge up and running and I'll get us a destination and cargo. Can you have us ready to sail in seventy-two hours?"

Nick brightened, "I'm in."

EAST BOUND AND DOWN

Without access to TradeNet, it would be very difficult to figure out who needed items moved from port to port. We had some value in our share of the ammo and it wouldn't be overly difficult for us, as independents, to find a buyer. It was substantially more complex to facilitate both sides of the transaction. First, we had to find someone with something to sell or move that could fit in our ship. Then, we had to find a way to connect them with a suitable buyer, preferably somewhere we could get to easily.

I spent the morning searching through online publications, want ads, and other sources. I started to appreciate why TradeNet demanded such a high fee. It was frustrating work. Some people listed mass and others listed cubic meters. I needed both.

I pinged Ordena to set up a meeting. *"Working on filling a cargo run."*

His reply was nearly instant. *"Why don't you stop by? I have some ideas."*

"When?"

"Why not now?"

"Where?"

"I am at my office, sending directions."

The address was in The Down Under. That hadn't worked out for me very well last time, but I rejected the idea that there was anywhere on this station I couldn't go. This time I wouldn't leave my flechette at home. If it came to that, at least I'd make sure someone was pulling darts outta their ass for a few days.

"I'm headed out," I informed Nick.

"Wait, I'll come along."

"Nope. Get the ship ready. I can handle it." I pulled on my

shoulder harness and ejected the magazine clip. Thirty-two darts. If I needed more than that, I would be seriously in over my head. I headed out the airlock with a sense of security nestled under my left arm. I was also wearing my AGBs. I hadn't practiced much with the military prosthetic and arc-jets, but it felt pretty good as I bounded over to the public access lift.

It took me better than twenty minutes riding different lifts to make my way to Ordena's address in The Down Under. The lift dumped me out into L-2 space so I could lower my mask, but I decided to run with a high reflective surface on the face mask. Between that and the holster under my arm, I felt reasonably safe.

The hallway leading to Ordena's office was neglected and the lighting wasn't all working. I had to turn down the mask filter so I could see. It reminded me of the condition of *Sterra's Gift* when we entered for the first time.

His office entrance was only a door cut out of the hallway. There was a pane of peep-glass allowing someone on the other side to see visitors. On my side, I saw my own reflection and thought I looked kind of bad-ass with my holster and reflective face plate.

I knocked and after a few moments, Xie Mie-su opened the door.

"You are very quick. So, not selling her, eh? Worth a lot of money." Xie took a breath, but before she could get going again, Ordena called her name.

She turned and led me down the hallway. I obviously hadn't paid enough attention when she was on the ship before, but Xie was gorgeous. Her straight black hair hung down her back, settling just above her waist. She walked with a very slight sway that was mesmerizing. I mentally chastised myself for looking, given how I had left things with Tabby, but Xie sure made it hard to ignore her.

I pulled my eyes up just in time to make the turn into Ordena's office. I looked guiltily to Xie, who had a small knowing smile on her face. I'm sure my face burned a little with shame.

"Thanks for coming down, Liam." Ordena sat back in his chair smiling. His office was disorganized and there were piles of different things all over the place. He gestured to a chair in front of his desk. "Have a seat." I had to move a small stack of boxes.

"Just put 'em anywhere. So, how is ship ownership treating you?" he asked.

Xie Mie-su pulled up another chair and positioned it to the side of the desk so she could see us both easily. I was momentarily distracted.

"Uh," I swiveled my head back to look at him. "Good. Lots of work."

"Well, I have something you might be interested in."

That got my attention. "What's that?"

"Straight up offer for your ship. Two hundred thousand."

"We valued it at two-forty a day ago without fuel and ammo. We've put in quite a bit of work since then." The offer caught me flat footed.

"Okay. How about three hundred?" His hands were steepled in front of him. He clearly enjoyed the negotiation.

"Not really for sale, Mr. O."

"Could go as high as three fifty."

I was taken off guard. While the ship was undoubtedly worth more than that, splitting that between Nick and me could go a long way. We wouldn't be able to get a replacement ship, but we could afford to go to school. Could we really give up the dream or maybe even postpone it?

"Give me a minute?"

Ordena nodded his head at me. I stood up and raised my face shield, walked out into the hallway, and initiated a comm with Nick.

"You'll never believe this. Ordena just offered us three fifty for the ship."

"You sound interested. What do you want?" Nick answered without skipping a beat.

"I need to know what you want. Could pay for school, we could go to the same place."

"That what you want?"

"Frak Nick, I'm asking you."

"Understood. Call the play." Nick terminated communication.

That little shite could be so frustrating. I walked back into the office.

"Good offer Mr. O., but we have to turn you down. Just not ready to sell."

"The offer is solid. Worth more than that ship. You should reconsider."

"You want to buy it?"

"No. Someone I represent."

"Who?" I asked.

"Can't say. They will be pretty disappointed. You should reconsider." He raised both eyebrows and sat forward with pursed lips. It felt more like a threat than disappointment.

"Sorry. Just not interested in selling."

He considered me for a few uncomfortable moments and then sat back again with a welcoming smile. "Well, heck. Okay, what are your big plans?"

"Trying to put together a load. Best price on the ammo is on Ceres at Baru Manush station and they are nice and close. It would be a good shakeout run for us. You would net fifty-two thousand."

"I thought we were a lot closer to sixty on that."

"That'd be gross. Buyer will give us two hundred for the lot. Your lot would go for fuel plus six." I had practiced this one a few times. I wasn't sure he would go for paying six thousand for delivery, but I wasn't going to ship his ammo for free.

"How about fuel plus four?" he immediately countered.

We haggled for a while and ended up at fuel plus fifty-two hundred on delivery. I suspected he negotiated bigger deals all the time, so I felt good just hanging in on this one. Six thousand was more than a fair price and I should have gotten at least the fuel deposit up front. I also should have started higher so I could get pulled back to that number. I realized that all too late.

"You have any more room to Baru Manush?" he asked.

"Two hundred meters," I said.

Ordena smiled. "Here I thought you had a full load and that was why you were stonewalling on the ship. How about I take all two hundred for fuel plus thirty, and one passenger."

I knew I had to separate these ideas. Passage to Baru Manush was worth ten by itself, but we weren't set up for it.

"We aren't set up for passengers right now. Can do the cargo for fuel plus thirty, fuel up front."

"Even if the passenger is Ms. Mei-su?" Ordena came as close to leering as a person could without being obvious.

He thought he had me on that. I did want the extra ten though, and she would definitely make the trip more enjoyable. It felt like he'd overstepped.

I looked at Xie, "It will be a pretty gnarly ride. You know the condition of the ship." I turned back to Ordena, "Fuel and ten up front for passenger. Thirty for the cargo." I stood and held my hand over the desk.

Ordena looked a little startled at my standing up, but he stood and shook my hand, "You drive a hard bargain, Mr. Hoffen. Hold on a minute. I will punch it up and we can get it signed."

I sat back down while he typed. I knew I would need to be a little careful since he was a lawyer. I fully expected him to write it up with some gotchas in it. I read it as carefully as I could and didn't find anything glaring. The fuel numbers felt low but I could see his reference to standard rates. I hoped this wasn't a colossal mistake, but it looked good to me, so I signed it.

"We will be at the loading bay of your choice at 0600 in three days. Ms. Mie-su, you can meet us there as well. I hope you will not be too uncomfortable. We expect to be approximately two hundred hours under sail." Total trip time was more like one eighty with the burn plan I had worked out, but Big Pete had always said, "Under promise, over deliver." Words I planned to build a business on.

"Look for my communication. Good doing business with you, Mr. Hoffen. I hope we will have a chance for more in the future." Mr. Ordena had an odd look on his face, but it quickly cleared to his normal professional appearance.

"Mind if I accompany you back to the ship? I would love to check out your progress." Xie hadn't said a word during the entire negotiation and that was odd, given her normal chattiness.

I looked at Ordena, who had busied himself with a spreadsheet on his vid screen.

"Anything else?" I shot his direction.

"No. You kids have fun." He leered again.

Xie and I walked out and headed toward the lift. It felt like I would be rude to mirror my face shield so I kept it down.

"What are you doing on Baru Manush?" I asked.

"Business trip. Had a deal go bad and need to get it fixed. I have to do it in person."

"You do that a lot?"

"What, fix things?"

"No. Sail between the colonies."

"Yes and no. It takes a lot of time, but sometimes there is too much on the line not to show up in person."

"I thought you were an engineer. You sure know your way around a ship. What kind of business are you into?"

"Trade mostly."

She didn't want to talk about it. Maybe I had her wrong, she wasn't that chatty now. We approached the lift and entered a wide area where several hallways intersected. I felt a sharp stabbing pain in my shoulder. Something had pierced my vac-suit. Then the material healed around the wound and my shoulder was on fire.

"Get down," Xie said loudly in a commanding voice.

I didn't need to hear it twice and dove to the floor, rolling clumsily away from the direction of the attack. On the way down I closed my suit's face mask. Big Pete's security program showed the warning blips of two people who had entered my safety perimeter. Frak.

On the ground, it was a lot harder to get my flechette pistol out of the holster, but I managed it as I kept moving. I wouldn't make an easy target if I could help it. I heard darts hitting the floor forward of my position.

Xie had rolled to the ground, but with more grace. She came up in front of one of the two attackers and slammed her elbow into the side of his mask. I fired in the direction of the other attacker. My darts weren't even getting close, although he did take cover in the hallway from which he had emerged.

We were completely exposed. I looked back to Xie and watched with awe as she dropped low and spun a leg, sweeping her attacker's legs out from under him. He fell heavily, but was agile enough to bring a foot up and kick her squarely in the chest. She was flung backward, so I took aim and shot him twice in the abdomen. The darts pierced his suit, the tails protruding. Blood splattered just before his suit started healing over its own wound.

"Look out," Xie exclaimed.

The other attacker was rounding the corner and lining up to take a shot at me, so I swung my pistol toward him and started firing. He got a couple of shots off but didn't appear interested in seeing it through. He turned tail and ran.

I looked back to the attacker Xie had knocked to the floor. He was getting up, so I aimed again and shouted, "Stay right there!"

He lunged for Xie, but she was ready for it and twisted gracefully. She grabbed his arm as he lunged, causing him to awkwardly fall back to the floor while she danced out of the way.

"I'm calling the Sheriff," I said to her.

"Not a good idea," she returned.

"What. Are you serious?"

"You won't take off in seventy-two hours if you do. Let's just go back to the ship. These guys won't be back anytime soon. You have a med kit on board?"

"No idea."

"You'll live either way, but you need a quality med-kit before you sail."

Xie didn't seem too upset about the altercation. I was pissed. My injuries were adding up. Jumping on the floor with cracked ribs and darts in my arm completely sucked.

"Give me your weapon," I demanded, holding my pistol to the guy's head.

"Lower," Xie said.

"What?"

"Lower. Aim at his chest. If he moves quickly, you will never get the head shot, but if you aim at his chest you can plant three or four before he does too much."

I lowered the weapon to point at his chest. "Hand me the pistol."

He carefully handed the weapon to me and said, "You're in deeper than you want to be kid. You better run and run hard." With that he pulled up and ran, gambling I wouldn't shoot him in the back. It was a good gamble.

"Won't the sheriff see this on the vid-feeds?"

"No vid-feeds down here for years. Apparently, they keep getting shot out." She seemed pleased by her statement.

When we got back to the ship, Nick wasn't too happy about me getting shot, but he seemed pleased we had a load lined up. Xie turned out to be excellent at removing darts. It was all about getting the barbs to lay flat before extracting them. Turns out there was a tool for that in the med kit. Xie layered a generous amount of glue on the wound and pronounced me as good as new. The glue burned like fire for a few minutes, but didn't hurt much after that. I was starting to think flechette guns might not have enough stopping power to be a successful deterrent.

"Where did you learn to fight like that?" I asked her.

"Where I grew up, you learned to fight."

"Where was that?"

"How about I'll show you some stuff when we're underway?" she evaded.

"That'd be great."

Nick showed Xie the repairs we had made, although he skipped showing her the new turret.

"You boys have made great progress. I was a little worried you might try to fly her without a nav system. This is probably better than what they had in it before." She glanced around. "Any chance you gonna get some better sleeping mats and linens? I didn't see a suit freshener either and are we eating meal bars the whole way?"

Xie was back to her normal self. I was glad Nick couldn't kill with a look because that was what he was trying to do.

"Hold on there, tiger. Xie is a paying customer." I pled my case and Nick narrowed his eyes. I wasn't out of danger yet. "Ten thousand up front."

"Hmm, I suppose we can make that work," Nick replied.

"So, bed roll and suit freshener?" Xie pushed.

"You install the freshener?" Nick countered.

"Agreed. How about some fresh food?"

Nick passed the buck to me.

I answered, "Sorry, Xie, that's what we have, although we do have coffee. I will make a new pot each morning after 0400 watch."

The promise of coffee seemed to mollify her.

"Is there coffee now?" she asked sweetly, turning on the charm.

When Xie left, she let us know she'd be back at 0600 on the day of departure. I definitely enjoyed being around her when she was more relaxed, but I wondered if I could take her constant chatter on a long trip. For ten thousand Mars credits though, I figured I'd make it work.

I couldn't escape the guilty feeling that thinking about Xie gave me, though. Tabby had made it crystal clear that she didn't have expectations about our relationship, but it was hard to sync that up with how I felt about her. Xie was at least ten years older than me, but she definitely had my attention.

Nick and I spent the rest of the afternoon working on the bridge. My first task was to remove the broken feet from the pilot chairs and unbolt the broken fittings from where the vid screens had been torn off. Every bolt was so rusted in place that I had to use an impact wrench and more than half of them sheared off when I applied force. I was left with the unpleasant task of drilling them out and re-tapping the holes. Each frakking bolt took at least thirty minutes. It put me in a grumpy mood.

I felt a sense of accomplishment when we got to 2300 and I had a good sized pile of fittings and broken vid mounts. Nick spent that same amount of time working on the port side flight yoke.

There had been no other option but to manufacture an entirely new one and the cost had been high due to the pattern's complexity. There was only one replicator on station that could handle the job and we had to pay to bump up our priority. There was nothing to be done about it. Without the yoke we weren't going anywhere.

"I have an outfitter coming tomorrow," Nick said from the captain's bunk, "Replacing the fabric on the chairs is too difficult without the right tools. I figure they can also fix the couch. I checked and it extends into a bed. The mattress is too messed up for tonight, but tomorrow you can sleep in style."

I lay on the couch after moving some of the ripped up stuffing around and then stared up at the ceiling wondering what the next couple of weeks would bring. So far, adventure had meant getting the crap beat out of me. With all of that, it still felt pretty awesome to be lying on my couch in a ship I owned, with a load of cargo waiting to be delivered.

"What's on deck for tomorrow?" I asked Nick.

"I'm about done with the port side yoke. We couldn't afford to manufacture the one on the starboard side. I have two vid screens coming and we are replicating the chair legs tonight. I also found a suit freshener." He was quiet for a moment and then asked, "Any idea what those guys wanted?"

"Not really. They made some comment about being in over our heads. It seemed like they could have done a lot more damage but they didn't. You should have seen Xie. She was awesome."

"I don't get it. What is that all about?"

"I think they're trying to scare us. Somebody wants their ship back. That offer wasn't from Ordena, he was representing someone. It pissed him off when I turned him down. Then he kind of forgot about it and offered the load. He didn't even negotiate that hard."

"Weird. Have you lined up anything out of Baru Manush?"

"No. Worse case is we sail back. We should have eight to ten days to arrange a load. Do we have any creds left to buy some precious metals from Big Pete?"

"Aren't those all contracted to M-Cor?"

"Sure, but there is always wiggle room. Partial ingots, cast offs. We could pay 120% of what M-Cor price gives them and double our money with gold or platinum."

"We are going to end up with fifteen thousand once we top off fuel, atmo, water and meal bars. By the way, do you want some blueberry?"

I laughed at his joke. "Take ten thousand in precious? I know Big Pete can get us that much in platinum from his buddies. It will hardly weigh anything."

"Does he deliver?"

The next morning, 0700 felt too early, but we had a big day ahead of us. There were forty-seven hours before we sailed and an impossibly long list of things that needed fixing. I received word from Gregor Belcose that the *Kuznetsov* would be departing later that day. He'd heard about the attack in the transfer station and wanted to make sure we were taking reasonable precautions.

"Please contact me if you run into further pirate activity," he said. "Use the encrypted comm equipment. Remember that boat of yours is all about speed. Trading slugs with anything near your size will be a lose-lose proposition. If they can't catch you, they can't hit you. Good trading, Captain, and Godspeed." Lieutenant Gregor Belcose signed off.

I contacted Big Pete and asked him about finding loose platinum for us. He showed up just after lunch. Ten thousand m-creds of platinum turned out to be just over 500 grams and roughly twice the size of the palm of my hand. Nick made a small shelf up under the bulkhead that held the bridge's starboard pilot's vid screen. After placing the brick of platinum on the shelf he welded it closed.

"Been practicing with those flechettes?" Big Pete asked.

I suppressed a grimace. "Some. We've been pretty busy though. It doesn't seem like they have much stopping power."

"That'd be true. They're a non-lethal weapon, made for deterrent. Plenty of people been killed with 'em though. How about I check you boys out on this turret?"

"What do you know about turrets?" I asked.

"They aren't much to operate. Just a couple of things to keep your eye on." Big Pete pushed on the entry panel to the armory. I knew from experience, he was being sarcastic. Apparently, operating a turret was a big deal.

The lock panel flashed red, denying Big Pete entry.

"Sorry, Mr. Hoffen." Nick punched a code in and opened the door.

"Good precaution, Nicholas. A slug-thrower is a big responsibility."

The room had closed shelves around the outer walls and a slim metal ladder in the center leading to the crow's nest. Mechanical conveyers on the shelves kept the turret loaded. It was a fully automated system with more robotic parts than I could imagine.

Big Pete climbed up the ladder, through the hatch, and fell easily into the webbed chair. His hands found the joystick and he tipped it over with anticipation. Nothing happened.

"You mind unlocking the travel?" Big Pete called down.

"Let me show Liam how," Nick replied.

He gave me a code and helped me navigate my AI to the control system for the turret. Releasing the travel on the turret was easy, although with the hatch open it wouldn't operate. I could also see the target projection out into space. There were lots of different numbers, but a red line projected straight out from the turret.

"Good. Can you see that red line?"

"Sure," Nick and I replied at the same time.

"If you pull the trigger, that's where the bad stuff will happen. Watch the line as I spin." Big Pete slowly rotated the turret. The line turned, showing an arc away from the direction of spin. "It's a prediction line of where your rounds are going. If we were firing live ammo, the slugs would be rendered in your vision. The barrels you have installed have a rate of fire that is pretty significant. For short periods you can override it to cause more damage. If you keep overriding you will most likely slag your barrels. In an emergency the extra firepower might be worth it."

"Why don't you hop in here, Liam?" I waited for him to come down the ladder and then I climbed up and slid into the chair. My ribs were feeling better but they still complained when I twisted.

I tipped the joystick all the way over to get an idea of how it worked. Bad idea. The turret spun at a crazy rate and it was all I could do to pull it back up. Dad and Nick were laughing down below.

"If you let go, they will reset to neutral. Full speed is not for the uninitiated." Apparently Dad was now into stating the obvious.

I spun the turrets around slower this time and watched the red line move along, estimating where we were pointing. Then, I got a ping on my comm marked urgent. It was from Gregor Belcose. I released the joysticks and connected.

"Hoffen," I answered.

"We are tracking a free turret on top of the station but no new ships. Are you tracking any bogeys?" Gregor skipped the normal pleasantries.

"That's us, Lieutenant."

"You need to stow 'em. We'll have to report that to the station. We record all potentially hostile acts when we are at a station."

"Crap. Okay." I replied.

"Don't worry. Sometimes our reports take a while to get filed, say next week?"

"Okay, thanks. We'll stow it. Appreciate the heads up."

"*Kuznetsov* out." Gregor closed the channel.

The afternoon was filled with the arrival of new mattresses and the outfitter. Between the chairs on the bridge, the couch in the captain's quarters, and crisp new sheets on the new mattresses, *Sterra's Gift* was starting to come together. Nick replaced the broken suit freshener in the hallway next to the secondary head.

Nick helped me pull the couch sleeper out and then hopped up onto the new mattress above the captain's cabinets and small desk. I lay down on the new mattress and it was the most comfortable bed I had ever been in. All of the bending and reaching was extremely tiring and we both sighed in relief.

"Any deliveries tomorrow?" I asked.

"No. Got a pretty big work list though. Why?"

"I'm thinking shakedown cruise. We have yet to fire up those engines for real," I said.

"We can stop by and load up the fuel, atmo and water. I was thinking with all the problems we've been having that maybe we shouldn't stay on station any longer than necessary."

I rolled over and sat up, "Why not leave now?"

Nick didn't reply immediately, but finally said, "Aren't you tired?"

"Not too tired to fly!" I grabbed my suit and started pulling it on. I stopped a moment to look at my prosthetic foot. I had become so used to it that I no longer thought that much about it. The military upgrade was incredible.

"I suppose we can sleep once we get underway," he said.

Nick grabbed a reading pad and handed it to me. "This is what I've come up with for a pre-flight checklist. We can automate most of it over time, but I think for safety we probably want a routine."

"Hmm, wouldn't have thought of that." I looked through his checklist. It was mostly common sense stuff, but it was pretty detailed. I was game.

It took the better part of an hour until we finally finished Nick's pre-sail check list. Nick was in the engine room and I sat in the pilot's chair.

Inform Perth Zero of launch plan. The security control tower was just above us. I imagined them staring down at us once they learned of our imminent departure.

The video screen that Nick had installed on the console lit up with a green glow. An approval code displayed and my suit sent an affirmative chirp.

"Ready for gravity push?" I was letting Nick know that I would first lift the ship off the skids.

"Go for push," Nick replied. We were acting more professional than we felt, but I had heard 'fake it 'til you make it,' more than once in my life. I eased arc propulsion downward at the station. The feedback from the skids counted the load backwards in kilos. When it reached zero, I started lifting the skids and felt the ship sagging toward the station. I wasn't sure what that was about, so I overcorrected the lift and caused us to bounce upward with a little jerk.

"Crap. Sorry Nick. My fault." I continued to lift the skids and reduced the arc-jet lift slightly, allowing the station's gravity to hold us down. Once again I let off too much and we started sagging into the station, I had to overreact to avoid contacting the station. Compared to my ore sled, *Sterra's Gift* seemed to over-react. It would take some time to get used to working with it. I hoped I would learn quickly enough not to plow into the station.

"Okay, I got this, Nick." I lowered the skids back down and used what I had learned and settled the ship back onto the station without too much bounce. I then spooled down the engines to an idle.

"Ready for gravity push?" I asked again. Nick hadn't said anything. I appreciated that about him. He would let me work through this.

"Go for push," he replied just as professionally as the last time. I spooled up the engines and directed the arc-jets to push against the gravity of the station. At zero kilograms I nudged gently at the throttle and lifted the giant skids. This time the ship started to skitter sideways to port. Fortunately, I had experienced this with my ore sled and knew that a small adjustment on the port side arc-jets was all we needed. We skittered ten meters before I was able to control it. My adrenaline was pumping.

"Ship is free," I said, as calmly as I possibly could.

"Roger. We are free. Engines normal." Nick sounded like he did this every day.

I eased forward and up and *Sterra's Gift* sailed free from the station. We were flying at ten meters per second, which was the speed I used to zip through the pod-ball court. I arced away from the top of the station at thirty degrees and increased our velocity. I was using almost none of the engine's available power. I desperately wanted to mash it, but figured that would have to wait. I needed to be responsible.

I accelerated to a hundred meters per second over the space of ten seconds. The acceleration caused me to sit back into the chair harder than was reasonable.

"Nick, are you running inertia damping?"

"Negative. Wait one," he replied.

I let off the thrust and coasted along. There was no noise other than a low thrumming of the engines. It was hypnotic and I wished Tabby was here to share the moment.

"Bridge." Nick broke my reverie.

"Go ahead," I said, totally loving every moment.

"Dampers online and added to the checklist."

"Roger that. Strap in, Nick. Gonna push it a little."

"All secured," Nick replied. It might have been my imagination, but I thought there might have been some dread in his voice.

We weren't clear of the stable asteroids near the station, but I had navigated us down to pass by the P-1 refinery. At one hundred meters per second, we passed it at a decent clip. I rolled the ship over for a better view as we passed by. It was 0030 in the morning, but I still saw an ore sled on approach to the refinery.

I pushed the thrust control forward to 20% and the ship responded immediately. The gravity systems on board compensated for all but a small amount of what would have otherwise been life-ending inertia.

"Engine Room. Status?" I asked over comm, noting that our current speed of four thousand meters per second was faster than I had ever gone in my life.

"All systems nominal."

"Are you watching this, Nick?"

"Yeah. Got it on my screens down here. We just passed five thousand meters per second, relative to P-Zero. Check the course I plotted. It's a clean exit past Perth perimeter." My family's claim was twice as far out as we currently were and it normally took us twenty minutes to get this far instead of five.

"High speed maneuvers incoming."

"Roger that."

So far I had kept the stick relatively flat, only causing the ship to rotate on the axis of acceleration. Now I was going to change direction at a high rate of speed. I started easy and accelerated into a slight turn. It pushed me down into the chair slightly and our relative speed to the station dropped. I was familiar with the mechanics from flying the ore sled and many other large machines that were common to a mining colony. What I wasn't used to was how quickly it occurred.

I nosed the ship back over in the opposite direction to put us back on our original directional vector. This time I pushed the thrust harder to get my speed back. The ship responded immediately and as it lurched forward I was pushed back into the chair a little harder.

"Captain we are at four times perimeter distance from station." Nick's voice came over the comm.

"Hah, Captain, I like it. Nick, we're sailing!"

"Let's zero our acceleration with the station and shut it down. We burned a thousand in fuel."

"Really?"

"Okay, more like three hundred."

"Can I shoot the turret?"

"Liam." Nick used his stern voice.

"Okay. Okay. But you know I'm not going to be able to sleep now."

"I have a scrub brush you can use. We need to start working on the grime," he said.

"Way to bring a guy down. Two minutes ago I was Captain and now you want to hand me a scrub brush."

I woke up the later that morning at 0930, pulled a cup of coffee from the galley, and made my way back to the bridge. Nick was already there, sitting in the starboard pilot's chair. I looked out to a new view. I couldn't see the station at all. It was funny that we had picked our seats already. Nick's place was the engine room, starboard chair and the captain's bunk. Mine was the bridge, couch and port side pilot's chair.

"Crazy, huh? So what's on the list today?" I handed Nick a pouch of water, since he had no interest in coffee.

"Believe it or not, I think one of us should drill on the slug-thrower while the other sails an easy zig-zag pattern. I figured out how to get the turret into simulation mode. We have a few more things to fix, but they can wait until we're underway. If we're going to fly with a turret, we better make sure we can use it."

I got Nick comfortable with the flight systems and headed to the armory. I entered the code, climbed up the ladder, and settled into the chair. I tested the operation of the turret and it swung around easily. I had quite a lot of freedom and a great view of everything on this side of the ship. "Go ahead Nick, I'm all set."

"Roger that." Nick accelerated on a zig-zag pattern and my AI projected a simulated attacking ship. I dragged the red line of the projected slug path along the side of the ship. It was hard to orient to the target, but after a few minutes I finally began scoring hits. After thirty minutes, we switched positions and I zig-zagged our way back the same way we had come.

"I scheduled a fuel-up at 0400 tomorrow morning. We'll top off water and atmo crystals, too. Your list is in your inbox," Nick informed me.

We worked the rest of the day. Nick was a task master. Most of the jobs required considerable direction by my AI, but I was pretty good at following instructions. That night we lay on our beds, completely exhausted. I wouldn't have thought I'd be able to sleep before such a big day, but Nick had worked us hard and we hadn't slept that much the night before.

It had become our routine to talk about the next day as we decompressed, waiting to get to sleep. "I sent a comm to Xie Mie-su to remind her to meet at the loading bay at 0600 tomorrow."

Nick replied, "Oh, good, I forgot about that. Alarm is set for 0330, I even programmed the coffee brewer to fire off shortly before that."

"I'm gonna need that," I agreed.

Confusion coursed through my brain as I heard the warbling sound. I hated waking to an alarm. Nick bounced out of bed and hit the lights in the room.

"Shoot me now," I muttered.

"Coffee's up, Captain. Let's meet our destiny." Geez he was

cheerful this morning. Nick was normally reserved, always thinking and almost never annoyingly cheerful.

It took me nearly ten minutes to get my suit on. I was starting to smell a bit. I wondered how I had ever thought that not having a suit freshener might work. I stumbled aft to the galley and poured a cup of coffee. At least that smell was amazing. What was I going to do when we used the last of it? That single kilo wouldn't last forever. I made my way forward to the bridge and found Nick in his normal morning position.

"We need to be at the fueling station at 0400. Engines are online and all systems are go," he said.

I sat in the port pilot's chair. "How about dampers?"

Nick grinned at me. "Roger that, Captain."

I followed Nick's navigation plan and we arrived at the fuel station within a minute of 0400. I eased *Sterra's Gift* into a fueling bay. A robotic attendant expertly connected the hoses, topped us off, and I watched our account balance dwindle. Now, we were pretty much carrying our entire net worth with us.

I eased back from the fueling station and made my way to the open door of the docking bay. Even though the bay was twice as tall as *Sterra's Gift*, it was a tight squeeze for the ship. I came in as slowly as a ship could be sailed, but I didn't care. I wasn't about to dig a crater into the station with my entire net worth. I extended the landing skids and set the ship down. I set the perimeter system to chime when it noted movement and leaned back into the chair, closing my eyes.

I woke up to a chime. The time was 0555. Xie Mie-su made her way across the docking bay with a duffel over her shoulder. She saw me through the armor glass and gave a small wave. I met her at the airlock and attempted to grab her duffel, but she wasn't having any of that.

"Ready for some coffee?" I asked.

"Oh, hell yeah," she responded.

"Cups are in the top cupboard. I'll drop your duffel in your bunk room. You have it to yourself."

"Oh, that's a shame," she replied slyly.

That got my attention, but I ignored it. Was she flirting? Okay, for now I would ignore it. I heard another chime and looked out the window to see four guys pulling large, loaded grav-carts toward the ship. I strapped on my holster and checked the magazine. I had reloaded and was holding thirty-five rounds. I raised my helmet and loaded the security routine.

"Nick. Look sharp. Stevedores are here." Colony 40 didn't have a stevedore union, but there were a couple of companies who specialized in loading ship cargo.

"On it."

The ship layout was simple. The two cargo bays were located in front of the engine room. Next came the galley and airlock on the port side, opposite the armory on starboard. Forward of the airlock on the port side was BR-3, the main head, and then the captain's quarters. Xie would be using the BR-1, opposite the captain's quarters. We were already using the other two bunk rooms to store overflow cargo.

Each of the two cargo bays held ninety-six cubic meters, provided they were packed tightly. The value of the cargo bays was they had an exterior loading platform that lowered from the ship. They also had the added advantage of having an audit record of access which prevented pillaging by a crew. We would have to overflow forty-five cubic meters or better of cargo into BR-2 and BR-3, depending on how well the crew did their job.

I stood several meters away from where Nick was talking with the stevedores. There was a lot of nodding and pointing. In the end, Nick lowered the cargo lifts to the loading bay floor. The cutter wasn't specifically made for hauling cargo, but like most long-haul ships, it needed to have some capacity. Its real advantage was that it was well protected with both missiles and the turret. Of course its primary defense was superior acceleration.

My job was to make sure no one got out of hand. We had too much on the line at this point and I couldn't afford for someone to make trouble for us. The plan they came up with was to put the overflow onto the starboard lift first and move it through the hallway into the bunk room. We would have to vent all of the atmo from the hallways to make it happen, but it would save us two hours of cycling through the ship's small airlock with the extra cargo. I moved inside the ship to watch the stevedores load the bunk room while Nick oversaw the loading of the port lift.

The crates were all loaded by 0730 and we had signed paperwork accepting responsibility for the load. Since this wasn't a bonded load, Ordena would have to bring a civil or criminal suit against us if the cargo wasn't delivered.

With the stevedores gone and the paperwork signed, we were significantly heavier by twenty metric tonnes than when we had landed. This was only 20% additional weight to the ship, overall. I grabbed a reading pad and loaded the pre-flight checklist. It just took twenty minutes to get through the checklist, mostly because I was familiar with the process.

"Pre-flight complete," I said into the comm.

"Roger that. Pre-flight complete," Nick replied.

Public Address. "Xie, we are about to get underway. Please have a seat."

"Ready gravity push."

"Go for gravity push," Nick replied.

Xie stuck her head into the bridge. "Mind if I sit up here?"

"Grab one of the two stations back there if you don't mind." I answered, still watching systems status stream by on the vid-screen.

Xie Mie-su dutifully sat in one of the chairs at the back of the bridge

I gently brought the thrust up, not wanting to knock into the ceiling of the loading bay. I felt quite a bit of stress, given my lack of experience. The pressure on the skids reduced to zero kilos and I gave it a small bump to lift off of the floor. For some reason, seeing the top of the ship in relationship to the ceiling made it easier to figure out how much thrust to add to the arc-jets beneath the ship. I decided to back out along the same path we had entered on instead of trying to turn around and fly out straight. It seemed to take forever before the armored glass cleared the lip of the docking bay. The good news was that by the time we got there the entire ship was out of the bay. For good measure, I continued backing until I was a ship's length away from the station.

I turned the ship on a familiar heading and steadily accelerated.

"Captain, are you looking at the navigation plot I set?" Nick called up from the engine room.

"Not yet, just want to do one thing." Free of the congestion around P-Zero, I accelerated a bit harder and felt the same joy at being pressed back into my seat.

Hoffen Channel One. The AI connected me to my family's primary channel. "Hey Dad, Mom, look up."

I spun the ship over as we passed over the top of Big Pete and Silver's claim number forty-two. We were moving pretty fast at that point.

"Godspeed," Big Pete said over the channel.

"Love you," Mom said.

"Good luck and see you on the other side," I said and closed the channel.

Nick had joined us on the bridge and took his spot in the starboard side pilot's chair.

"Alright, east bound and down," I said and pushed the stick to line us up on the heading Nick had laid out in the navigation system.

"East?" Nick asked, confused.

"Old movie from Earth history." *Play East Bound and Down on Bridge.* My ever listening AI caught the command and piped the audio of a twangy sounding singer named Jerry Reed.

East bound and down, loaded up and truckin',
We're gonna do what they say can't be done.

PASSAGE TO BARU MANUSH

Engage Automatic Burn Plan A.

The flight control stick slid forward automatically and came to rest in a slot in the bulkhead directly in front of my chair. The insistent pull of the stick initially startled me until I realized it was purposefully sliding out of the way. For the next 178 hours, the auto pilot would coordinate with the navigation system to most efficiently reach Baru Manush. We would experience 14 hours of hard burn, 150 hours of free sailing, and then 14 for deceleration.

Hard burn was not extremely well named. The experience is relatively pleasant compared to the motion felt during combat maneuvers. During a hard burn, the gravity and inertia stabilizing systems work together to redirect the effects of acceleration into vertical g-forces. As passengers, we feel as if we are walking around in 1.5 gravity. The effects are quite different if you are used to .6 gravity. We wear our vac-suits to help with circulation, but we can move around, even if it is a bit sluggish.

I grabbed the console as the ship jerked beneath us. For a second, I thought it was possible the auto pilot might have broken. The vid screen display to my left was unfamiliar to me, since this was our maiden flight. I finally located the acceleration display and realized we were okay. The ship was still accelerating, but the auto pilot was choosing significantly different settings than the ones I had been using for manual control.

"Fourteen hours of burn. Gravity at one point five," I announced to the bridge. Nick had designed the flight plan, so I was really giving the heads-up to Xie Mie-su.

"When will we make Baru Manush?" she asked.

"Plan calls for 178 hours, give or take," I answered.

"You told Ordena 250 hours."

"I did. Under promise, over deliver."

Nick handed a reading tablet to me. "Here is your task list. I figured four hours of productivity each twenty-four hour cycle. I prioritized cleaning public spaces first since we have a guest."

"Two hour watches?" Nick and I had previously discussed making sure we always had someone on the bridge.

"Yup."

I scanned the list and the very first item on my list was the head. *Sterra's Gift* was like most other small boats. Each head was a combination shower and toilet with zero-g attachments. While in-station, I had carefully avoided bringing up the subject, but both heads were completely wrecked. I found the idea of Xie using either one embarrassing.

"Did we remember to get cleaning supplies?" I asked.

"Panel G-14," Nick replied.

The first letter of a panel indicated which room of the ship and the number kept things unique. In this case G stood for galley and I'd have to search for the 14th panel. Paint was missing from the panels and it was unlikely I would find it without referencing the ship diagrams. I was glad I had first shift on the bridge.

Nick stood and walked up the small ramp to the back of the bridge where Xie was still seated.

"Ms. Mie-su, if you don't mind, I would like to clean out your bunk room during my first shift," Nick said, sounding all professional.

"Let me get my bag out of your way." Xie stood up in front of Nick, barring his way out of the bridge.

"It should be fine, I can move it if necessary," Nick replied.

Xie laughed like Nick had told a joke. "Don't be silly, I will just grab it and hang out with Liam while you do your work."

"It's not a ..." Nick started.

Xie reached toward Nick and put her index finger on his lips, effectively stopping him from talking. "Never you mind a girl and her bag." With that she turned and exited the bridge, presumably to fetch her bag.

Nick looked over his shoulder as if I might offer some help. I just smiled.

I turned back to look out of the armored glass. The view hadn't changed significantly from what I was used to at home, but it felt completely different. We were hurtling through space at speeds I had never gone before and we would continue accelerating for the next fourteen hours. It was mind boggling.

I spent the next two hours rearranging the vid-screen displays so that I was comfortable. *Sterra's Gift* had a lot of unfamiliar systems, but I had every confidence in my AI's ability to prioritize issues and present solutions. At some point we would need to upgrade software for advanced ship controls, but for now I hoped we had things reasonably under control.

Nick's voice broke my concentration, "Ms. Mie-su, your bunk is ready." It was weird to hear him be so formal, but it made sense. She was a paying customer. "You can use either of the foot lockers to stow your personal items. Can I carry your bag for you?"

Xie had been very quiet for the last two hours. I realized she had been sleeping in the chair and I'd completely forgotten she was there. She answered Nick with a subdued, just-been-sleeping voice, "Oh, no. I have it. Thanks." She stood before Nick could reach her bag and picked it up. "I think I might take a rest, I haven't slept much the last few days." Xie gave me a polite smile and exited the bridge.

Nick didn't feel that needed a response, so he turned his attention on me. It was then that I realized his vac-suit was covered in grime.

"What in the frak did you get into?" I asked.

"I think they transported animals," Nick answered without humor.

"No way." I felt a little sorry for him, but I also remembered that he had me signed up for cleaning the head and I knew it wasn't in any better shape.

"Glad we got that suit freshener. I don't think I've ever smelled this bad. I know I asked Xie to install it, but I think I will take that one on next shift."

"Are you sure you don't want to do that now?" I glanced from his filthy vac-suit to the pristine fabric of the pilot chairs. He followed my eyes and nodded his head with a look of understanding.

"Yeah, it will probably take me less than an hour. I was thinking of putting it in the galley."

"Sure. Come up when you are done."

An hour later Nick showed back up on the bridge. While he was gone I set the ship to alert my AI for any issues that were lower than a green status. Unfortunately, this showed twenty yellow issues that I had to filter out. Most of these were related to missing ship systems and a general lack of combat readiness. I set up a filter to prioritize life support and navigation issues. They were all green, so I relaxed.

Nick's vac-suit looked and smelled better than it had in weeks. His thick black hair was still a mess, but the rest was a vast improvement. Nick sat down heavily in the chair I had just vacated. I had already sent him my ship system's query while he was installing the suit freshener.

"I am showing important systems as green. Let me know if you think we should be watching anything else. I set it to ping me if there is a problem. Why don't you see if you can get some rest?" Nick looked pretty beat. He had been pushing hard for days to get *Sterra's Gift* launched.

"I'll be okay. Feels good to sit down. 1.5 G is rough, but at least we only have nine hours left. We might want to change the work schedule under hard-burn." Nick started working on the vid-screen displays to show a running status of different systems. I didn't mind. I had my preferences saved off. "Left the cleaning stuff in the head. Have fun with that." Nick didn't sound like he thought I would.

I sighed and turned to walk through the door of the bridge. "The bridge is yours."

"Aye, the bridge is mine."

I supposed that we needed to adopt some sort of formal bridge hand-over protocol. I had read that military and corporate ships required strict control of who was in charge of the bridge. It was one of a million things we would have to work out.

I had been sitting for an extended period of time and I could use a trip to the head. My vac-suit could be configured to take care of liquid waste, but I didn't have the software for that yet. I think it also required some additional material - possibly nano-bot upgrades. I didn't like the idea of using my suit that way.

The main head was on the port side and positioned between the captain's quarters and BR-3. There was a secondary head forward of the armory on the starboard side.

The walls, ceiling and floor of the room were one continuous surface of a low-gloss silver-colored alloy. Integrated into the walls were a few strips of lighting that could be dimmed depending on the sleep cycles of the passengers. The floor's higher friction surface had a definite propensity for holding onto grunge.

The shower head was broken off and it looked like someone had simply compressed the end of the tube to give it a level of spray instead of a constant stream of water. The toilet wasn't in any better shape. It was dinged, dented and covered in layers of things we won't discuss. The null-gravity attachments hung loosely and I suspected they weren't working, which would explain some of the grime that coated the walls. The sink looked like it might have been used for the wrong purposes. In short, it was nearly the worst possible scenario that I could come up with.

I decided grime was the first order of business. My tools were straightforward - a brush and heavy duty cleaning powder. Before I started, I decided to check the filtering system. Growing up on a space station and in habitation pods, I knew water was always reclaimed. It was too expensive to simply allow it to go to waste.

The overall design of the water reclamation and filtering system was familiar enough. There was black water reclamation and gray water reclamation. Gray water was the drain from the sink and shower and black was the toilet. The most critical was the black system because while we could all make it ten days without a shower, we certainly wouldn't make it more than another couple of hours without the toilet.

I browsed through the ship's systems and found the main head and its black water system. I discovered that this was one of those non-critical systems with yellow warnings I had filtered out. Not good. The black water system was operating at five percent and on the verge of total shut down. The closest access panel, PH-3, was beneath the floor of the hallway.

The hallway floor was caked with grime and even finding the star-headed bolts was a task. I retrieved a tool set from the engine room and pulled a panel off the floor. The bolts were in terrible shape and I ended up breaking one off in the process and had to drill it out. Half an hour into my job, all I had accomplished was to make the hallway nearly impassable.

Working in 1.5 gravity is not enjoyable. I was getting grumpy again. Fortunately, no one bothered me. I thought I heard Xie's door open once, but she must have had the good sense not to try to talk to me.

Beneath the hallway, running the length of the ship, was yet another meter high hallway. I broke even more bolts pulling panel PH-3. Most were completely corroded with rust and suspicious goo. I was going to have to re-weld the brackets all along the bottom of the panel. Once I pulled off the panel, an awful wave of stench hit me full-on. I wretched and then didn't breath again until I could raise my vac-suit helmet.

The compartment beneath the main head was also only a meter tall, though it was the same width and depth as the head. I pulled a couple of magnetic lights out of the tool box and placed them on the walls for illumination. There was a mass of plumbing filters, pipes and tanks in the small space and there appeared to be at least a three inch layer of semi-frozen black sludge on the floor.

I fired up my AI to overlay the individual components as I looked at them with a green, yellow or red glow indicating their current status. The display provided by my AI made things pretty obvious. There were only two green glowing components. The rest of the system was overwhelmingly yellow and red.

Limit status overlay to black water waste.

This command eliminated components related to the shower,

sink, and the supply side of the toilet. The sludge problem was most likely limited to just the waste side. I had seen this type of thing before, but it had always been Big Pete's problem to solve. I had helped, of course, but ugh, it was never good. As a rule of thumb, you never ignored the head's maintenance schedule unless you wanted to deal with messes like this.

Show aft head status.

Two yellow components appeared on the display and otherwise everything else was green. Perfect. It was much closer to being operational than the main head. I would switch gears and get that sorted out first.

I grabbed the tool box and made my way to the aft hatch H-4. The bolts on this panel came off intact after some work. There were no working lights back here either, but my suit was capable of lighting the area up reasonably well. I grabbed another magnetic light and stuck it inside the small space.

The black water system is designed to take the solids and hold them in a series of pipes with membranes to help filter liquids and solids. Specially designed bacteria break solids down, generating a small amount of energy. The primary benefit of this engineered bacteria is that it consumes a vast majority of the volume of physical waste while also consuming carbon dioxide. The small amount of remaining waste is periodically removed and placed in a frozen cartridge. The resultant waste is basically sand and has no real value, having been stripped of all its useful nutrients.

I could see the waste tubes running beneath the grated floor of the crawlspace starting aft of the bridge for twenty meters. Both the main head and the secondary head dumped (pardon the pun) their waste into one central pipe that zig-zagged back and forth under the floor. That pipe contained filtering membranes and it was supposed to connect to the storage canisters somewhere near the secondary head. Once filled, the cartridges were designed to be removed or flushed out and re-attached.

Pulling off the panel in front of the secondary head, I saw with some dismay, that the cartridges were completely missing. Shortsighted didn't begin to describe the stupidity of this.

Cartridges weren't even remotely expensive to manufacture and were reusable. On station, I could have replicated one for less than thirty m-creds, but I had no way to manufacture one right now.

If I wasn't able to get this fixed, we were in for a long ride to Baru Manush.

The job turned out to be less of a nightmare than I thought it would be. Whoever designed the waste system must have, number one, been a frakking genius, and number two, spent a lot of time sitting in crap. I discovered I was able to remove the sections of pipe in front of where the cartridges attached and clean them out by dumping their contents into waste bags. I strapped bags in place of where the cartridges would normally attach. It would get us to Baru Manush. I added a reminder to check the waste bags every forty-eight hours and replace the cartridges once we got to our destination.

I lugged the filled bags down the crawlspace and tossed them up into the hallway. I didn't have the energy to replace all of the panels I had taken off, so settled for tacking in the hall floor with a couple of new bolts. I dropped the bags into the pressurized airlock and programmed the space to freeze and run at low pressure. I lowered my mask and, sure enough, that ugly sewage smell persevered. There was still a puddle of half frozen goo underneath the main head and, possibly, some overflow under the secondary head as well.

I stepped onto the bridge. Nick turned to look at me. "You smell bad," Nick stretched the last word out for several seconds.

"Solids were backed up. No cartridges either. I need another hour to get the secondary head cleaned up."

"You sure? Want me to switch out with you?" He didn't sound excited about the prospect.

"Nah. I'm smelly but I think the secondary head will at least process now. The main head is pretty well gunked up though."

I jumped back down into the crawlspace with another bag, a scraper, and a stiff brush. It took forty-five minutes, but I was able to peel up the mostly frozen goo under the main head and get it into the bag. Pipes were obviously backed up with sludge, had lost their seal, and would need replacing. If we avoided using the toilet, the shower would most likely work. I finished below by replacing the panels and added a maintenance item in Nick's master list to re-weld the corroded bulkheads.

The aft head was only two meters square with a generous sink, toilet, and a broken null-gravity head adapter. I removed the head adapter first, figuring it wouldn't make sense to clean something that was broken.

It was made of the same material as the main head and was every bit as disgusting. It was as if a room full of monkeys had been fed prunes and let loose. I started at the top and found, to my surprise, that once the cleaning paste was wet, it did an amazing job of removing grime - a pleasant word for what I believed was all over this room. Buoyed by success, I kept at it for another hour and left the room, proud of the job I'd done. I also noticed with satisfaction that the toilet successfully processed the waste and the sink drained well.

In the captain's quarters, I peeled off my vac-suit and suit liner to run through the suit-freshener. While I was pulling on a fresh liner, my back was to the door and I didn't notice Xie leaning on the door frame looking at me.

I had my suit liner up to my waist when I finally saw her.

"Hey, do you mind? I'm changing here," I said, embarrassed.

"You get all of that from when we got jumped in The Down Under?" Xie asked, perusing the different bruises and scrapes on my torso. With all of the excitement of getting the ship going, I had nearly forgotten about getting jumped twice by goons.

"No, ran into some other trouble the day before." I finished pulling my liner over my shoulders and zipped it up.

"What's all that about?" Xie asked.

"Well, to be truthful I was hoping you might be able to shed some light on why we got jumped," I responded.

Xie looked shocked. "Me? What would I know about it?"

"No idea, that's why I asked." I couldn't understand why she was getting defensive.

"Dunno." Now she sounded annoyed.

"Well, you took care of that one guy pretty neatly. You have some serious moves." I sat on the couch to pull my vac-suit on.

Xie gave me what I could only describe as a lecherous look. "Oh, I have moves."

She had to be at least ten years older than me, but I had to admit she was very attractive. Her straight black hair hung forward over her left shoulder and draped down over her chest. Her lithe frame was slightly more filled in than Tabby's and her hips were shapely without being thick. Even with that, I wasn't the least bit interested in her not-so-veiled flirtation.

I realized I had been staring at her, obviously considering her proposal. She stared back, enjoying the tension.

"Oh, sorry. I have a girlfriend." I felt a bit flustered.

Xie crossed the room and sat next to me on the couch and placed her hand on my leg a little too far up for my comfort. She leaned in and suggested, "She wouldn't need to know a thing. Isn't she headed to school anyway?"

It was hard to think with her sitting that close, especially when I felt her breasts pushed up against my arm. I gently picked up her hand and placed it back in her own lap and then stood up to pull my vac-suit over my suit-liner.

"Yeah, no. I can't, Xie." The sucky thing was I wanted to. Xie was right here, warm and smelling really nice. Then I felt guilty, like I was betraying Tabby by just thinking about it.

Xie looked disappointed, even going so far as to push her lips forward in a pout. I wasn't prepared for female drama. It was one of the things that attracted me to Tabby. I needed to change the subject.

"Any chance you would show me some of those moves you used on that guy in The Down Under?" Her graceful handling of one of the thugs, even though he had a flechette pointed at her, was impressive.

Xie lost some of her pout and held her hand out for a little help out of the couch. It made sense. I had struggled under the 1.5 gravity we were currently flying with. I offered her my right hand.

Xie grabbed my hand and as she came to a standing position, gripped it hard, crunching my fingers together at the same time she twisted it into my body. I naturally turned away from the pain, putting her directly behind me. She quickly followed by grabbing hair on the back of my head and pulling downward.

"What the frak!" I cried, pissed at the turn of events.

"Lesson one, Liam. Always assume you are at risk."

Xie pushed my head and arm forward abruptly, causing me to stumble into the couch. I turned to watch her stalk out of the room and head aft. I felt like calling after her and asking what her problem was, but I wasn't sure I wanted to know.

I found Nick on the bridge. "Ready to change shifts?" I asked.

"Yup." Nick jumped up.

"Anything going on?" I had read it was standard operating procedure to get a status report before taking over a bridge watch.

"We are still under hard burn. All systems are nominal," Nick said.

"You are relieved." I said, mostly joking with my formality.

Nick nodded in approval. "I stand relieved."

"Let's move to four hour shifts," I said. "I think it's impossible to get anything done in a two-hour shift." Nick was already heading off of the bridge. I suspected he had something big to work on. He hadn't stopped working for days and, after what I ran into with the septic system, I could only imagine how bad the other systems were.

"Roger that," he replied and exited the bridge.

Update displays to Hoffen One. Automate changing displays when I assume bridge watch. The AI responded with a positive chime.

Add septic system status to main display. Maybe it was because of my recent efforts, but it seemed a mistake not to consider the septic system critical. It still showed as yellow, but I knew from experience it could take days to get everything flowing correctly. Next shift I would have to hit the main head and at least get the shower running. For now, however, it felt great to just sit in the pilot's chair.

It was not unreasonable to nap while on watch, especially for poorly manned ships like ours. The navigation computer would automatically make adjustments for objects, like debris, that passed nearby. If, however, the object had any sign of life, the AI would immediately warn the standing watch. It would be unusual to find an uncharted object out here, but it wasn't unheard of. Even more unlikely would be for us to encounter another ship, but if we did the AI would know about it well in advance.

While I dozed in and out, I thought about my last day with Tabby and wondered what she was up to. She wouldn't make it to the Naval Academy by the time we arrived at Baru Manush. I really needed to send her a recording. We were too far away to communicate two-way without the Navy's communication equipment on the *Kuznetsov*. I wondered if the equipment the Navy had installed on *Sterra's Gift* would be able to initiate that level of communications, but I wasn't about to find out.

"Permission to enter the bridge," Nick asked from outside the bridge's open door.

"Enter." I replied a little groggily. I was starting to believe that Nick was training me on ship etiquette. I still had an hour left. "What's up?"

Nick handed me a pouch of water and a meal bar. I was both hungry and thirsty, so his timing was good.

"Nothing much. I need to do some reading on the atmo generator."

"Anything bad going on?" I hated to think what would happen if our atmo systems failed.

"Yes and no. Nothing to worry about with three of us, but the algae systems are completely down. We're running on crystals," Nick said and dropped into the starboard pilot's chair.

I was surprised my display didn't show a failure in such a critical system. *Show atmospheric systems.* My vid-screen showed a solid green display on top, but the next line showed a red failure. I drilled into it and discovered it was the algae regeneration system. It seemed incomprehensible that the algae system wasn't considered critical.

"That's weird, the algae isn't a critical system." I said.

"I knew about it and downgraded it for the trip. Our atmo crystal system is in great shape and we have enough crystal for ten trips."

"Think you can get the algae system running?"

"No chance. Best I can do is get it cleaned out and start a regeneration process once we reach Baru Manush. We need seed material and I didn't have any place to put it. All of the plants are dead and we're missing parts."

"I am starting to guess those pirates didn't fly this thing very far." I had been trying to work out what *Sterra's Gift* had been used for. "Where's Xie?" I hadn't seen her since I started bridge watch.

"Must be in her bunk room. Haven't seen her." Nick studied my face. I could tell he was wondering if there was something going on between Xie and me, but I also knew he wouldn't ask. Nick knew I wouldn't tell him and so he would try to read it in my face. It was a mental game we'd played before.

I got up from my chair and pushed the bridge door closed. I had Nick's full attention now.

"Have you given any thought to why the ship was torn apart?" I asked.

"Yup, someone was looking for something. Didn't find it though."

"Why do you think that?" I had learned to trust Nick's intuition.

"The ship was systematically tossed. The item has to be small, too." I was about to ask how he knew that, but he held up his hand to hold me off. "Even small spaces were torn up or had panels removed. Why would you rip open the padding on the pilot chairs? Why would someone bring something that valuable or secret on a raid?"

"I pretty much assumed they were scuttling the ship. You know, if they can't have it then no one can?" I was beginning to doubt my obviously simplistic view.

"Why would a pirate scuttle the ship? Plus, where did the equipment go? They were stuck in the ship until the sheriff's department got 'em out and locked 'em up." Nick sounded certain.

"Knock, knock." Xie's voice came through the bridge door as she pushed it open. "What are you boys up to? Am I breaking into a secret meeting?"

There was a small hint of panic in Nick's face. He wasn't one for intrigue.

"Nope, come on in. We were just doing a little planning. Nothing we can't get back to. What's up?" I asked.

"I was wondering when you thought the shower would be up and running. Do you have anything on this tub other than meal bars? And, do you plan to make coffee more than once a day?"

I chuckled, "Wow, that's a lot of wondering. Let me give it my best shot. Shower tomorrow, but I suspect it won't do much more than get you wet. Meal bars are it and coffee will be ready every morning at 0400. We don't have enough for multiple pots each day. A luxury ride, we aren't."

"Well, I suppose I knew most of that before I booked the ride. You guys play cards?"

I looked at Nick. We had been running pretty hard for the last few days. Cards sounded like a good idea to me.

"You have cards?" I asked.

"Thought you would never ask." Xie sauntered over between us and sat up on the bulkhead under the armored glass. It was an unusual place to sit but I didn't see any harm in it. "The game is five card draw ..." I had a feeling I was about to be taken for a ride.

I wasn't disappointed. Xie was excellent. She bluffed and bullied her way through game after game. I considered myself a good card player, but Xie gave me a run for my money. We were playing for m-creds and had decided on a twenty-five credit buy in. We configured three reading pads to hold our chips and placed them in front of us.

Xie and I traded hands and Nick slowly gave ground. In the end, Nick played a short hand and went out in a blaze of glory with a final big bet. To his disadvantage, I could read him and knew when he was bluffing.

After a couple of hours, the engines cut out. They don't make a tremendous amount of noise, but they cause a substantial amount of vibration and a low hum. When they turn off, it is a difficult sensation to describe. My stomach fluttered, but for whatever reason, I wasn't overly bothered by it.

Nick's stomach, on the other hand, took great exception to the sudden change. He set his cards down, jumped up and ran toward the bridge door, making it just past the already ruined carpet and hurled into the hallway. I caught up with him before he had the chance to completely steady himself. I tried to help him stay standing, but he pushed my hands off.

"I'm okay," he said shakily.

We were standing right outside the captain's quarters. "Hey, it's already 2000, how about you sack out and relieve me at 0500?"

Nick considered it for a minute and I noticed sweat beading up on his forehead. I didn't wait for an answer and walked him through the door. I didn't think he was going to make it into the elevated bed so I helped him lay down on the newly repaired couch. He immediately closed his eyes and appeared to be quite a bit more comfortable.

Set alarm for oh-four-thirty, Nick mumbled. I heard the faint chime of his AI responding. On the way out, I reduced the lights in the cabin to normal sleeping level and made my way to the galley for the cleaning kit. It wasn't lost on me that I'd spent most of the day up to my elbows in the septic system and I was once again cleaning up something gross. Oh, the joys of ownership.

I finally made my way back to the bridge and found Xie lounging in the starboard pilot's chair.

"How's he doing?" she asked.

I was happy she had given up on her pushy bad-girl routine. "He'll be fine. He's always had a bit of a problem with motion. It used to get him in pod-ball, so he stopped playing."

"Tough for a spacer, but he might get used to it. Mind if I hang out for a while?"

"No problem. Hope I don't bother you, I'm working on lining up a run."

"Where are you headed next?"

"Not sure. Looking for the best load, I suppose. We talked about setting up a counterclockwise run through the colonies and ending up on Puskar. We aren't set up for a long haul, so we're just looking for a load to the next location."

"I haven't been there for years. I miss the night life of Puskar Stellar," Xie said wistfully. "Well, Baru is all about fuel, calcium and oxygen crystal products. But, just like Perth, M-Cor has Baru miners tied up with contracts. Gray market transactions like that are pretty risky. It's hard to line up buyers. No one wants to piss off M-Cor. What have you found on TradeNet?"

"Once we complete this delivery we can afford the TradeNet subscription, but we won't have enough for the minimum bond."

"How much is all that?" Xie sounded only mildly interested.

"A subscription with thirty minute delayed notification is fifty thousand annual and minimum bond is two hundred. So we need 250 just to get started."

"Yeah, that's a problem. For ten points I might be able to help you set up a gray-market load. You would pay TradeNet that anyway."

"Have to think about it," I replied.

Xie was offering to help me set up a smuggling run where she took ten percent off the top. I was suddenly concerned about the load we currently had on board since I hadn't paid much attention to the bill of lading.

Search commercial feeds for Baru Manush. Find available shipping contracts.

I was encouraged to see a list of twenty items show up.

Restrict to one-hundred-fifty cubic meters or less.

The list shrunk to half a dozen. Not so good, but still in the park.

Show destination, deliver-by date, bond requirement, destination, volume. The list returned, including stops at Hygeia Prime, Perth, Terrance and Puskar Stellar. In a month and a half of travel we could gross eighty-two thousand. The problem was that we needed over six-hundred thousand in bond which we didn't have.

Bonds were going to be the death of us. We had five thousand to our name and when we finally delivered to Baru Manush we would end up with thirty thousand from Ordena and another fifty-two hundred for selling his ammo. If we sold all of our remaining slug-thrower ammo, we would gross one-hundred-forty thousand. Put it all together and we had a maximum of a little over one-hundred-eighty thousand.

We could ignore Perth, since it was in the wrong direction. The high bond was something we couldn't deal with, so that left us with Terrence on the way to Hygeia Prime and then on to Puskar Stellar.

Plot route Hygeia, Terrence, Puskar Stellar from Baru Manush. Arrange with delivery schedules. Normal burn plan.

The list looked better, but was still not right. We didn't have enough available cargo space and were short on bond by thirty thousand. One cargo jumped out at me: one-hundred-twenty thousand bond and payout of only ten thousand m-creds. Hah, only ten thousand. It was more money than I had ever worked with before and now I was turning my nose up at it.

Remove cargo from Hygeia with the one-hundred-twenty thousand bond requirement and redisplay last. Record plan as Puskar One.

Xie had listened quietly to the exchange. "What is that? Twenty-five thousand over three stops?"

"Twenty-eight, I believe." I had always found it easy to do the quick math.

"Since you aren't full, you will have to make up some of the fuel too." Xie continued. "I can get you a two-stop that will net fifty thousand. I bet your net is closer to twenty-two thousand after consumables."

"That was my first try. I'm not turning you down, just want to work it out for myself." She was right. If we didn't add cargo in Terrence we would sail with fifty cubic meters empty and have to cover some of the fuel ourselves. I didn't think it would end up being six thousand, but then she wanted to get a cut. I couldn't blame her. Nothing wrong with that.

Xie stood up. "Alright, I think I will get some sleep. We can talk later. Just don't get yourself contracted before we talk it through, okay?"

"Good night then." I wasn't about to commit anything to Xie. Then again, I wasn't about to enter a contract tonight either.

Record message, focus on my face.

"Heya Tabby, welcome to *Sterra's Gift*. We just dropped out of hard burn and it appears that Nick's motion sickness isn't any better than it used to be." *Pan camera forward, edit commands out of feed.*

"It's so beautiful out here in the deep dark. As you can see, all we have is a gorgeous view of the stars. What I wouldn't give to have you with me right now. We named the ship *Sterra's Gift*, in honor of Commander Sterra. We are en-route to Baru Manush and won't get there until 08.11 which, if I am right, is still a month before you arrive at the Naval Academy. So let me show you some of the things we have been working on."

I spent the better part of thirty minutes taking Tabby through the details of the repairs to *Sterra's Gift*. I didn't leave out any details and relished describing the grossest parts of the septic system.

"Well, that's all I know for now. I miss you." *End Recording, send to Tabitha Masters.* Tabby would receive the message once the freighter she was on picked up a transmitting source. We weren't further apart than an AU (astronomical unit), so Tabby could get the message anywhere from eight minutes to who knows when. Freighters were notorious for not being able to receive transmissions while they were under hard burn and they were almost always on hard burn, since time was money.

I grabbed a cup of coffee. It wasn't as good as it had been this morning, but I found it comforting. The solitude of being on the bridge by myself, looking out at the stars was intensely satisfying. We were sailing at an incredible rate, so fast that I was able to see a visible change in the star field that had always been so constant back home.

Mom had taught me to enjoy quiet moments by practicing yoga and I'd brought along my yoga mat for just that purpose. I slipped into the captain's quarters and noticed Nick had climbed up into the captain's bed, which was his now. I grabbed my yoga mat and re-entered the bridge.

I was very glad I had a yoga mat to practice on, the floor was not in very good shape. I placed my mat behind the two pilot's chairs, took up a meditation position and worked to clear my mind, a difficult task with all the excitement of the last several days. I started by working through my deep breathing exercises and followed up by systematically relaxing all of the muscles in my body. I hadn't practiced yoga for a number of weeks and it felt good to get back to it. Looking out at the stars in front of me, I felt a deep sense of gratitude.

After meditating for nearly forty minutes, I worked into a series of stretching poses. My flexibility wasn't where it had been and so I pushed it. The pain of my tendons stretching was both intense and almost pleasurable. After meditation and stretching, I started a work-out and was disappointed that I had also lost much of my conditioning. It would take a while to get back in shape. No matter, that's why I had returned to it. Ninety minutes later, I was sweaty and wished I had fixed the shower earlier that day. I returned to our cabin and changed suit liners.

While I was cleaning my liner in the galley, I thought I heard a noise below in the maintenance cat walk. I looked up and down the hall and couldn't see that any of the panels had been removed. Either I imagined the noise or something had shifted and fallen. I'd check it out in the morning since I didn't feel comfortable leaving the bridge unattended for more than a few minutes.

I programmed the coffee brewer to run the next morning at 0430. There were only dregs left but I decided to take them and a pouch of water forward.

Nick gently shook my shoulder and I came awake to the same scene I had left the night before. We were gliding through space without the constant thrum of the engines. I had finally fallen asleep well after 0200 and it was now 0500.

"Anything to report?" Nick asked softly.

"All is quiet."

"I relieve you," he said.

"I stand relieved." I was still pretty groggy so I got up and made my way to our cabin and saw with joy that Nick had transformed the couch into its sleeper configuration. I lay down and didn't re-awaken until 1000. I felt great.

I grabbed a cup of coffee and headed up to the bridge. "Good morning, Nick."

"Morning."

"How would you like to run shifts today?"

"Sorry about last night." Nick didn't turn around.

"No worries." It was best to ignore the whole thing. He'd do the same for me. "I probably have a solid six hours of work on the main head, but I think I can get the shower up in a lot less than that. I can't fix the main head toilet and the zero grav components are completely shot. Thoughts?" I asked.

"Okay. I am prepping the atmo system for repairs once we get to a class three replicator. I found a public one on Baru and we have the IP."

Getting the IP rights for *Sterra's Gift* had been absolutely brilliant on Nick's part. Running a plan through a replicator wasn't terribly expensive but the plans for anything could be astronomical. It wasn't uncommon to have to purchase a single run plan.

Commander Sterra hadn't been foolish. She had marked our plans to General Astral Cutter, specifically *Sterra's Gift*, as non-transferable. We could use the plans as long as we owned the ship. The plans were worth more than the ship if we had been able to sell them.

"How about I take a four hour shift after I grab a meal bar and then we can switch back?" I offered.

"Grab me one, too."

"Coffee?"

"Sure."

Once I was back in the pilot's chair, I reran the queries I had built from the night before. Nothing new. I added similar searches to the intermediate ports of call and was able to find a single good load from Terrence to Puskar Stellar Fair. We'd still have fifty cubic meters of space left and would end up on Puskar with forty thousand additional m-creds.

Calculate a final credit balance on Puskar, keep 25% of existing ammunition, top off consumables at each port. Include taxes and fees. Include five days of docking at Puskar.

The number came back at one-hundred-forty thousand. I had hoped for more but we still weren't full. It made me nervous not to tie down the contracts but with our five thousand m-cred balance we couldn't commit to any of the bond requirements.

The rest of my shift went without interruption. Xie got up and went back for coffee, but didn't join me on the bridge, which suited me.

"Permission to enter," Nick said from the doorway.

"Enter. You know I feel weird asking for permission to enter the bridge of my own ship, right?" I said to him as he walked forward.

"Technically you wouldn't have to since you are the Captain. It is the responsibility of the officer of the deck to announce your arrival," Nick informed me

"So you own this ship as much as I do, why are you doing that?"

"We are going to have to take on crew soon. Sailing this short-staffed is dangerous. If I do it right, then I can expect them to do it right."

Nick's logic was solid but it annoyed me to have to think about it. Fortunately, it was why we were a good team. I pushed us forward and Nick kept us organized. I couldn't imagine doing it without him.

"Anything to report?"

"All systems normal and nothing to report." I wanted to show Nick that I was willing to use his approach.

"I relieve you."

"I stand relieved."

I pulled off my vac-suit and left it in the cabin since the better part of my shift would be spent working on the main head. With the cleaning kit from the galley and a tool belt from the engine room, I made my way with some dread to the head. I chuckled to myself, doubting that I was the first to experience 'head dread.'

The smell hit me hard when the door was opened. I was probably overly sensitive from my previous day's exercise, but this job wasn't getting done by itself. It made no sense to clean the anti-grav components, so they were removed first. The components came off easily which was surprising. Everything else was completely frozen due to a lack of regular maintenance. I was happy enough to have a job go my way, for once. After a solid hour of work the entire main head and surfaces were clean, if not sparkly. It was annoying to have to keep running back to the secondary head to dump out the slime I was gathering in my bucket but I couldn't justify leaving the surfaces so disgusting.

I must have been quite a sight, or maybe it was the smell, because when Xie exited her bunk room, she stepped back to keep clear of me. "Ooh, you smell bad, Liam." She waved her hand in front of her nose. Her hair was tousled and she had obviously just woken up.

"All in a day's work. Fresh coffee in the galley, if you are of a mind." There wasn't much to say about my present condition, so I focused on the positive.

"Sounds good," Xie replied but then shut her door. I don't think she had expected to see me in the hallway.

If Xie was going to be up and running around, I decided to gain access to the maintenance cat-walk from the engine room. I hated to have her stumble into an open panel in the hallway. The floor panel I chose came up easily and I suspected it had been removed more often than other panels. Accessing engine compartments would be a constant occurrence, even for pirates.

I found a couple of panel bolts on the catwalk that might account for the noise I'd heard the night before. I didn't think they had been there yesterday, but in my exhaustion, they could have been overlooked.

The panel leading to under the main head came off easily today since I had freed it up yesterday. I felt fortunate that the majority of the gunk was cleaned out of the compartment already, but it still reeked of sewage and wasn't going to get better. All of the seals between the head and the septic system were ruptured and the lines were completely blocked. As a result, the drain for the shower did nothing.

I spent my entire shift freeing the drains of the shower, toilet, zero-grav head and sink. It was a simple idea, push a flexible rod down each drain and allow the junk to fall on the floor of the compartment below.

At the end of my shift I was within an hour of finishing up, so I stuck my head into the bridge. "Hey, Nick, mind if I keep at this? I think I can finish up in an hour or so."

"Any chance of getting that shower running? I can smell you from here," he replied.

"I think we might get it all back online. I will have to use some repair tape to seal the plumbing but the parts are shot anyway. It will probably get us to Baru."

"Do it and make sure you take a shower."

"Roger that." It wasn't lost on me how bad I smelled.

I cleaned the main head and wiped down the surfaces that had become contaminated in the process. Once the water was running and the drains connected, it would require a more thorough cleaning, but this was a start.

Back in the compartment below, I started to swab up the refuse from the floor that had fallen down from the drains when I saw a small spherical object a centimeter in diameter. I didn't want to reach down and touch it, but it was so out of place. I used a rag to wipe it off and I was surprised to find that it was some sort of offline data device.

Connect to device, list contents.

Crap. I wasn't wearing my suit and hadn't thought to bring a wrist connector. My AI was unable to make a connection to the device. I pushed the marble sized device into my pocket and then wondered if this could possibly be what they were looking for when they tore up the ship. It was a heck of a good hiding place, to be sure.

Showering was still a priority, so I swabbed out the compartment and reconnected the fittings. I had to use a copious amounts of sealer tape but, in the end, it all held water very well.

The main head compartment looked clean for the first time and I was proud of the job I'd done. It was a shame that most of the drains, pipes and tubes were wrapped in sealer tape. It was made to fix vacuum leaks in armor glass and nano-reinforced steel and once it was applied, it wouldn't come off without ruining the underlying components. The lightweight material used for plumbing fused to the tape upon application, but it was a worthy sacrifice to get a working shower.

Topside again, I turned on the water in the shower and was satisfied to see it run into the drain and disappear. Another trip below and I discovered a couple of key spots had been missed and were leaking. I hastily applied more sealer tape. I would have to do another check later to make sure nothing else had been missed.

I replaced the panel to the compartment and realized corrosion had rendered much of the lower part of the panel useless. It was important to fix, as the compartment panels needed to be able to be sealed in case of decompression. That made me wonder how many sections in our ship would actually hold vacuum. The ship wouldn't be able to isolate this compartment if the cat-walk became decompressed.

I grabbed my clean suit-liner and a tube of personal cleanser, then locked the door to the main head and ran water through the nozzle of the shower. It was deliciously warm. The water ran dark with grime from my body and for the first time in a number of days I felt clean. I had to scrub my prosthesis by hand and took the time to inspect the stump of my leg underneath the medical cuff. It was still weird, but at least there wasn't any pain or swelling. I figured I would just do my best to put it out of my mind.

I wiped down the surfaces and put on my prosthetic foot and then my suit liner. I felt a hundred times better than I had an hour ago. You don't know how much you miss a shower until you're up to your neck in grime.

Xie caught up with me while I was running my dirty suit-liner through the freshener.

"You smell good. I like that." She pressed close and placed her hand on my chest suggestively.

I gently grabbed her arm at the wrist and pulled it away. "Shower is running. It needs a new nozzle but it beats not having one at all."

Xie didn't pout at my rejection this time. I guess she figured this was how we were gonna play it.

"Oooh, I am ready for a shower." She returned to her bunk room.

I grabbed a water pouch and a couple of meal bars. I had missed lunch and was starving, but felt awesome about getting so much done. It was, however, 2000 and Nick had been on bridge duty for six hours.

"Anything to report?" I asked as I entered the bridge.

"Main head is showing yellow. Quite an improvement. Otherwise, critical systems are nominal."

"I relieve you."

"I stand relieved."

It didn't feel quite as weird this time. I sat down in the chair and reviewed the systems, noticing one of the septic runs had shifted from red to yellow. The influx of my shower water was probably helping things move along.

"How about I take it until 0600 tomorrow? I'll set an alarm if anything changes while I'm dozing."

"Sounds good. I think Xie wants to play cards again tonight. You game?" he asked.

Sure enough, around 2200, Nick and Xie showed up. We finally quit playing around 0100. I was too tired for exercise, but still pulled out my yoga mat and meditated for half an hour. It felt wonderful to clear my mind and simply relax, if only for a short while. I resumed my watch and started thinking about the jobs ahead. The floor of the bridge needed a complete overhaul and somehow I had to find a way to clean the short-piled carpeting, or replace it altogether.

Next thing I knew, my alarm was warbling at 0530. I had wanted to do several system checks before Nick came in. I drank a little water to get the bad taste out of my mouth and saw that all systems were in the same shape they had been the day before. I was working on three hours of sleep.

When Nick entered the bridge, I was more than a little satisfied that he had forgotten to ask permission. We did the rest of our dance and I headed back to my bed on the couch. I fell asleep almost instantly and didn't wake until 1130 when my alarm warbled again. I had been doing a terrible job of eating on time, so I grabbed a couple of meal bars, rinsed out my coffee cup and relieved Nick on the bridge.

"What's the schedule today?" I asked, once I was comfortable that all systems were in good shape. Seeing that the other septic line had moved from red status to yellow made me happy.

"I have at least three more days work on the algae system to get it ready for when we get to Baru," Nick said.

"Okay, I have small things left on the heads to work on. I'll need the welding/fabricator down on the catwalk and we may need to replace several corroded panels. I also question how well any of the compartments will hold against vacuum loss. The crawlspace is in pretty tough shape."

"Do you still have your list?" he asked.

"Yup. Looks like more scrubbing for me."

I pulled out my mat again and spent less time meditating and more time stretching and exercising. Xie entered the bridge while I was in a vulnerable pose, but to her credit, she didn't take advantage of it. Instead, she grabbed a towel, put it on the floor and joined me.

"Thank you, Liam."

We were both pretty sweaty, but I would have to wait to take a shower until after my shift.

Xie continued, "How about we work a little on your self-defense skills."

"That'd be awesome," I replied.

"Self-defense is all about awareness. You walk around in a

bubble, like there is no one around you. That's dangerous. Fighting should always be the last thing on your mind. Avoidance should be number one. Escape should be the second. How are you healing up?"

"I didn't put any med patches on this morning and the bruises are all but gone."

"Good. So, I practice Aikido. I am not a master, but I've been practicing for many years. The value of this to you is that Aikido is designed to be practiced with partners. Even if you decide not to continue with it, I will enjoy teaching you what I know. It will help reinforce my own training."

I almost wanted to ask who she was and what she had done with the Xie Mie-su that I knew, but since she was being serious, I left it alone.

"Our first lesson will be to learn how to fall safely and then we will learn a kata." Xie started.

She showed me a forward fall. It involved correctly rolling forward onto my hip and then back up. It looked deceptively easy when she demonstrated it, but I found I wasn't able to execute it with any degree of confidence.

"You used this fall when we were attacked in the hallway," I blurted out at one point.

"*Mae Ukemi*, yes. It is the most basic fall in Aikido," she said patiently.

"How do you sweep the legs out from under someone?" I was getting excited.

"We will not be learning that today. It would be dangerous if you have not first learned how to fall correctly."

I accepted this with some disappointment, but I also understood that learning Aikido might take some time. We continued to practice and Xie introduced me to the concept of the *uke* and the *tori* - or the defender and the attacker. After an hour of practice I was exhausted, but Xie didn't look any worse for wear.

She left to shower and I returned to my chair and tried to towel off. I wasn't sweating that badly, but I would have appreciated a shower.

Run shipping search Puskar one. No changes.

Check messages. Nothing new.

I shot off a quick message to my parents, letting them know what we were up to. Silver replied within twenty minutes and filled me in on their current mining cut. It was going okay, but nothing terribly exciting. She told me how happy she was that I had struck out on my own, but let me know I would always have a place in the family business. I was less than two weeks away from that life and couldn't imagine ever going back. It was good to see her face, even on a small screen.

Nick relieved me at 1600 and I stayed to eat dinner with him.

My first set of repairs were to bring the weld/fab machine down onto the catwalk. I pulled the panel under the main head. It was completely dry. What a great feeling. I programmed the machine to rebuild the supports that the removable panel attached to. It was a fairly quick job and I returned the weld/fab machine to its storage location in the engine room.

I greeted my old friend, the cleaning kit, and got to work on the galley. It wasn't anywhere near as bad as either of the heads, but it could still use some help.

Connect to Nick. "Aren't there bots that would clean this grime?"

"Yes, cheapest is twenty-five hundred, but it has bad reviews. More like ten thousand for one that would do the work we want and if you want it to be able to lay down a paint scheme, it is eighteen thousand."

"Okay, I will get back to it. But let's get that on the list. I am not a big fan of this." *Hoffen out.* I closed the channel. I could do some cleaning to save eighteen thousand, but someday soon we would need to get one.

2200 came and I focused on cleaning the hallway all the way up to the bridge and over to the airlock. I had removed all but the most tenacious grime and we would need repeated cleaning or stronger brushes to get anything more. I felt good about it.

I went up to the bridge with a couple of meal bars and wasn't surprised to see Xie sitting in her normal card-playing position when I got there.

1005 at the top of the bridge.

"No cards tonight, Captain?" she asked in a mocking voice.

"Sorry. Cleaning duty called."

"I'm beat," Nick explained as he headed off of the bridge.

"That's all I got," Xie said and she left too.

The next thing I knew my 0530 alarm was going off and I reviewed the status of the ship. The septic system was completely yellow on both sides. My efforts hadn't gone to waste.

I had meant to discuss the offline storage device I'd found with Nick yesterday morning. Morning was probably the best time to avoid Xie being awake and listening in. I was determined to show it to him before I headed to bed.

Nick checked in and I held the small device out to him.

"What's this?"

"I found it in the main head, buried in sewage. Gotta wonder if it's what someone was looking for when they tore the place up."

Access device. After a couple moments Nick shook his head.

Bring up console. Nick typed rapidly on a virtual keyboard.

"Locked up pretty tight. It appears to be completely un-addressable, possibly turned off or maybe completely passive. Maybe it needs a cradle." Nick said after a few moments.

"Agreed. I will keep it safe. Probably best not to mention this to Xie." I stuffed the marble into a small pouch in my vac-suit.

Nick gave me a strange look and turned back to clear his console.

Cleaning, yoga, Aikido with Xie, and cards summed up the next few days. I made no progress in understanding what Xie was teaching me with Aikido other than to recognize that it would take a very long time to get any good at it.

We had a couple of short bursts from the engines as the navigation computer kept us away from an object in space. I had programmed a conservative path that didn't bring us closer than one thousand kilometers from any object. Once we got closer to Ceres, there would be a lot of adjustments to make, but we would also be going a lot slower at that point.

The date was 498.08.11 at 1005 and we had been sailing for over seven days. I was sound asleep on the bed in our quarters when the cabin ceiling started pulsing yellow. A soft female voice I had never heard before started repeating, *Significant acceleration adjustment in fifteen minutes. Please take reasonable precautions.*

My heart hammered into my throat and adrenaline surged through my body. I hurriedly pulled on my vac-suit and threw on my AGBs for good measure. By the time I made it out of the cabin, I finally realized that this was all part of the original burn plan. I had failed to notice the night before what day it was. One more rookie mistake.

"Captain on the bridge," Nick called out when he saw me enter. Xie was already sitting in a chair at the back of the bridge.

"Good morning, fuzzy head," Xie taunted in a not unfriendly manner.

I sat down heavily into the starboard pilot's chair.

"Battle stations?" Nick asked when he noticed I was wearing my AGBs.

"Kind of caught me off guard," I replied.

At 1026 the ship started a gentle maneuver, turning the ship 180 degrees. The ship could apply only 20% thrust forward and we would need to go to hard burn for ten hours to match the ship's velocity and trajectory with that of Baru Manush.

At 1027 the main engines cycled up and applied thrust. The change made was very subtle and lacked the gut wrenching transition we had when we exited full burn.

"I like your burn plan adjustment. Maybe we should do that when we transition off too," I said.

Nick nodded his agreement.

"How about I take 1100 to 1300 and then 1600 on?" We were scheduled to arrive at Baru at 1830 and I wanted to be in the chair when we got close.

"Roger that," Nick replied.

I cleaned up a little and grabbed a couple of meal bars and a cup of coffee and then it was time to relieve Nick. I ran updates to see if the shipping opportunities had changed. With my current filter, a few of the deliver-by dates had been updated into the future. Whoever wanted the goods shipped was trying to sweeten the pot, though they hadn't changed the price. It felt like that meant there might be some negotiating room available. None of that would matter until we completed this delivery and sold the slug-thrower ammunition.

Nick relieved me at 1300 and I found it impossible to concentrate on anything. I decided to work on yoga in my cabin and clean the linens on my couch. It felt like I saw every minute on the clock before 1600 came.

Relieving Nick didn't make anything better. I checked system statuses and not finding any problems, watched the clock count down to 1810 when *Sterra's Gift* exited hard burn and turned toward Baru Manush. I'd decided I didn't want to see Ceres until we turned around. I could see it with our sensor package and, without zoom, it was still very small. It would be exciting to see it grow through the armored glass and I didn't want to ruin that.

Yellow diffused light started pulsing from a horizontal light source that ran around the entire ceiling of the bridge. A moment later a soft alto voice, clearly designed to not inspire panic, announced that we would be reducing thrust from our hard burn in fifteen minutes.

I pulled my vac-suit helmet up so I could have the HUD displayed onto my eye. We were still traveling in excess of fifty thousand meters per second, relative to most objects around Ceres. This meant I would only have one second to avoid an object if we found it at fifty kilometers away. Give everything a wide berth. The closest object currently was to our starboard at two thousand kilometers or forty seconds if we were on a direct line with it, which we weren't.

Nick joined me on the bridge and sat in the starboard pilot's chair. I expected to see Xie but she hadn't arrived yet.

"Xie?" I asked.

"I think she is going to ride it out in her cabin. She wants to make some last minute arrangements."

"Does she have a transmitter?"

"Probably nothing special, but even a low power transmitter should be able to reach half a million kilometers through space."

I shrugged. It wasn't a big deal to me either way. We were under a million kilometers away.

We had slowed to ten thousand meters per second relative by the time Nick's new thrust reduction algorithm completed and we had turned around. *Sterra's Gift* rotated on two axes so that the nose of the ship appeared to drop down onto Ceres. We were twenty-seven thousand kilometers away.

Ceres was the size of the end of my pinky finger held out at arm's length and its surface glowed from the reflection of the Sun. It wasn't bright by any means, but sailing through the darkness of space gives you an appreciation for even small amounts of light. It was both beautiful and thrilling to have traveled through space and arrived at a place I had only seen in pictures.

The view was awe inspiring. At one thousand kilometers in diameter, Ceres has 25% of all of the matter in the asteroid belt. P-Zero on Colony 40 would be a pinhead on the surface of such a large body. Even so, the diameter of Mars was seven times larger. I wondered what it would feel like to approach Mars or even Earth. I had heard that the first approach to Earth could make grown men cry.

We continued to slow down on approach and it would take us the better part of an hour to dock up with the station.

Release flight controls. The flight stick, which had spent the better part of the last seven days tucked in the console, released from the forward bulkhead.

Set up collision warning on thirty seconds. Automated collision avoidance at five seconds.

The navigation system would continue to decelerate at our predefined burn plan, but now I had the ability to maneuver around the more numerous objects we would encounter once we were within a hundred kilometers.

"That sure went better," I said to Nick.

I looked over to Nick, who was staring at the door of the bridge with concern. My stomach dropped. There was a bright red dot on his forehead. My eyes followed his to the door of the bridge.

PIRATES OF BARU MANUSH

Xie stood framed in the doorway, casually holding a laser pistol aimed at Nick.

"What are you doing?" Nick asked. I started to rise up out of my chair to face her.

"Nothing personal, lover. Just need my ship back. Now sit down or I drill a hole in you like you did Gaben."

I caught a bit of sadness in her voice. I couldn't make sense of what I was seeing, but it didn't matter. She had a laser aimed at Nick's head and was threatening to use it.

"Who is Gaben?" I knew who Gaben was but needed to buy time to come up with a plan. Gaben Fuse was the pirate I had killed with the mining laser when I punched it through the armory into the slug-thrower turret.

"Don't play dumb, Liam. You never forget your first." Xie was now three meters behind us, well out of arm's reach.

"What do you want?" I needed to buy time to figure things out.

"Turn ship control over to me." Her voice was calm and had lost the girly edge I was used to hearing from her.

"Won't work," Nick grunted.

"What's that, lover?" Xie asked mockingly.

"We can't turn control over. You pointed a weapon at the bridge crew. The ship AI is a combat AI and you are now locked out as an enemy combatant." Nick replied.

"Well, I don't need two of you to fly it," she responded. There was no more mocking, just anger in her voice.

I needed to attract Xie's focus. Nick was good at a lot of things, but negotiation wasn't one of them. I wondered if he was bluffing. If so, it was fabulous, because even I believed him.

"Look, you kill either of us, I guarantee this goes south." For me, this was no bluff.

"Who said anything about killing?" Xie asked and calmly shot Nick in the shoulder.

I had never seen a hand laser fired and my mind reeled as I saw the flash. Nick fell forward toward the bulkhead. If he wasn't dead, he was unconscious. It was more than I could take. I jumped from my chair and charged Xie. I was considerably stronger, but my martial arts skills were no match for hers.

Xie easily caught my charge and threw me to the side. I attempted to roll, the only thing I'd come close to learning in the last few days. I managed to break my fall and come back up to my feet, stumbling a bit drunkenly, but upright.

She looked at me impassively, waiting to see what I would do next. I didn't disappoint her, I wasn't thinking very well. She had shot Nick and I wanted to rip her head off. I don't believe I'd ever felt so much rage.

I charged again and attempted to change it up when I reached her, knowing she would leverage my force against me. Unfortunately, the result was much the same. She adapted easily and this time threw me to my back, causing the breath to expel from my body. She retained control over my arm and twisted it cruelly.

"If you would like to keep the use of this arm, I suggest you get up and attend to your friend," she said.

I struggled, but her hold was such that with a small amount of pressure she was able to cause me no end of pain.

"Please let me know when you are done." She was infuriating but she was also right, I needed to see to Nick.

"Okay, I'm done. Let me fix Nick."

She released me and I opened a panel on the back of the bridge and reached for the medical kit.

"Careful sweetie. Nice and slow with that." Xie was pointing her gun at me, the laser dot steady on my chest.

Nick had fallen out of the chair and lay in a heap between the forward bulkhead and the starboard pilot's chair.

"Careful buddy. I gotta turn you over and take a look here." I spoke to Nick in a soothing voice, trying to calm him if he were conscious. He groaned unhappily as I rolled him onto his back. The entry wound looked like a nasty burn.

Access medical triage program.

I lifted my face shield to look at the heads-up display. The numbers weren't encouraging, but the only thing I could do was cover the wound with a disinfectant medical patch. It would clean his wound and soften the charred skin and tissue. Without help relatively soon, Nick would lose the use of his left arm.

"You bitch," I said, mostly to myself.

"Don't be a child, Liam. I had to establish a new pecking order. You are too pig-headed to believe that a laser pistol makes me the boss, so you needed a demonstration. Now pick him up, put him in the chair and sit down. We have places to go and people to meet. The next demonstration will be permanent."

I was angry but she had definitely made her point. I grabbed Nick, trying to be as gentle as possible, and helped him up into the chair. I had my arms around his torso to lift him. My head was next to his and I clearly heard him say "Loose Nuts." He wasn't in good shape, but more awake than he was letting on.

"Let me put him back on a bunk," I pleaded with her.

"Can't risk him waking up unguarded. Need to keep an eye on you both. Don't worry. This will all be over in less than half an hour. Now back in your chair, Captain. Your new heading waits in your message queue. Please make the necessary course adjustments and don't get cute. I would hate to have to arrange for another demonstration. Oh, and your back roll is definitely improving."

Xie moved to a chair at the rear of the bridge and sat down. She had indeed messaged me both a heading and speed. I was to pick up the pace to fifteen thousand kilometers per second and follow a line to the other side of Ceres, away from Baru Manush.

After thirty minutes of sail, Xie instructed me to reduce speed and then gave me a new heading. We sailed another twenty minutes and entered a small cluster of asteroids.

My heart sank into my stomach when I saw another general astral cutter fly up alongside us. It was a mirror of the *Sterra's Gift* except that it still retained two missiles. The gunner fired several rounds past the armor glass - a shot across the bow. Visual bridge alarms flashed red, indicating we were taking fire.

"Hail the ship and put it on an open channel," Xie demanded.

"Heave to and prepare to be boarded," a gravelly voice demanded.

"Stand down, Boyarov," Xie replied.

"Who is this?" the voice asked.

"Commander Mie-su."

"Give me a minute," Boyarov said. The ships glided along silently for a few moments. The view out of the armored glass was beautiful, but mostly lost on me. The glass framed the cutter against the backdrop of Ceres which occupied 25% of my view. I had to put it out of my mind. The next minutes would likely determine Nick and my life's story.

"Verified. What's the play, boss?" Boyarov's voice replied.

"The boys here locked us out using a military protocol. If you attempt to board, it will automatically blow the airlock and shut down all of the systems. We will follow you back and set down. We can fix it back at base. If Liam here gets cute, blow the engines and try not to kill me."

"Prinyal."

"Okay, Liam, form up on my buddy Alexander there. I suggest you don't get cute, since I am the only thing between him and a promotion," Xie informed me.

Follow cutter at five hundred meters. I instructed the ship.

"What's the end game here, Xie? I set this ship down and what happens to Nick and me?"

"We are always looking for recruits," she chuckled. "You're green but you seem to be resourceful."

She could be serious and it would certainly be better than being dead, but if I didn't get Nick some help, he would lose his arm. This was a bunch of crap and rage rose again.

"I found your toy." I stood up slowly from my chair.

"Easy there big boy. I don't want to blow this ship but I will if I have to. What is it that you think you found?" Xie calmly put the red dot back onto my chest.

Gotcha. We had played enough cards for me to know that one of her tells was that she got real calm when she was focused on something. I raised my hands passively.

"What's Ordena's role in this?" I wouldn't have another opportunity to discover this.

"He doesn't ask too many questions."

I must have pursed my lips at this because Xie defended Ordena. "Oh don't be too hard on him. He's a survivor. You never know who's going to be in charge out here, so it's best to not make too many waves." Xie rationalized. "I think the question is, are you a survivor Liam? You know we aren't any different than Mars Protectorate. They allow you to steal our stuff. What do you think a Letter of Marque is? License to steal from enemy combatants."

"Who are you?" I was genuinely interested.

"Red Houzi. We are a corporation, Liam. I own the local franchise, and I'm always looking for good employees. So what is this toy you referred to?"

"I need to get help for Nick," I pushed.

"We have a combat med tank. You play ball with me and I will get him his turn in the tank." I believed her and it concerned me how much sense it made. "About that toy?"

"You probably don't know it but I have always enjoyed playing ball. How about you lower your gun a little? I will pull it out real slow. I'm not packing."

Xie lowered the pistol and I could see the dot on the floor in front of me. It was probably as good as it would get. I lowered my hands and drew back the seal of the small pocket at my waist holding the marble. I pulled the marble out between my forefinger and thumb.

"I think this is what you have been looking for."

Xie's eyes narrowed on the small object in my hands. This was the moment.

I underhand-tossed the marble to her, but aimed just within

reach of her gun hand, causing her momentary confusion whether to catch it or let it drop. I was counting on the value of the object as being greater to her than her concern for keeping me under control.

I yelled "LOOSE NUTS!" Nick had given me the clue and I hoped I understood what he meant.

A lot of things happened all at once. The gravity of the bridge dropped to 5% of normal and the lights dimmed. I fired the arc-jets on both my hands and boots and Nick lurched across the chair and pushed the flight stick hard to port. I had made it halfway to Xie when the rolling ship caused me to slam up into the ceiling. Random laser fire lanced through the bridge. It was information I didn't need and blocked out.

It was a crazy gamble on Nick's part. I heard him slam into the starboard side armor-glass, but more importantly, Xie flew into the bulkhead behind her with the gun still blazing. What she didn't realize was that I was in my element. This was no different than a pod-ball game. I recovered quickly, rolled off the ceiling and fired my arc-jets in unison. Xie might be an expert at Aikido, but I was certain she was no sort of pod-ball expert. I rolled over on a direct line and saw her lining up for a shot.

"Not gonna happen." I fired my palm jet hard as my arm passed her head, slamming the back of my hand into her face. To her credit, she raised her face shield in time, absorbing the majority of the impact. We were in virtually zero gravity though, so her body was no longer tethered to the floor. The rule that every action has an equal and opposite reaction pretty much ended up with her head dragging her body backward into the wall.

I was used to collisions on the pod-ball court and turned with my other hand and brought it across her wrist with an arc-jet burst. Booyah! The laser pistol came free and flew away harmlessly, clattering into the ceiling.

Xie wasn't without zero gravity skills, however. She recovered quickly and launched back at me. I had the advantage of my arc-jets but she had grappling skills that I couldn't fathom and I was in close. She grabbed my arm and used her legs to hold onto me, then pulled me into a choke hold.

I felt the pain before I could understand what had happened. My left arm felt like it was on fire and I realized that the laser pistol had been fired and I'd been shot. Xie's reaction was considerably more profound. She let go completely and sagged away from me. I pushed her away with both arms to better understand what had occurred.

"Sorry, Liam," Nick said.

I looked back at him, now holding the pistol. Understanding dawned on me.

"You shot me!"

"Bigger problems," he said.

The ship we had been following had rotated in place and was heading back toward us. We were too close for them to not be right on us. I fired my arc-jets back to the pilot's chair.

"You got her?" I asked.

"Yup."

Inertial dampers on. Combat avoidance now. I tried to sound calm, but I'm pretty sure I screamed it.

The ship's gravity returned and we all sunk back to whatever was between us and the floor. For me it was the pilot's chair. My arm hurt, but I had use of it so that was all I cared about. *Sterra's Gift* peeled off on a close vector to the approaching ship and fired the engines hard.

We only had a few moments before the pirate cutter would turn around and likely fire missiles at us.

Burn rate max. Override now!

I was slammed back into the chair. The inertia and gravity systems could barely keep up with the amount of thrust I was pouring into *Sterra's Gift*. We took off at an alarming rate and were putting considerable distance between us and the pursuing ship.

Find objects within 10 seconds.

My heads up display showed a few nearby asteroids. Good. I headed toward a clump of them.

Missiles inbound, the ship warned me.

Countdown missile impact. Override engine safety burn, one twenty percent.

Six ... Five ...

Max thrust. The ship lurched forward again, we were accelerating even faster. I hoped that Nick was well tied in. The g-forces were insane and my vision was starting to narrow. Frak, what a rush.

Six ... Eight ...

We were just about to the asteroids, but were moving insanely fast.

Turret control heads up display. Constant fire. Track reticle to eye.

My heads-up display showed a red glowing field which was the range of the turret on top of *Sterra's Gift*. The slugs started tearing up a smaller asteroid we were headed directly for, with no effect. I switched to another asteroid next to it ... same ... switch ... same. Finally, on the fourth asteroid I saw what I was looking for. Parts of the small asteroid were chipping off.

Reduce thrust. Keep missile at three seconds.

The ship didn't seem to slow much.

Five ... Four ...

I kept firing into the asteroid and just before I overran it, the asteroid burst apart into thousands of small parts.

"BITCH!" I exclaimed.

I thought I heard Nick say "frak," but I wasn't sure and I was pretty busy.

Asteroid pieces impacted the ship and alarms sounded. The bridge door slammed shut. I must have holed the ship and we'd lost vacuum. I was thankful that the bridge hadn't decompressed. More importantly, the missiles also exploded behind us on impact with the ice chunks we had flown through.

"Are you frakking crazy?" Nick yelled.

Reduce thrust 80%. Where is that other ship?

Twenty kilometers and closing in forty-five seconds.

Keep them at twenty kilometers.

I watched for our thrust and saw they were running at 100%.

So they weren't willing to damage their ship. Good to know.

Hail Baru Manush authority. "This is the ship *Sterra's Gift* en-route from Colony 40. We are actively being pursued by pirates and request assistance," I sent.

I received an immediate reply, "Wait one."

Set course for Baru Manush. Keep pursuit ship at twenty kilometers.

The pirates seemed to be content to keep us in range and follow. We were burning an insane amount of fuel, but no way was I interested in them catching us. The navigation computer showed a series of course corrections that would take us around Ceres and match velocity with Baru Manush. We were fifteen minutes away at our current speed.

Five long minutes later, a woman's voice came over the channel I had opened with Baru Manush. "This is Lieutenant M. Bertrand with Ceres Defense. What is your sit rep and who am I talking to?"

"Captain Liam Hoffen of the cutter *Sterra's Gift*. We are actively being pursued by a hostile ship and request assistance."

"Aye. Be advised we have no craft capable of intercepting. Uploading our defense boundary grid. Those bastards won't follow you into the grid. You will need to stow your turrets once inside or you will be fired on. Copy?"

"Roger that," I replied.

The pirate ship must have either intercepted the transmission or could see our new course and turned within a few minutes of that conversation. I didn't want to be fired on, so I stowed the turrets once the pirate cutter was comfortably heading away.

"Captain Hoffen, I am showing you are no longer being pursued. We request a weapons lockout now that hostilities have ceased."

"Granted." I didn't think we had much of a choice. Baru Manush was asking to take control of our turret now that we were within their boundaries. It was a reasonable precaution.

"Captain Hoffen, do you require further assistance?" Lieutenant M. Bertrand asked.

"We have two wounded. One prisoner and my first mate. I

JAMIE McFARLANE

believe my ship is holed. Do you have a pressurized bay available?" It would be difficult to move wounded people through a zero pressure environment.

"Aye Captain. Uploading now. We will have to impound your ship for an investigation."

"Understood."

I got up and reviewed the state of the bridge. Nick was propped into his chair leveling the laser pistol at Xie's still unconscious body.

He looked at me. "I think I killed her."

I moved over to her and retracted her suit's helmet. She had been thrown around the bridge a fair bit, but she wasn't dead. The aftereffects of adrenaline were still leaving my body but I didn't care about her condition. I was really tired of getting shot at and beat up.

"She was going to kill us, Nick. How is your arm?"

"I can't feel my hand and the rest of it hurts like you can't believe."

I backed away from Xie and took the laser pistol from Nick. "Hang in there for a little longer."

Xie moved, opened her eyes, and looked around. Nick had shot me through the outside of my left arm. I had full movement and while it burned like the devil, it didn't otherwise seem to be causing any problems. Xie, on the other hand, had a wound below her right breast. She wasn't breathing very well.

"Point Hoffen." I said unkindly to her.

"You're never getting out of here alive, pal." Claws out and fully extended.

When we crossed the boundary into Baru Manush defended space, the ship's AI relayed a request from Baru Manush Defense to pilot our ship into a quarantine bay. I accepted. I sincerely hoped M. Bertrand would not be a pain in the ass.

I didn't want to let Xie know what I was doing, so I pulled up a virtual keyboard. I punched in a message to Gregor Belcose on the *Kuznetsov*. When we left Colony 40 he had asked to be kept up to date on any pirate activity we might run into. I sent him our bridge log from the last hour with no other information. I figured he could do with it what he wanted.

"Did you see where that marble device went to?" I asked Nick.

"Nope, easy to find though." *Show bridge log last half hour,* Nick ordered. *Center on Hoffen. Speed four times.* Nick was watching on his helmet display. *Stop. Reverse. Stop. Zoom in on Hoffen's right hand. Forward quarter speed. Stop. Select spherical object in Hoffen's hand. Trace forward to real time.*

"It's in her suit," he informed me.

I looked down at Xie. "Pull it out and put it on the ground."

"Why don't you grab it yourself?" she said silkily.

"Sorry Nick, I am going to need you to grab it. Xie, I will not hesitate to shoot you if you make a move."

"You are making a big mistake, boys." Xie said and pulled out the marble-sized device. She handed it up to Nick.

"You keep saying that. Just toss it away from you. Then lie down."

"On this floor? It's disgusting."

"Last warning." It really was. I was prepared to shoot her right there and then, because I still believed she could jump up and kill us both. I later found out she was holding on by a thread and was a much better bluffer than I realized. I turned my attention to the approach to Baru Manush.

The space station was a large, man-made rectangular structure in geo-synchronous orbit above Ceres. It was home to twenty-two hundred colonists who were mostly involved in gas and ice mining ventures on Ceres. A space station isn't much to look at when you come upon it. There are lots of flashing lights and various bays and landing pads connected to each side.

The computer-controlled flight brought us to an upper level and we sailed neatly into an open bay. The docking bay door closed behind us and atmosphere was pumped into the bay.

Incoming hail from Baru Manush Defense, Lieutenant M. Bertrand. Accept.

"Captain Hoffen, I hope you understand, but for our safety, we must be armed when we board your ship. Will you comply?"

"Yes. We are on the bridge and I have a wounded prisoner under guard. I will not be able to lower my weapon until you take control of the prisoner."

"Okay, Captain. I guess we are going to have to trust each other here. Will you release your airlock?"

Release airlock.

"Careful of those bags, they contain waste," I warned.

I heard a loud rapping on the door of the bridge and walked over, keeping my gun on Xie's prone body. I pulled the door open to see the muzzle of a laser rifle. A large woman in armor stood behind the rifle.

"Please stow the weapon, Captain." I recognized the voice of Lieutenant Bertrand. In my mind I had seen her as a slight-framed spacer type. This woman was my height, just shy of two meters, and had the build of someone who had grown up in full gravity and then some. Put an armored vac-suit on her and she was absolutely intimidating.

I stammered slightly. "Yes ma'am." I placed the laser pistol onto the bulkhead of the port side back wall of the bridge.

Bertrand didn't lower her weapon, but pushed her way onto the bridge and swung her weapon first to Nick and then down to Xie. Bertrand was followed by a smaller man, also dressed in armor and carrying a laser rifle. He pointed the gun directly at me.

"Secure the prisoner, Feitz." Lieutenant Bertrand said.

The smaller man pushed his rifle at me and said gruffly, "Hands on the wall dumb ass. Spread 'em."

I started to turn away when Bertrand interrupted. "Not the Captain. The woman on the floor."

"Sorry boss." Feitz pulled Xie's arms behind her back and cuffed them at her wrists.

"Come on in, Doc," Bertrand said into her communicator.

An older man with a small spacer build, entered the bridge a couple of moments later. He was graying and wore a harried look. He carried a bag I had come to associate with doctors. The doctor made his way directly to Xie and pulled an instrument out of his bag and held it on her chest. He was wearing glasses that were obviously connected to the instrument and providing him information.

"She'll make it, but she's in pretty bad shape," he said after a couple of minutes.

"Lieutenant, she is very dangerous."

"I think we can handle it, Captain," Lieutenant Bertrand replied.

"Doc, can you take a look at Nick's shoulder?" I asked.

The doctor looked at me and I nodded to where my friend was sitting. He made his way over to Nick and put the same device on him. After a few moments he said, "He will need a few hours in the medical bay, but the first aid he received was sufficient to keep from ruining his shoulder. Lucky hit, really."

"Fietz, get this woman over to the infirmary. I want you personally to keep guard on her until I relieve you. Copy?"

"Copy that boss," Fietz said.

"Is it okay if my First Officer, Nick, follows them to the infirmary to get patched up? I am at your disposal until this is resolved," I said.

"No problem that, Captain. Doc can you take care of Mister ..." She looked at Nick expectantly.

"James. Nicholas James." He followed the doctor off the bridge.

When they loaded Xie onto the floating gurney, I objected. "Not my job to tell you your business but you should cuff her. If she comes to, she is very dangerous."

Bertrand looked me over and made a decision. "Okay. I suppose you would know. Fietz, keep her cuffed, even if she sweet talks you. Got it?"

The bridge finally cleared of all but Lieutenant Bertrand and myself. She filled the room. It wasn't that she was that big, it was just she was packed with energy, or more accurately, power. The armored vac-suit added to that impression, but where most spacers are lithe, Bertrand looked like she had been chiseled from a granite block. Her armored legs were bigger around than my waist. It was hard for me to take my eyes off of her.

"Done?" Bertrand asked catching my stare.

I was embarrassed at being caught, "I... I haven't seen that many Earthers."

For the first time since she'd entered the bridge, she smiled. "Don't worry about it, Captain. I get that a lot. When you grow up a big girl, you either get comfortable with yourself or you cry."

I didn't know how to respond. It felt like there were too many traps in this social conversation. I decided to keep it all business.

"Mind if I grab a med patch for my arm?" I'd had a chance to look at it and it was just a burn.

"Sure, pull down your suit and I will put it on."

I handed her the patch and unsealed my vac-suit. "How do you want to do this?" I paused for a moment then caught myself. "Your investigation that is." My face flushed.

"Haha, you are a sweet one aren't you," she said, causing my face to flush even more. "Would you be okay with me watching your bridge recordings?"

Bertrand's hands had long fingers, but they didn't lack a delicate touch. I pulled my suit-liner over the med patch and then the vac-suit back over the top of that. The suit-liner was ruined, I should probably invest in a few more and right now an armored suit felt like it would be a good investment, too.

"How far back do you want to go?"

"How about the first six hours out of Colony 40 and the last twenty-four hours?"

"Do you have to keep them?"

"Yes. Anything you give us will be kept forever."

"We might have a problem."

"Oh?" The atmosphere turned menacing.

"You trusted me when you came on board, Lieutenant. I'm going to trust you with something. Can I show you a sequence? I will let you be the judge. We had problems with Red Houzi infiltrating the Sheriff's office at Perth. I think you will see why it is important that this not go any further than it has to."

Bertrand relaxed again. "Fair enough. I need to establish that you have a right to detain the prisoner."

On port vid-screen, show bridge log starting from when I tossed a small spherical object to Xie Mie-su.

Backup three minutes.

The screen showed the scene where I was offering to hand over the marble sized device to Xie. I let it play up until the point where I launched myself at her.

Stop video.

"Loose Nuts?" Bertrand laughed, though not unkindly, then she said, "What do you think that sphere contains?"

"Not sure, but I know the Red Houzi were willing to kill us for it. I believe they also offered us a couple hundred thousand m-creds for it, in a roundabout way."

"Okay. I will watch the logs here on your bridge and make a determination. Give me access?"

Grant Lieutenant M. Bertrand view access to bridge logs. No time restrictions. I hoped that she would see we were aboveboard.

"Coffee? I'm starving too. Trust me enough to get coffee and some bars?"

"Nope, not yet, but I will accompany you. I haven't had coffee in months."

Bertrand drank nearly a liter of coffee and ate no less than four meal bars over the next two hours. She rolled the video back and forth and finally finished.

Ship Sterra's Gift is released from impound and crew probation is lifted. "You guys are in the clear. Thanks for the coffee. Sorry about your ship."

"Any chance we could buy you a drink? I'm pretty sure if you hadn't let us fly in, they would have hunted us down."

"Sure. I'm off duty at 2200 tonight. You can buy the first round. How 'bout Wuzzies?"

As I watched her walk off the bridge, I couldn't wrap my brain around how big she was. She was nearly as big as Gregor Belcose. Over the last couple of hours, I had also come to appreciate how she had worked with me instead of making trouble. She could easily have demanded the storage device.

WUZZIES

I wanted to take advantage of our docked status to refill our bank account. I pulled open the contract from Ordena and sent a message to the customer. I received a reply indicating they would have the local stevedores unload the following morning. Then I pulled up the open contract for the slug-thrower ammo. The contact listed was one Marny Bertrand. M. Bertrand. It couldn't be a coincidence.

I sent a message to the listed address and asked to fulfill the contract. I had decided to keep 30% of our share of the ammo and wondered if I would come to regret selling the rest out here in the Wild West.

"I'm on my way back." Nick's voice came out of my suit collar.

I left a message for one of the two station refuse companies to pick up the bags I had pulled out of the airlock and dropped next to the wall in the docking bay. They would come by sometime after 2100 and requested pictures of the trash, no doubt for their robot to recognize what to pick up. I replied with pictures of the bags.

Nick crawled around the inside of the ship while I arranged for the manufacture of the septic and main head parts. The replicating came to under fifteen hundred m-creds, including delivery. Then I leased a top-of-the-line surface cleaning bot. We didn't need to own one, but we desperately needed to clean up the floors. It was an inexpensive order.

Nick found me sitting on the couch with the table raised, using my reading pad.

"How bad is it?" I asked. I was prepared for bad news.

"Pretty good gashes, took out a piece of one of the sensor strips.

We got lucky though. If we replicate three armor panels we can be as good as new, which is saying something."

"How much do they cost to manufacture?"

"In this case, material is a factor. They have an industrial replicator that is free to use, but we need help installing it."

"Bottom line?"

"Fifteen thousand m-creds, give or take."

"We will get our thirty thousand from Ordena tomorrow and the ammo sale will happen at roughly the same time. We should be sitting flush at 182 or so. This ship saved our lives. Let's treat it right."

"Agreed, but there's more."

I wondered if I had spoken too soon. "Okay, give it to me."

"We burned through some of the couplings in the engines. They weren't in great shape to begin with and you were running at 122% for a while."

"How much?"

"We need to hire a mechanic. It's beyond what I can do."

I was starting to worry we wouldn't have enough.

"Seriously, how much?"

"Forty-seven thousand."

My heart sank. Our fund for bonded loads was diminishing quickly.

"All that from one short period of overload?" I asked.

"No, the engines are old. You just pushed them over the top. We were going to have to replace them at some point."

I felt a bit better. "It doesn't change anything. If I hadn't overloaded, we wouldn't be wondering about money to fix 'em."

"Roger that, Captain."

"I'm glad you're okay Nick. I would never forgive myself."

"Back at ya. Sorry I shot you."

"You feel like taking a break? We're meeting Lieutenant Bertrand at Wuzzies tonight."

"What's a Wuzzies?"

"Not sure but they have drinks and I gotta say, I sure could use one."

I grabbed a fresh suit liner and took a quick shower in the main head. It was amazing how much better I felt. I wasn't messing around anymore, however, and loaded Xie's laser pistol into my shoulder harness. I was meeting with the police and if she had a problem with it she could tell me to my face. I also put my AGBs back on.

Nick had his AGBs on, too and was packing one of our flechettes in a hip holster. We had learned some hard lessons and neither of us wanted to deal with a new one tonight. We fired up the ship's security protocol and I ran Bit Pete's security program.

The hallways of Baru Manush were considerably narrower than that of P-Zero. It had to do with the fact that they were constructed out of steel instead of bored out of huge iron rock. The entire station was considerably smaller, although the regular shape of the rooms and hallways allowed for a much denser population.

We didn't need to go very far to find the entertainment district. When we reached it, our hallway turned into a four meter wide balcony that was twenty meters above the ground. It was the second of five different levels overlooking the courtyard below. We had been hearing music for quite a while, but here it was much louder.

Nick and I leaned over the railing like a couple of tourists. Above us, people were running along an exercise track in a clockwise direction. The levels other than the first appeared to be non-commercial. At ground level, there were live trees growing, reaching up several levels and a meandering stream that ran from one end of the level to the other. Shops of all different types with well-lit signs were advertising their presence.

I had to yell to get Nick's attention.

"This is nice and cheery," I said, more loudly than I wanted.

"Do you know where we are headed?" he asked.

"I think we're down there." I pointed at a large green sign with outlined letters that spelled out Wuzzies.

Nick nodded.

We stepped up to the elevator. When the doors opened, several people rushed off and hurried down the hallway. I looked after them questioningly, but we took their place inside and pushed the button for the lower level. When we exited the elevator, it became clear our presence was causing something of a stir. People hurried out of the way and refused to make eye contact. I felt bad, but didn't know how to stop it. Maybe it was our weapons, but even on Perth you wouldn't get this much attention for a holstered pistol.

Wuzzies was pretty active and we got the same sort of looks we'd received in the courtyard. Apparently, the patrons of Wuzzies were made of slightly sterner stuff than the average citizens of Baru Manush, though, because few patrons ran out the door. The bar was a single room with a U shaped counter made of some wood product. There was a brass-colored foot rail along the bottom of the bar and a huge collection of bottled liquor on the far wall.

A balding, dark-skinned man with a white apron tied around his waist approached the end of the bar next to the door as we walked in.

"Help you boys?" he asked in a friendly but pointed manner.

"Just going to grab a table. That okay?"

"Sure thing. Just so you know, this is a trouble free zone."

"That'll be refreshing," I said, probably too quickly.

He gave me a long look and made a decision. "What are you drinking?"

"Nothing too strong. Do you have anything to eat?"

"We have a pretty good burger and real potato fries. Add my home brew ale to that and you are in for fifteen m-creds a piece. How does that strike you?"

We found an empty table next to the wall at the back of the room. It was made for four people, but we sat down anyway. Lieutenant Bertrand would be here within half an hour.

The brew arrived in frosty glass mugs. It was a light yellow color and tasted bitter on the way down. I can't say it was delicious, but I had never been much for beer. It did have the nice effect of relaxing my nerves.

Halfway through our mugs, we were still waiting for our food. Nick and I hadn't said more than three words to each other as we watched the activity in the bar. I saw Lieutenant Bertrand making her way to our table, so I stood and motioned to the open chairs. She'd changed out of her armored vac-suit and was wearing blue jeans and a loose, nicely cut shirt.

"Greetings, Lieutenant," I said.

"Good evening, Captain. I'm off duty, so that's Marny." The loose shirt and jeans showed her thick Earth body off in a more flattering way than the armored vac-suit had. She was still a big woman, but it was nice to see her features softened up. No question about it, she was all woman.

"Sounds good. Call me Liam, then. You didn't get a chance to meet my partner. This is Nicholas James, or Nick as we call him."

Marny reached her hand across the table and I enjoyed the expression on his face as he took her in. The last time he had seen her he'd been suffering from the shock of being shot. Now he was spending time in her presence, I knew what he was feeling or at least I thought I did. Marny wasn't just big, it was more that she radiated power. Her brown hair was closely cut on her neck and longer bangs were swept to the side.

I elbowed Nick since he was staring. It caused him to jump and he looked away, embarrassed.

"Might give a girl a bit of a complex," Marny responded to the awkward situation.

"Sorry, its ... well ..." Nick stuttered.

"I know. For you spacers, I'm a big girl."

Nick shook his head, "Not that." He was having trouble getting it out.

"Okay, out with it." Marny was amused. I suspected she had this conversation once in a while.

"You're just so beautiful." Nick's face flamed red as he said it.

"Oh man. I'm gonna keep this one." Marny rubbed her hand in Nick's hair. He smiled back at her. I couldn't believe what I was seeing, they hardly knew each other.

The bartender saved us all. "You know these boys, Marny?"

"Yup. Just in from Colony 40. Got jumped by Houzi pirates on the way in."

"Hmm, rumor is they shot one of their own crew."

"You know about rumors, Reggie. Liam and Nick are just good hard-working folk like the rest of us."

That seemed to be enough for Reggie Wuzzie. "What are you having tonight? Boys just ordered burgers. Same?"

"Perfect. Got any of that lager left?"

"Just for you, dear." He winked at her and showed a smile that we hadn't seen a few minutes earlier.

"People aren't overly friendly here," I said.

"They've had it pretty rough. In the last nine months, four raids got past the outer defenses and we've had open combat in the station's halls. If not for the colonists, we couldn't have repelled the pirates. Don't let the bright lights fool you. This is a war zone. A year ago this bar was so crowded you couldn't get a table. Look around, more than half of the tables are open."

"Man, I didn't know it had been so bad. I swear that's not what the news feeds are saying."

"I know. The Indian government is suppressing it. They won't help and don't want anyone to know about it. The station is pretty cut off."

"Man that sucks," I said.

"Good people here, but it's kind of a crap-hole. There is some word about the Indian Government selling the whole station to the Chinese."

"How would that work?"

"It makes sense if you think about it. Chinese have the second biggest fleet and they are trying to expand. Baru produces more fuel than the next three biggest stations. Big money."

"Speaking of. Did you get my message about the ammo?" I asked.

"Yup, we will bring a grav-pallet by in the morning. I hope we won't leave you too short."

"Not at all, we need the money. We're just getting started." I said.

"Do you really have a Letter of Marque with Mars Protectorate?"

"That in the news feeds?" I asked.

"No, I read some of the report. Mars Navy was pretty complimentary toward you fellas."

We talked for a while about the attack on Perth. Marny had a pretty good understanding of what had happened but was interested in some of the finer points. We were all too happy to share our exploits. Nick especially enjoyed describing how we used mining gas bags to launch containers at the pirates. I enjoyed relaying how fierce Tabby could be in a fight.

"That was genius," Marny said. "Those are some stones you're carrying, to be sure."

Reggie Wuzzie arrived with three plates piled with food. I knew I wouldn't be able to eat half of what was presented. The strips of fried potatoes caught my attention, though. They smelled unbelievably good.

Wuzzie caught me eying them. "You're gonna want some of this. Dip 'em in it." He picked up a bottle off of the table and squirted a small pile of thick red fluid.

I looked back at him skeptically. Marny caught the interaction.

"No. Seriously, it's only ketchup," she said.

I picked up one of the potatoes and had to drop it immediately. It was extremely hot. I licked my fingers because the grease was still burning a little and I was surprised that they tasted salty.

Marny chuckled. "Blow it off and try again. I'd ask what rock you crawled out from under, but I'm afraid you'd tell me."

"What's that supposed to mean?" I wasn't really offended, but clearly there was something I was missing about the food.

"French fries and ketchup? How do you get to your age without even knowing what they are?"

"I don't know ..."

"So blow on it and then dunk it. Man up," she chided.

I followed her instructions and was delighted by the taste explosion. Salty, sweet and crispy all at once. They were delicious. I wondered if we could make these on the ship.

"Right?"

"Frak, I wish Tabby was here. She would love this!" I said in an unguarded moment. It was probably the beer, but the unoccupied chair reminded me that our group was one friend short. Enjoying a night out, laughing and sharing stories and new experiences was great. I just wished Tabby was there to share it with us.

"Sounds like a real pip, that Tabby. She'll turn that Navy on its head, I'll bet."

"Tell us. How did M. Bertrand become a Lieutenant of the Baru Manush Defense department?"

"Not much of a story. I came out of the North American Federation, originally from Winnipeg, Manitoba. I was a Marine, did a couple of tours on the ground in South America where things got dicey. Signed up for a tour with the North American Navy and happened to be on Baru Manush when my term ended. They gave me the option of re-upping or hanging out here. I have a bit of a temper and believed they were trying to trap me so I stayed. Baru Manush offered me a job to help organize their defense systems. Been here the last couple of years."

"You were in South America. As in the Amazon War?" Nick asked.

"Was and is. Probably the most scared I've ever been for fourteen months. It was all ground combat. Drones no bigger than a bird that'd get you, given half a chance. Nothing clean about fighting in a jungle either. When I got a chance to go into space I jumped at it. Never want to sleep on the wet ground again. Gotta say, I miss wide open skies. Don't miss that jungle though."

"Any experience in a turret?" I asked.

"Oh yeah. That's what we Marines are good for on a ship."

"Any way to get your hands on any missiles?" I pushed further.

"Maybe. What you cooking over there?"

"What if we took the fight to the pirates? If they had more than one ship, they would have brought it out to chase us down. I think we could take out their ship, maybe even capture it. Our odds are more than even. When we overloaded our engines, their ship couldn't keep up. I guarantee it wasn't because they were being cautious, it was because they didn't have another choice. *Sterra's Gift* was once one of theirs, and I'm telling you, it was in terrible shape. I don't think they have the resources to give us much of a fight."

"You got rocks on you, Hoffen. You serious?"

"Wouldn't that be worth something here? Stop all the pirate attacks?"

"Yeah, of course, but personally I'm not into an even fight."

"See if you can get a line on some missiles and maybe Baru Manush would front 'em. We would have surprise on our side. I bet Nick here could coax a little more out of our engines, at least for a short period."

"Let me talk to my boss."

"Any way you could avoid that?"

"What? Talking to my boss? You know something I don't?"

"They owned our sheriff on Perth. Not saying anything about the authorities here. But, the fewer people who know, the more chance we keep the surprise."

"You might have a point there. Let me see what I can dredge up. Anyway, thanks for dinner. I better get going. I gotta buy some ammo from a guy tomorrow." Marny stood up and winked at Nick, who was staring again.

"You got it bad, my friend. Let's get some sleep," I said. The bill came up to over eighty m-creds. We couldn't afford to eat and drink like that every night, but it wasn't every night you avoided getting killed by pirates.

FORTUNE FAVORS THE BOLD

By the time we made it back to the ship, the sacks of garbage had been removed. I was OCD enough that I needed to see them gone.

At 0730 my alarm went off and I got up and stumbled to the galley for a cup of coffee. My head was pounding and I remembered the common wisdom that said drinking lots of water would offset the effect of alcohol. I sucked down a pouch of water while waiting for the coffee to brew. I wasn't a bit hungry, having eaten too many fried potato strips. It sounded so simple, but they were so tasty and went so well with beer. What a racket that Wuzzie had. You pay for food that makes you want to drink. Not a bad business model.

At 0800 sharp, the stevedores showed up and quickly unloaded the ship. It turns out unloading takes only a fraction of the time that loading takes. It has something to do with not having to figure out where to put stuff. It also helped that we didn't have to vent and pressurize the cabin since we were already in pressurized space.

At 1000, Marny, who I had to remember to call Lieutenant Bertrand when she was in uniform, showed up with grav-pallets and two uniformed men. Nick and I helped them off-load the ammo we had sold Baru Manush. Marny didn't disappoint. Her size wasn't just for show. She easily lifted twice what anyone else could and didn't complain or brag about it. That's just the way it was. She was particular about how things were moved and careful to point out when someone was lifting dangerously. I was used to moving things in low gravity, so I was a little amused to see such a strong person worried about bad posture when lifting. Lieutenant Bertrand was insistent and it was easier to do it right.

I was pleased that by lunch, our account had filled up nicely. Nick was in charge of the master parts list and had them lined up to be manufactured at several different replicators on the station. He also paid extra to have fitters available to install the armor panels. The biggest problem was that the mechanic said it would take at least four days to install the couplings and he couldn't start until tomorrow. The delay couldn't be helped.

The floor cleaner bot showed up around 1300 along with a box of septic parts. I installed the shower head first - easy fix, big result. I didn't feel like getting into the slop again, so I left a message for a plumber to see what they would charge to install those parts. I hoped their price would be good.

At 1600, Lieutenant Bertrand sent a message requesting our presence at Baru Defense Headquarters. The note mentioned a secure communication and I had an idea what that might be about. I took a shower and noticed I hadn't replaced my torn liner.

"Mind if we hit a chandlery on the way back?" I asked Nick.

"No problem, is there more than one?" The majority of the people here lived on the station and commuted to the ice and gas mining rigs. As a result, The Strip, as it was called by the locals, was significantly livelier than any one location on Perth. I had made a mental note that I would like to explore that a bit more tonight. Getting home last night had been a bit of a blur.

The Baru Manush Defense headquarters was very close to the quarantine docking bay we had landed in. I imagined we weren't the first suspicious ship that had been inspected in the bay and wondered what additional scans *Sterra's Gift* had endured. Once we got the armor plates installed, we would have to re-dock at a less expensive location.

We walked up a couple of levels in a stairwell and came out less than a hundred meters from the headquarters. It looked like any other municipal office I'd seen.

The lobby itself was small, only three meters deep and five meters wide. I recognized the man sitting behind the counter as one who had helped us move the ammunition from *Sterra's Gift* to the grav-pallets.

The brown-skinned man, still in his light blue uniform vac-suit, looked up with a smile. I felt fortunate to have an easy recall of people's names. "Heya Majeed. We got a call from the lieutenant."

"Okay, check your weapons and have a seat. I will tell her you're here," he replied.

I was still packing the laser pistol and Nick was carrying a flechette pistol. We slid them across the counter. Majeed pulled the slide back on the flechette and put a trigger lock on the laser pistol.

"You can have them back on your way out," he said, still smiling. Apparently this was common on Baru Manush.

Before we could sit, the door to the right of the counter opened and Lieutenant M. Bertrand filled the doorway. I expected a smile, but she was all business. "Come on in fellas, we are in the conference room." We followed her into a room where comfortable chairs surrounded a simulated wood grain table. Nick and I sat down.

Secure room. Initiate communications. Bertrand instructed. The room lights dimmed and a green light encircling the top of the room in acknowledgment. At the end of the table, a hologram of Lieutenant Gregor Belcose appeared. I could imagine the large naval officer sitting in one of the rooms on the *Kuznetsov.*

Gregor Belcose began. "Thank you for setting this up, Lieutenant Bertrand. Might we be allowed a private conversation?"

"Aye, Aye," she replied, leaving off the honorific 'Sir.' She closed the door after leaving the room.

"I'll get right to the point." Gregor looked at us intensely. "As you probably know, you are not in Mars Protectorate space. Baru Manush is under the protection of India and we have absolutely no jurisdiction. We are not authorized to render you any direct assistance." He paused to let that sink in.

"Okay, what do you need from us?" There must be more, since Gregor could easily have sent that in an open communication.

"We need Ms. Mie-su and that device in Mars Protectorate space."

"Can't the Indians help?"

"No. We have exhausted that particular avenue. They are sympathetic, but frankly, it is too small of an issue for them to send their limited assets all the way from Mars orbit to Baru Manush. The Indians are, however, interested in Ms. Mie-su being removed from the station."

"And?" I wasn't going to make this easy for him.

"And we need you to bring her back into Mars Protectorate space. We are not in a position to violate their space." He seemed a little annoyed at having to spell it out for us again.

"We don't have the capacity to haul a prisoner."

"We might not have the ability to directly assist you, but we are in a position to offer you a contract."

"Hmm ..." I wasn't ready to bite on this yet.

"What would it take to outfit your ship with a brig and hire sufficient crew?"

"Is there a prize for the prisoner and for the device?" I felt greedy, but if I was going to be a successful businessman, I sure as heck wasn't leaving money on the table. I felt Nick squirm next to me. In my mind, there were two points of business here. Hauling a prisoner and the prize for an asset.

"The contract would be for the prisoner, device and transport. Depending on the contents of that device, it could be of significant value."

"Quite a bit of risk for us. I was hoping we could dump the device off here, real public like."

"Tell me what you need," Gregor countered.

"Mind if I get back to you on that? I need to check out some things first. What do you know about Lieutenant Bertrand?"

"Nothing in-depth. Marine Sargent. Decorated in Africa for valor. Bit of an attitude problem. I can pull a file for you if that helps us get this going."

"That'd be great. How soon do you need a response?"

"You need to make it quick. Something out there has Red Houzi's attention. We are tracking four ships headed in your direction right now."

"When will they get here? And what do you mean too small of a concern for India. Four pirate ships heading to one of their stations?"

"Probably less than a week. We believe Red Houzi activity is being sanctioned by the Chinese and the Chinese are looking to buy Baru Manush. You put it together."

"Got it. I'll get you something in a couple of hours. Savvy?"

"What? Yes. Use that communications gear we installed, it's secure. *Kuznetsov* out."

The room lit back up and Lieutenant M. Bertrand re-entered. "Have to say that was a first. Never been kicked out of a meeting by Mars Protectorate." She sounded a little peeved.

"Buy you dinner tonight?" I asked.

"People will talk," she replied playfully.

"I have a business proposition for you."

"2000? I'm off early."

"Wuzzies?"

"Nope, important businessmen like yourselves can afford better than that. Tipped Kettle at 2200. Dress up a little and try to blend in."

"Still gonna be packing. We've had some bad experiences."

"Get a sport coat then."

Bertrand escorted us to the door and we retrieved our weapons from Majeed. We hadn't been in the conference room for more than fifteen minutes.

We made our way down to The Strip and Nick located a clothier. I'd never been in a shop dedicated to selling clothing. For that matter, I only owned one pair of jeans that I wore when I was in school. Most of the time I just wore a suit-liner.

A round, balding man in a dark suit wore a disapproving grimace and greeted us dryly. White walls and white shelves held glass vid screen displays on three walls and were accented by two tall bright green gloss tables. Upon our entrance, the vid screens started displaying different clothing ensembles on models that were suspiciously similar to Nick and myself. The cheery interior couldn't have been more different than the dour little man.

"May I help you?" he asked, trying not to sound bored.

"I am looking for jeans, dress shirt and a jacket that can fit over my shoulder holster."

His interest appeared to pique, "A blazer then?"

I hadn't heard the term so I figured I should be clear, "A dress jacket, something I can wear to a restaurant."

"Any thoughts about color or material?" He must have been disappointed in my answer.

"Really. I don't know. I want to look nice, but not like I am pretending."

"Well, step over here." He motioned to the floor where a pair of green feet were painted on the floor. I did as he bade and saw small red lights flicker over my suit.

"Look at these," he said, "and tell me if you see anything you like." The entire wall now showed me in a dozen different outfits. I pointed to one where I was in a black coat, white shirt and jeans. It also showed me in some sort of boots with a heel.

"Conservative, but you are young enough to pull it off. Let's explore that a little." He gestured and the screens all showed different versions of jeans, dark coats and different light colored shirts. I didn't have a strong opinion.

"Uh, well, what do you think?" I looked first to the man and then to Nick.

"I might go for cream instead of white. Your coloring goes well with a very basic palate. I think your first instinct was good. How about a nice linen weave on the jacket. It breathes beautifully and is guaranteed never to rip or wrinkle."

"How much for that and the boots?" I had never owned a real pair of shoes, having always just used my vac-suit's boots.

"Cowboy boots. I pegged you for the cowboy look. The entire ensemble will cost 350. We replicate them here and will deliver within the hour."

"Could you add four navy blue suit-liners too?" I asked.

"Yes, the cost for a basic synth-cotton liner is 50, but we are having a special on a new fabric that stays fresher longer, only 75 each or four for 250. It's quite a good deal."

I wasn't in the mood to change material. Synth-cotton was very comfortable. "Let's stick with the synth-cotton," I requested.

"Swipe here, please." He indicated a payment terminal.

Nick interjected, "These are together."

The man turned a greasy smile to Nick. "And you were looking for a couple of shirts."

He convinced Nick to also purchase a light brown blazer that looked nice over the black shirt he had chosen. He didn't cave to the pressure to purchase a new set of shoes.

We worked our way around the nearly empty first level of The Strip to a weaponry shop. I was disappointed with the performance of the flechette gun that Nick was carrying and had no idea what I was into with the laser pistol I had appropriated from Xie Mie-su.

Apparently, Nick and I were just the proprietor's type of people. We received a much warmer reception than we had anywhere else in Baru Manush.

"Welcome, friends! What brings you to my humble establishment?" The woman clearly had a spacer build with spindly legs, but had thickened around the middle with age. She had a disarmingly warm smile.

"Wondered if you could tell me about this pistol." I pulled the laser pistol from my holster and handed it butt-first to her.

"Ruger, long-laser 15, commonly known as the Ruger LL. See here, the barrel is three centimeters longer than your standard. Nice gun. You shouldn't leave it turned on though, it's hard on the power cell." She had a calm teaching cadence to her voice.

"Uh, could you show me?"

"Right here next to the trigger guard. Need to feel a little click to turn it on, shows red on the side when it's live." She held the gun so I could see the small stud that stuck out below the barrel. "Push it again and it turns off." She demonstrated and a small swatch of metal below the barrel turned from red, back to the same gray-silver color of the rest of the barrel.

"Cool. Can you check it out for me? I need to know if it's in good shape."

She pulled up a stool up and pushed her body onto it. "If a man's going to hand me his gun, I feel like I should at least know his name." She winked at me. I was sure I didn't want to know what she meant.

"Liam Hoffen. This is my buddy Nick," I said.

"Liam and Nick. Good enough. I'm Gladys. Let's see what we've got here." She put on a pair of glasses and then pulled on the pistol in a couple of strategic locations and the barrel popped off. She laid the barrel on a soft cloth towel on the counter and seconds later had the pistol stripped down into parts.

"See, you gotta love the Rugers, they are so well built. You know they won't release these to the replicators? Yeah, you gotta get this from Earth. Hmm, hasn't been cleaned for a while, got a little bit of carbon build-up. This baby has seen some action, but I can clean it right up for you. Wonder if that sight is lined up or not. Got yourself a real beauty here."

"How long to get it cleaned?" I asked.

"Five in the cleaner should be good. Need anything else? You got a charger?"

Nick replied to this. "Need an adapter for a P12 shelf."

Gladys gave him an appraising look, "Oh, got a gun cabinet then?"

"Yup, pretty much."

She pulled an L-shaped bracket from under the cabinet and set it on the counter, then placed the disassembled pieces under the counter. I heard the click of a cabinet closing and the slight whir of machinery. She pushed her glasses up to rest on her forehead.

"Let that run a couple of minutes. Anything else for you boys? Can I interest you in a Remington 8701? Good for personal defense."

"No, but take a look at Nick's flechette. It seems almost worthless, barely does anything but stick through the vac-suit."

"Let me take a look." She pulled her glasses back down.

"Hmm ... it's a basic model, nothing really wrong with it. It's not designed for anything more than pissing people off in a bar fight. What might peak your interest?" She was looking at Nick.

He wasn't looking for anything but we needed protection. I decided to answer for him. "What would you recommend?"

"Self-defense?" she asked.

"Yeah, but we are on a ship. Need to be careful about puncturing the hull."

"Well, flechette or laser are your options, then. Laser is a good choice for pure offense, not gonna punch a hole in anything, but they're pretty lethal and not legal in most places. A nice high-powered flechette will knock down a charging rhino. Add a suit interface to that and you can shoot around corners."

While she was talking, she pulled out a sleek gun with a dark black barrel and a brown wood grain handle. It was a nice looking gun.

"How much is that?" I asked, drawn in.

"Twenty-five hundred," she replied.

"Wow, that's a nice gun." I was a little put off by the number.

Nick picked up his flechette and put it back into his holster.

"We'll think about it," he said. Message received, he wasn't ready to buy something.

"Okay, you boys talk it over. You wouldn't be disappointed," she said smoothly.

Gladys pulled the parts of Xie's laser out from beneath the counter and placed them back onto the towel. I couldn't see a difference, but she seemed happy enough to reassemble the gun.

"Twenty for the cleaning and twenty five for the bracket."

We made it back to the ship by 1800, two hours to spare before dinner. I wanted to put some numbers together before getting back to Lieutenant Belcose with a proposal. I wasn't sure what he would do if we came in too expensive, but I also didn't want to jeopardize our relationship either.

I was happy to see that a file on Sargent Marny Bertrand of the North American Federation was waiting.

The file showed Marny Bertrand had been born on 498.04.02. That put her at twenty-two years old. She had joined the North American Marine Corp at the age of seventeen, shortly after earning her EMC. Less than six months later she was fighting in

South America in the Amazon Basin. While in the jungle, she had been awarded a Bronze Star with Valor and then received another Bronze Star while aboard the North American Naval Cruiser, George W. Bush.

I found Nick working in the engine room. "Do you have a minute?" I asked.

"Yup." Nick looked at me expectantly.

"I think we need to hire Lieutenant Bertrand, she's a war hero for the North Americans. She can do a lot better than this shit-hole. I also want to take Belcose's deal. What do you think?"

"Do it. Marny is the right kind of person and I'm not just saying that because I kind of like her. We are running too thin on staff and need people we can trust. If she checks out with Belcose, that's good enough for me. As for the rest of it, I'm in. Just let me know what you need this baby to do and I'll make it happen."

Back in our quarters, I composed a message to Belcose. We would bring the device and Xie Mie-su to Mars for 360,000 m-creds. We would be spending every m-cred we had to get her out of here alive. I wanted my 180,000 back and doubled. Then, I messaged a metal fabricator and requested a meeting for the next morning. I wanted to turn BR-2 into a temporary brig.

"Can you see if that mechanic is willing to work overtime? Tell him we will double his rate if he can get the engines up and running in three days," I said into my communicator and worked my way back to where he was.

"Let's run it down, we have 180 less 62 for engine and armor repairs. How much for fuel, oxy and repairs for atmo system?"

Nick replied, "Another twenty, give or take."

"Okay, puts us at ninety-eight, take out five for parts we have been replicating. Think big, what else?"

"First Mate's flight stick and a compliment of vid screens for the bridge. Add a heads-up display and replace carpet in the bridge. Refrigeration and a galley pro." Nick listed off, looking at his tablet.

"What's a galley pro?" I asked.

"Re-hydrates meal-packages that we get from the chandlery.

Can do eight at a time. If we are going to have crew, we will need one. Not everyone wants to eat meal bars."

"Okay. Got it. How much damage are we talking and can we find any coffee on this station?"

"Leaves us at roughly seventy-two thousand and we will have to load up on the food at the Chandlery. Also probably our best bet for coffee. They will have synthetic at a minimum."

"Do it. We may not make it out of here, so we might as well give ourselves every chance. Don't take us any lower than sixty thousand without telling me, okay?"

"Agreed. I'll get someone to install the septic repairs too." Nick offered.

"Oh, thank Jupiter, yes! Ready to head out for dinner in half hour?"

"Yup."

Leaving the ship, I felt naked without my vac-suit. My boots had heels on them which made me stand a little taller and I liked how they came to a point in the front. I had seen cowboy boots in vids before, but this was the first time I had ever worn them. I had all sorts of firsts happening to me these days. The white linen shirt let a lot more breeze through than I was used to and the black blazer pulled along my shoulders. I wasn't comfortable, but Nick assured me that I looked good.

Nick had on his jeans and a black shirt. He had opted to wear the light brown coat and switched to a shoulder holster also. He is considerably smaller than I am with dark black wavy hair. It gets out of control pretty quickly, but he had showered and even shaved, which was something I didn't need to worry about. He had brown eyes and I could always tell what he was thinking by how his jaw was set.

Without a vac-suit, I wasn't able to run my security program. This station had recently hired up a lot of defense personnel due to the pirate attacks. We saw their presence in the hallways everywhere we went. Aside from the suspicious glances and hostile glares from the inhabitants, we felt pretty safe.

The Strip was playing an upbeat music set that echoed back

into the hallway on our approach. We stopped at the railing and looked down. The Tipped Kettle was on the first level, not far from Wuzzies.

I nudged Nick when I saw Marny. She was wearing a loose, colorful tunic with a wide black belt. The tunic hung to mid-thigh and she had tight black pants on beneath that. Her hair style hadn't changed, close cut on her neck with longer bangs swept to the side. She had high cheekbones and a wide jaw, which gave her a striking look. It was hard not to stare. As a man, I would have to be dead not to find her interesting. She was a lot of woman. But, honestly, thoughts like that just made me miss Tabby. I found myself wishing she would respond to my message.

Marny must have been watching for us. It didn't take long before she turned and looked directly up at us and waved. We waved back and grabbed an elevator down.

"You boys look great! I love the new clothes. Cowboy boots?" She looked at me.

"Always wanted 'em," I replied.

She turned to Nick. "Nice coat, Mr. James. You are a handsome little devil, aren't you?"

I grinned internally. That comment would keep Nick spinning for the rest of the night.

"You look really nice, Lieutenant. Where did you find that shirt?"

"Marny, remember? Lieutenant when I'm working. Back when independent trade ships were here more often, I got this from one of their bazaars. Nice old lady. Said she wove it herself. "

Nick nodded with a dumb smile, poor guy. We walked into the Tipped Kettle and were stopped by a young woman manning a podium. She escorted us through the dimly lit dining room to a table topped with a white tablecloth and a small light in the center.

"Wow, this is nice," I said.

"Don't be too impressed. I like the food better at Wuzzies. Atmosphere is better here," Marny said.

"You want to take care of ordering for us?" I asked.

"Will do. They have a nice set of Italian dishes here. Do you like lasagna?"

I looked to Nick. He answered, "Never had it, but that sounds good."

"Let me get to the point," I said.

Marny fired back without missing a beat, "Perfect, that's how I like it."

"We are going to take Mie-su back to Mars and we don't have enough crew. There are four Red Houzi ships on their way here right now, will be here in less than a week. If we aren't gone by then, I don't think we are going anywhere."

Marny started to stand up, "I need to tell my boss, Captain Stabos. He can notify the Indian Navy and send some help. We can't hold off five ships."

"It's already done. Mars Protectorate informed them and they aren't sending help. By all means though, call your captain, but I'm sure he knows about it."

Marny left the table and was gone for twenty minutes and we had to ask the waiter to give us a few minutes. The restaurant wasn't busy, so he didn't seem to mind. When Marny rejoined us at the table her normally pale skin was bright red, like she had been exercising.

"You okay?" I asked.

"You're right. He knew all about it. He said to do whatever I had to do to help you guys get off the station. You have seventy-two hours to clear out. "

"Ouch. That's not enough time to get our engines repaired."

"It's gonna have to be," Marny said unhappily.

The waiter chose this moment to come back. He wasn't bothered by the fact that we were talking and asked if we were ready to order. Marny ordered lasagna and some sort of wine.

"So what do you want from me?" Marny was wound so tight, she seemed ready to explode.

"Why do you think the Indian government would allow pirates to converge on one of their stations?" I needed Marny to put it together.

"Clearly they don't have the assets available. Maybe they're not worried about it. Shoot straight. Do you know something?" She was getting hot and I didn't want to let her keep spinning up.

"Nothing specific. I know general things. Why would the Indian government allow a group of Chinese pirates to raid their station? Rumor has it the Chinese are controlling the Houzi at some level or at least allowing them to exist and they're keeping the Indian government at bay."

Marny wasn't buying it. "So you want me to believe the pirates are part of the Chinese government and the Indian government is just allowing all of this to happen?"

"Work with what we know. The Indian government isn't sending help when a credible threat is headed to this station. The why and how of that seems secondary to me."

That seemed to mollify her and she sat back, deflated. The timing was good because the waiter brought out three steaming plates of an incredible smelling dish.

"Careful," the waiter warned. "It's very hot. Will there be anything else?"

"No thank you. We need privacy for a while. Could you leave the bill?"

"Swipe here and thank you." He was miffed.

Nick grabbed the pad and swiped payment.

We ate in silence. It was important that Marny be the next one to talk. She could take as long as she needed to process what she had just learned.

She finally broke the silence, "Hard to enjoy food with all that."

"Sorry," I said.

"No, not your fault, not really." She wasn't as self-assured as she had been. "How do I fit into this?" she asked quietly.

"Gonna shoot you straight, Marny, put all my cards on the table, no bull. Okay?" She nodded. "Nick and I need you. Come be part of the crew. With you we have a chance. We need someone who understands weapon systems and can handle a prisoner. Xie Mie-su eats us for lunch."

"Quit my job here?" she asked.

I gave her a few moments to process. "Be part of something new. Something important. Mars Protectorate needs Mie-su to help break these bastards. That device might have a critical piece of information on it that helps them do that. We can't do this without you."

"Why me?" she asked.

"When the chips are down, you do the right thing. I've seen your file, Marny."

"After this job?"

"Marny, we're looking for a partner, not an employee. What Nick and I are trying to build is bigger than the two of us. It's bigger than even the three of us. With the right people, there's nothing we can't do, but right now we need your help keeping us alive."

"Let me think about it. What does partner mean?"

"I'm not sure. How about 33% of whatever we earn on this run and a free ride to Mars. That should be around fifty thousand. If you want to get off there, then we part as friends. If you choose to stay on, we will give you stock options and a salary that you set."

"You're crazy." She looked over to Nick. "You on board with this?"

"Ever since I was seven years old," he replied.

ESCAPE FROM BARU MANUSH

0800 came earlier than I would have liked. Nick, Marny and I had polished off a bottle of wine and I had another headache to remind me of the night. I was starting to wonder if wine was such a good idea.

I checked my queued messages and was excited to see a message from Tabby. She wore a cobalt blue suit liner and was sitting in a small cubicle. The suit must have been new because I had pretty much memorized all of her clothing. Her buzz cut still took some getting used to, but I was dealing with it.

"Hi Liam. Gratz on your first load. I knew you would get out of that place! I just didn't think you'd do it before I even got to school. There is absolutely no privacy aboard this freighter so I grabbed one of the offices. We're almost constantly on hard-burn, either accelerating or decelerating, so I've spent the entire time in 1.5 gravity. It's a workout just walking around. They have a nice gymnasium so I am keeping in really good shape. Wanna see?"

Tabby had a mischievous glint in her eyes and she stood and zipped her suit liner down the center to below her belly button. If she didn't have my full attention before, she certainly had it now. It frustrated me that she was somehow able to keep the suit strategically covering a mystery I wanted to explore. I had to admit that she was in incredible shape, her abs were completely ripped.

"Alright. Enough teasing." She closed her suit back up and sat back down. She smiled, knowingly. "Hate to have you forget about me." Tabby continued to fill me in on life aboard a freighter with no luxury accommodations. It sounded a lot like life on *Sterra's Gift,* but without the pirates.

The next message was from Lieutenant Gregor Belcose, "Captain Hoffen, I have received approval for an open account on Baru Manush for mission supplies, repairs and personnel. Please make all haste to the Mobile Protectorate Platform Valhalla, coordinates embedded. Happy hunting."

I wondered what the Valhalla Platform might be and my imagination ran wild for a few moments.

"Nick, where are you?"

"Engine room."

I made my way back, "I heard from Belcose. Slight change of plans. Have we already paid for everything?"

"Like what?" he asked.

"Repairs, armor, upgrades."

"Oh, almost none of it. I paid for the clothes, carpet cleaning bot, and the replicator for the septic parts."

"Perfect. I have an account number for everything else. Belcose doesn't want to put a price on anything, but we have an open account to cover repairs, fuel, etc. We need to jump it to the next level with the repairs and improvements we can get done before we get kicked out. Pay premiums and bonuses to get it rolling."

"I see. Does that change things with Marny?" he asked.

"I seriously doubt it. You got this?"

"Yup."

My comm channel chirped and I moved into the galley so I wouldn't annoy Nick. "Hoffen."

"Got a present for you. How are you set for cash?" It was Bertrand.

"Solid. What do you have?"

"Four Samsung Maelstrom missiles. They want fifty apiece. It's a heck of a deal."

"You think about our conversation last night?"

"I'm in."

"Sweet. What's the best way to get those missiles? Will they deliver?"

"I'll take care of it. Who gets the bill?"

"Nick or me. When can you start?"

"Knock, knock," she replied.

I stuck my head around the corner and looked through the airlock windows. Marny's smiling face was on the other side of the door. I let her in and extended my hand, "Welcome aboard!"

Nick must have overheard because he came down the narrow hallway of the airlock. He sent instructions to the ship. *Add crew member Marny Bertrand. Add exterior access, bridge access, armory access. Make recommendations on security based on the role of gunnery officer. Accept.* The ship's AI was proposing security access. *Accept. Accept. Accept.*

"I got gear on the deck. Where should I stow it?" she asked.

"Probably the forward bunk room, BR-1. BR-2 will be converted into a brig for the trip. Meet me in the bridge when you get squared away."

"Aye aye," she replied.

A few minutes later, I heard her say, "Permission to enter the bridge."

"Enter." When she came in, I said, "Grab a seat."

"I just came from the station. They aren't budging. We have sixty-two hours before we become persona non-grata. Are we going to be ready?"

"With your help, yes. Nick will get the ship ready to fly, but I need you to get us ready to transport a prisoner and defend the ship."

"Wish you hadn't sold me all of that ammo," she said ruefully.

"Can you buy any of it back?" I asked.

"How much money do you have?"

"Mars Protectorate gave us an open account."

"I can buy it back. Captain Stabos is cheap. If I offer him a 50% bonus he'll load it himself."

"Do it. Let's see what open account really means. I don't want to die because we ran out of bullets."

"What else?"

"A crew is coming over to build the brig. Can you coordinate that? If you stick around, you own security. Coordinate with Nick, though. No sense double ordering things."

"Do you have a ship insignia or ship colors?"

That took me off guard. "How's that?"

"We need armor suits. Might as well get them to match. Who is doing the chandlery?"

"Figured we would go with meal bars."

"Probably not," she answered dryly.

"Can you put it on your to do list?"

"I'll take care of it."

"Need coffee," I pled.

A workman appeared at the door of the bridge. "Mind if we take over in here?"

"All yours," I said.

Lockdown flight controls. Open contractor access, Marny instructed.

By the middle of the third day, most of the work was wrapping up. Marny had outfitted the armory with half a dozen high quality blaster rifles. The missiles had been inspected, repaired if necessary, and installed. Sixty percent of the ammunition we had sold had been re-purchased and loaded back onto their original shelves. New armored vac-suits were stowed in our footlockers.

Nick had overseen the installation of all of the vid screens on the bridge and a fully functioning heads-up display. The HUD was tied into the ship's AI system and could display tactical and navigational information onto the retina of any person on the bridge.

Nick had also installed a refrigeration unit, the Galley Pro, a dish sanitizer, and our very own Class 2 Replicator. The replicator was large enough to manufacture moderately complex mechanical items with diameters less than twenty-five centimeters.

I sent a message to Gregor Belcose, letting him know when we would be taking off and asked for any up-to-date information he might have on the converging ships. He had sent a few updates and it looked like at least three of the four ships were close enough to be a problem by the time we took off.

We were exhausted, but I felt pressure to get off of Baru Manush. I wouldn't feel better until we were underway and out of range of the pirates. Baru's stationary guns could disable one or two attacking ships quite well. But the Red Houzi had enough ships coming to overwhelm the station's defenses if they made a coordinated effort. Somehow I doubted they would, though. The smarter move would be to spread out just outside Baru's defense system and wait for us to leave.

"I think it's time to get our prisoner," I announced to Marny and Nick over lunch. The food from the Galley Pro tasted great.

"How do you want to do this?" I asked her. Marny had done a great job turning BR-2 into a brig. An armor-glass wall with a narrow door and food-tray slot spanned the room a third of the way in. The larger section of the room had only a single bunk in it. A vent circulated air between the brig and the remainder of BR-2. Marny had explained the advantage of the design. By not using the entire room, we would be able to have someone inside, on guard if necessary, with the hallway door locked. The only point of vulnerability would come during trips to the restroom. Marny had thoughtfully provided a privy, which was nothing more than a bucket, for Xie to use in an emergency.

"Suit up. We are all going. Once we have the prisoner, she will be cuffed and Nick will have a shock cord on her. Liam will lead, Nick will walk beside her with the cord, and I will follow. Liam and I will be armed with blaster rifles. I wish we had spent a little more time training with them, but our armor suits will help with aiming if it comes to that." We had been through this plan a few times already and I had walked our route earlier that day. Marny didn't think we could be too prepared.

I felt a combination of pride and silliness as we walked through the hallway of the station carrying blaster rifles and wearing armored vac-suits. Just as I had come to expect, Marny radiated power. Her well defined legs were even more impressive with the extra bulk of the armor. She caught me looking at her and simply winked with a slight grin. I think she was used to getting some attention when she armored up.

Xie Mie-su had been held in a cell a kilometer away from our ship. I had tried to figure out if we could move the ship but Baru

Manush Defense wasn't interested in granting any us any new permissions, so we took the walk.

Nick looked like he might have swallowed a goldfish or something. His eyes were opened wide and I thought he was going to hurl. Marny noticed it, too, and moved over to walk beside him.

"Looking pretty fine there, Mr. James."

"I'm no good at this," he said.

"And yet when push came to shove you stood tall. Remember, I reviewed those vids."

"That was different, it all happened so fast."

"All you can do is prepare and then react. No amount of worrying is going to make it better. You gotta live in the moment. We're just taking a walk," she counseled.

"Just taking a walk. Fine." Nick still sounded unsure.

"Have a little faith. Shit hits the fan and I want you to do two things. Get flat on the ground and lay on that shock cord. It won't hurt her and if she doesn't move, it won't do anything. You aren't carrying a weapon, so she can't steal anything from you. That also means your job is to stay alive. Repeat those two things: hit the ground, hit the shock cord." Marny sounded like she was teaching school.

"I can do that," Nick said with a little more conviction.

"I know you can because you did it on Perth when your buddies needed you."

We walked in silence to the holding cell. When we got there, a man in a crisp new uniform greeted us at the door.

"Captain Stabos, I didn't expect you to see us off," Marny said with guarded humor.

"Sure you want to do this, Bertrand? Offer still stands. The path you are on ends poorly and you know it." Apparently the Captain wasn't one to mince words.

"Got to see this through, Cap."

"Your funeral. You're gonna need to leave those rifles here though. Station policy," he said smugly.

Marny's temper flared, "Since when?"

"New orders. Just came down. You must have missed the memo. You can fill out some forms and get them back of course. Majeed, confiscate their weapons."

We handed the rifles to Majeed, who looked a little cowed by Marny.

"Won't forget this, Cap," Marny said through clenched teeth.

"I'm sure of that," he replied.

"The prisoner?" she asked.

"Majeed, bring Ms. Mie-su out please," The captain commanded.

Majeed put the rifles behind a counter, then turned to open a door. Xie, dressed in her black vac-suit, walked unescorted through the door.

"I'll need to search her for weapons. Hands on the wall." Marny was still fuming.

Xie looked to the Captain who replied, "That won't be necessary, Bertrand."

"My prisoner, my call," By now, she was menacing enough to even frighten me.

"Suit yourself."

Marny searched Xie and didn't find a weapon.

"Satisfied?" the Captain asked.

"Yes."

"Good enough for me. You need to leave now."

"Need to put on cuffs and a shock cord, or are they illegal now too?" Marny was pissed.

"Hand over the shock cord, but the cuffs are certainly okay." The Captain was enjoying himself.

Marny nodded to Nick to hand over the cord and then grabbed Xie roughly, pulling Xie's arms behind her back and placing magnetic hand restraining cuffs on her wrists. Marny raised her face shield.

Security channel one. I heard her say and Nick and I obeyed.

"Nick, take lead. Liam you will have to escort her. If we take fire, listen for my instructions. We are going to jog back double-time."

Nick and I acknowledged. Once we made it into the hallway, we started walking briskly.

"Five hundred thousand m-creds if you release me right now. Otherwise, you'll end up dead." Xie said, once we started moving.

"Keep it quiet or I will gag you." Marny said menacingly. I had no doubt she meant it.

"Call off your dog, Liam. That's half a million m-creds. If you want to be a businessman, I guarantee you don't want to piss off Red Houzi like this," she continued.

Marny didn't waste time and pulled a black sash from a pocket and wrapped it around Xie's mouth. Xie struggled, but in the end was gagged.

"Might as well get us on the right path, right out of the box," Marny said humorlessly.

I would like to say we made it back to the ship without incident, but that wasn't the case. We hadn't made it more than a hundred meters when we picked up a tail.

"Get ready boys. The guy behind us is there to keep us from escaping. The main attack is coming from the front or the sides. Liam when it comes, sweep Xie's legs out. Nick, I want you to launch yourself at Xie and keep her down. And Liam, I need you to get the guy who is behind us.

We only made it another twenty meters. The attack came from a crossing hallway. I had just cleared it when two figures emerged, one on each side of us.

Knowing what to do and doing it when the crap hits the fan are two different things. I took two hits right away from flechette guns. Fortunately, the armored vac-suit prevented the darts from penetrating. I tried to sweep Xie's legs, but she was already in motion. She jumped before my leg swept around, so I fired my arc-jets and barreled into her, crashing us both into the wall. Nick was already moving and landed on top of both of us.

I rolled out of the pile and saw the rear goon rushing our way. He could tell Marny wasn't paying attention to him, but then he wasn't paying attention to me either. I could understand that. Marny was the real threat in our group.

He had his flechette drawn, but with all of the friendlies walking around, he hadn't taken a shot. We were in almost full gravity, so my arc-jets didn't easily make me fly, but they could still give me a significant boost. Assisted by the arc-jets, I blindsided the man while at a full run. His gun clattered to the floor and he slumped downward, stunned. I snagged his flechette before he came around, put the barrel two centimeters from his knee and fired five rounds directly into it. He woke, screamed and fell over again. I winced at the pain I had caused and may even have apologized to him. It was the heat of battle. Who remembers? It had been necessary, but I still felt bad.

I looked down the hallway and saw Marny down on one knee. Body language told me she was tiring or had taken a significant amount of damage. There were two bodies on the ground near her and two baddies still attacking. The rest of the crowd had been smart and scattered. I tried to calm down. I was too far away to jump in physically, but now I had the flechette. I dropped to one knee and swung the gun up as one of the guys took aim at Marny. I was going to be too late.

All of a sudden, Nick bounded up from his position on top of Xie. He collided with the gunman whose shot went wild. They both landed in a heap against the wall. This gave Marny enough time to turn her head and address the attacker behind her. Instead of standing up, she rolled, twisted and sprang up under her attacker's arms, grabbing his crotch with one hand and his neck with the other. The poor man screeched and went flying, headfirst into the wall. He didn't move.

Marny walked over to Nick and offered him a hand up. "My thanks, Nicholas, for protecting my flank." Neither Marny's words nor her smile faltered a bit as her foot shot out to the side, delivering a head blow to the guy squirming on the ground. My first thought was that she was one tough woman. My next thought was that I was glad she was on our side.

The fight was over, but we still had to get Xie to the ship. I'd kept her in my peripheral, so I wasn't surprised she'd managed to get her cuffed hands in front and was standing up. I was not in the mood for any of Xie's crap. I stepped forward and leveled the gun at her chest just as she was about to run.

"Xie. I swear I will empty this gun into you if you move," I said with as much vehemence as I could muster. I must have been convincing because she remained still. Nick collected the remaining guns and Marny limped over to where Xie was standing. She unlocked the manacles and then re-locked them behind Xie's back.

"Marny, can you make it back to the ship?" I asked.

"Aye, just a strain. We need to move now," she said intensely.

We made it to the ship without further incident.

"Marny, stow the prisoner. Nick, fire up the engines, then bring the med-kit to the bridge." I made my own way to the bridge.

Open bay doors. Show system's status. List new communications from Kuznetsov.

The disembodied female voice of the ship's AI replied, which was unusual. I didn't like to hear from the AI and preferred to read status.

You have a message from Baru Manush Defense regarding a security lock down of Sterra's Gift. One message from Lieutenant Gregor Belcose.

Relay Baru Manush Defense message to all crew.

"Captain Hoffen, you and your crew will report to Baru Manush Defense Station for questioning related to an incident during prisoner transfer."

Marny stopped short of the bridge door. "Permission to enter bridge."

"Enter." I would have thought that she would skip that given the situation.

"They are trying to delay us," Marny informed me.

"Without those doors open, we aren't going anywhere." I retorted.

"I can get those doors open," Nick said from the doorway, making his way onto the bridge.

I wasn't going to waste time questioning his plan. If he said he could do it, then good enough.

"Will they fire on us?" I looked to Marny.

"Not sure. Feels like that would go beyond the Captain's pay grade. I doubt he would want to blow up Mie-su in any case."

"Nick, do it."

"Marny, can you cover me?" Nick asked.

"I'll do better than that," she replied.

Activate ship defensive perimeter. Marny instructed the AI.

"Right behind you." She followed Nick off the bridge.

Play message from Kuznetsov.

The ship's AI started by displaying a map of the local 3D space. In the center of the display was Baru Manush. The view pulled back from the station and blinking lights showed a net of defense gun positions. The view pulled back even further and the station and Ceres continued to shrink until they were no longer visible. Four ships, magnified, were coming from three different directions. Deceleration vectors showed behind them, indicating both direction and change in velocity.

One of the ships wouldn't be a real problem. It was at least twenty hours behind the others. Two ships traveled together and were the closest to our path away from Baru. We would have to deal with them first. They were close enough that if Captain Stabos, or anyone else from Baru Manush Defense provided them with our departure information, they could easily overtake us.

Skirmishes in space can generally be measured in seconds. If two ships are equal, the fleeing ship only needs a few minutes of thrust to get well beyond range of the other. My concern was the two ships traveling together were small attack craft. The rendering in my HUD showed them as two-thirds the size of *Sterra's Gift*.

I reached up into the rendering and pulled the ships toward me. Apparently, the *Kuznetsov* had received high-def scans of the ships. I expected them to be low quality models, but these ships were extremely detailed.

Belcose didn't provide any narrative, but I appreciated the information nonetheless.

The two ships varied minimally in design. Both were narrow and long with engines all on the back, just like *Sterra's Gift*. They weren't made for dogfight style attacks like you see next to the large battleships in entertainment vids. These ships were built for chase and flee.

I started working on exit simulations to get us past the pursuing ships. Using my best guess as to their capabilities, the best case scenarios weren't looking good. We might be able to get out thirty hours before they caught up with us. Once they caught us in open space, they would shred us. We had less than even odds of survival.

It would have to be Plan B.

"Door will be opening in twenty seconds." Nick's voice broke my concentration.

"Roger that," I replied.

The normally well-lit docking bay had turned dark and red alarm lights were flashing everywhere.

Fire has been detected in Docking Bay. Recommend vacating. A yellow alarm pulsed in the bridge. The ship was fairly impervious to most fire, unless the temps got really hot and started to fry our systems. Fire was one of the most dangerous events in a space station, as it quickly consumed breathable atmosphere. I grinned. No system had a higher priority than fire suppression - not even security systems.

Inform me when all crew are aboard and the airlock is secure.

I grabbed the flight stick and thrust controls and watched with satisfaction as the docking bay door opened.

Crew is aboard and airlock secure, the AI informed me.

Assist flight controls. Quickest exit from station. Keep free of floor and ceiling. I couldn't afford to spend so much time getting out this time. A twist of my wrist caused the ship to spin and move quickly toward the opening doors.

Incoming communication from Baru Manush Defense.

Inform them that we are exiting station to protect our ship from a station emergency.

I pushed forward on the stick and we cleared the exit.

Prepare ship for acceleration. Cease telemetry link with Baru Manush.

A familiar lurch in my stomach let me know the inertia and gravity systems were once again communicating.

"*Sterra's Gift*. Return to Quarantine Bay 2 immediately and report to Station 1."

At full thrust we were less than thirty seconds to the defense perimeter.

Ship address. "Battle stations. Max acceleration in five seconds. Acknowledge!"

Nick and Marny both ran onto the bridge and threw themselves into their chairs.

"Go, go, go," Nick yelled excitedly.

I pushed the virtual thrust bar forward and twisted the flight stick to avoid an approaching ship. I hoped it was just a miner.

"*Sterra's Gift*. Return to Quarantine Bay 2 or you will be fired upon."

"Cap, he could do it." Marny warned.

I didn't reduce the thrust.

Hail Baru Manush Defense. "Baru Manush Defense, you are interfering in a legal prisoner transfer. We are under contract with Mars Protectorate Navy. We are transmitting this conversation. Please repeat last."

If he wanted to stop us, he should know what he was risking.

"Captain Hoffen, stand down. You have ten seconds before I instruct our defense perimeter to disable your ship."

Close communications. Show perimeter gun effective range and Sterra's Gift in one tenth scale.

The HUD showed an uneven sphere around Baru Manush.

Audible count down for Sterra's Gift exiting perimeter gun effective range.

Ten. Nine. Eight. Urgent communication from Baru Manush Defense. Six. Five. Four. Three. Two. One.

We were beyond the effective range of the perimeter guns.

"Remind me not to play cards with you," Marny said.

I nodded. I didn't see it as a gamble. They could have disabled our ship, it wouldn't have been different than us landing back on the station.

I continued, "Do we have turret control back now that we are out of the perimeter?" We had given that up to the station when we entered their space. It was a program that we would have a difficult time overriding in a reasonable amount of time. It would take a system wipe, boot, and restore process. While docked, this could be done very quickly but undocked, it was more complicated. I reduced our acceleration to 25%.

"I released it three days ago just before I took the job. Give me a minute to see if anyone figured that out." Marny turned her chair to face the new vid-screens that had been installed where she would be sitting.

"Nick, can you take the controls? I need to talk to our prisoner." I jumped up and headed back to the brig. The door opened to my touch. Xie was seated on the floor against the armor-glass. I suspected the acceleration had tossed her out of her bunk. At max thrust, the gravity system cannot absorb all of the inertia. On the bridge we were all slammed back into chairs that were designed to absorb the additional g-forces. The brig had no such chair. The safest thing for Xie would have been to lay against the armor-glass and allow her vac-suit to support her spine.

She turned her head to look at me with a scowl. "What do you want, Hoffen."

"Do you want to live?" I asked. There would be no bluffing Xie. She sneered. "Are you going to kill me, Liam?"

"Let me lay it out for you. We aren't going to stop for any of the four ships coming after us. There are two fast attack craft that will overtake us eventually. I will stand and fight," I explained.

"Why are you telling me this? I said you wouldn't be alive for long." She shook her head at me like I was a child.

"Our fates are now the same. I am willing to bet your friends won't hesitate to kill you to get whatever is on this little device." I pulled the marble sized storage device out of my pocket.

"I don't see how that helps you. We will both be dead," she said without expression.

"Tell me the location of the Red Houzi base and give me the layout of the station. That is the bargain I give you. In six hours the two fast attack craft will be on us. I suspect they will join up with the other cutter and it will be three on one. We can't survive that. I am willing to bet you want to live past today."

Her reply was venomous. "You would bet wrong."

"You have thirty minutes before we have to make a run for it. If you hand over those coordinates before that, I believe we have better than even odds." I turned to leave.

"You have another choice, Liam," she said.

"What's that?" I was skeptical.

"Join Red Houzi. We could use a young aggressive bull like you."

"So I can attack hard working colonists and steal their life's work? Never going to happen."

"You don't have to be so sanctimonious. It's not that bad."

"Thirty minutes, Xie. Choose whether or not you want to live." I walked out of the door and back up to the bridge.

"Marny, how bad are you injured?" I turned toward her and looked intently.

"I'll be fine," she responded.

"What if we need to make an incursion?" I asked.

"Board a ship?"

"Bigger. How's that leg?"

"How soon?"

"One hour."

"Help me get a patch on it. I have a combat patch that will give me a few hours of pain free operation. I will pay for it in six hours and won't be able to walk for a day or two. Will that work?"

"Roger that. Can we be battle ready in forty-five minutes?"

"Aye." Marny replied.

"Nick?"

"Yup. What do you have planned?"

Replay bridge log from combat action on 498.08.16. Create navigational vector from last heading of enemy cutter. Create a navigational plan to achieve same vector.

I explained the outline of my plan. We used every bit of the half hour I had given Xie. I was disappointed when she didn't contact me at the end of the deadline.

I pushed the door to the brig open again. Xie was sitting back on her bunk and watched me enter. "Have you made your choice?"

"It won't matter. You have killed us all," she answered.

"If it doesn't matter, then give me the coordinates and let's be done with this."

"Okay. If you are successful you have to let me go."

"Your choice is to live or not, freedom will be a decision for Mars Protectorate. We're wasting time."

"Fine, have it your way. I will provide them once I am on the bridge." She negotiated again.

"Not happening. Just give me the coordinates."

Xie conceded.

INCURSION

I followed Marny back to the galley. She had to remove her armored vac-suit so I could wrap a combat medical patch around her thigh. If I hadn't been so distracted I would have paid attention to the well-defined, shapely, heavily muscled, tanned ...

Okay, so I paid attention.

"You have two flechette darts in your back armor," she informed me.

"I'm making a statement. Let's get ready."

Marny loaded a sack with the supplies we needed. I grabbed a five meter length of cable and clipped it to my belt. We met back up on the bridge.

As soon as we had received the coordinates for the Red Houzi base, Nick set us on a direct path. It was imperative that we arrive well in advance of the approaching pirate ships. I was fairly confident there was only a single Red Houzi ship nearby and we knew *Sterra's Gift* was more than a match for it, especially after receiving the much needed maintenance. But Nick had just flipped us around to slow us down to the same velocity as the asteroid base. It had to be obvious to the pirates that we were on our way.

"Nick, how much time before we reach our launch point?" I asked.

Give us a count down at ten, five, two and the last thirty seconds, Nick instructed and then said, "About fifteen minutes. We have been synchronizing speed with the asteroid cluster for the last ten minutes. That will be done in six."

"Let's go over the plan one more time," I interjected. "If you don't hear from us in ninety minutes, then haul your ass back over to Baru Manush. Better for you to be locked up for a few months than dead, Nick."

"Not gonna talk about it," Nick replied.

Hostile ship detected on intercept course. I could have sworn the soft female voice sounded stressed.

When will they be in firing range? Nick queried.

One minute, twenty-three seconds. The ship had come upon us much faster than expected.

"Hold on!" Nick shoved the virtual throttle all the way forward and caused Marny and me to tumble back into the bulkhead at the back of the bridge. My ribs hit first and the air was knocked out of me. Fortunately, the armor vac-suit stiffened up and absorbed enough of the impact to prevent cracked ribs, but it still caused me to slump to the floor. Marny made it to her feet before I did and helped me up.

"Get in the airlock now! I will give you as much time as I can," Nick said over the noise of the engines.

Nick had taken the only action available to him. If we didn't slow down sufficiently, Marny and I would be unable to lose enough of our momentum as we propelled over to the pirate's enclave. I closed my face shield and instructed my suit's AI, *Give me a thirty second countdown to enemy ship firing range.*

Marny and I stumbled out of the bridge into the hallway. The downward or vertical force was at least 2gs, and that kept our feet on the floor. The backward horizontal g-force, however, was so strong that we had to bend our knees and dig in one foot to try and slow our slide down the hallway toward the back of the ship. I was worried we wouldn't be able to make the corner into the airlock. Luckily, Marny had thought ahead and left the two blast rifles we would need clipped to a shelf inside the airlock. Making a side trip to the armory was not possible.

Thirty. Twenty-nine.

Stepping up the timing on this little mission was going to make our jump a significantly more dangerous maneuver. Keeping Marny and me safe meant Nick would have to continue decelerating into the path of the oncoming enemy cutter, exposing

Sterra's Gift to more time in the pirate's weapon's range. We were hoping Nick could have dropped us off and been able to escape from the pirate base before the local Red Houzi cutter got close. I hated the thought of Nick being fired on, but there was no getting around it.

With Marny and me inside the airlock, I slung one of the rifles over my shoulder, grabbed the loops of cable and started the pump to cycle the air out. One end of the cable was already attached to me, so I clipped the other end to Marny.

Once we were outside the ship, I wouldn't be able to talk to Nick without advertising that we were on EVA (external vehicle activity). "Nick, when we are off, you need to accelerate on max toward that ship. They will get a strafing run on you, so give 'em your belly. You won't be able to fire back but there will be fewer critical systems for them to hit. Remember, once they are on you, keep curving up so if they get close enough you can get a shot at them from your turret. Keep firing at them up to that point, we can buy more ammo."

Five. Four. I opened the external door of the airlock.

"Engines are off for seven seconds. Go!" Nick shouted.

Acceleration shut down abruptly. I hoped Nick would be able to keep his lunch down. Marny and I held hands and jumped free of the ship. *Two. One.*

Establish closed communication channel with Bertrand.

Sterra's Gift gently swiveled around and I saw flashes as her turret started firing at the quickly approaching cutter. I hoped we weren't in its path because they wouldn't be able to see us until we were a smear on their armor-glass. The odds were infinitesimally small that they would hit us, but once planted, the idea stuck.

Nick applied thrust, gently at first, angling away from Marny and me. A couple of seconds later we were treated to a much-too-close view of the back end of three insanely powerful engines firing at max power. My face shield automatically dimmed due to the extreme brightness. Nick would have to survive at least ten seconds within gun range of the other cutter. I hoped they didn't have missiles.

I knew the enemy ship had raced by us, but it happened so fast that it was more of an impression than something I could actually see. I sure hoped Nick would be okay. I rationalized that *Sterra's Gift* should surely be able to take a few hits. As bright lights flashed in the dark, I knew guns were firing. It made me sick to realize those bullets were being fired at my lifelong friend.

"Snap out of it, Captain." Marny pulled me around so that we were face to face. "You gotta stay in the moment."

I stared back at her, frozen in indecision.

"Trust him. He is trusting us to get our job done. Trust him to do his."

"Okay." I was having difficulty pulling it together.

Marny and I fell toward the asteroid. It was twenty-five minutes away as long as we executed our planned burns at the right times and for the right durations. If Nick hadn't been able to slow down sufficiently, our vac-suit's arc-jets wouldn't have had been able to generate enough thrust to reduce our relative speed to the oncoming asteroid. The suits had a limited amount of thrust available and we were cutting it close as it was.

We would remain connected via the cable until the last possible moment. The danger of us becoming separated while moving through space was very real. Marny and I were two very small people in the deep dark right now. We couldn't reasonably expect a rescue if we messed up.

Back on our family claim, I would stare up into the vastness of space and imagine floating off. Occasionally, I even jetted off for short distances. Floating through the vast emptiness had always brought me a profound sense of serenity. I had never feared the isolation. I had heard talk of people freaking out in similar situations. Maybe it's because I grew up as a miner that I had a different perspective about floating, unattached, in zero-g. Attacking a pirate base, on the other hand, now that was crazy.

Thirty second burn in Five. Four. Our AIs helped us align our jets with the asteroid and we burned for nearly a minute. The line between us grew taut due to the significant difference in our masses and the differences between our thrust directions.

"Marny, you are pulling us off in the wrong direction," I said.

"Trying to adjust," she responded, obviously starting to become stressed. I had to remind myself that she was not space born and hadn't been doing this since before she could walk.

"That's fine. Stop making adjustments. We're connected and you are falling faster than I am. I can steer." Marny was almost double my weight. As soon as she stopped adjusting her direction constantly, I was able to keep us oriented on the navigational plan the AI was constantly updating.

"Good job," I praised.

"Crap, this is terrifying," Marny answered. She was still flustered, but the panic in her voice was gone.

We had decided to periodically slow down instead of doing it all at the end. It would allow us to make adjustments over the entire twenty-five minute fall instead of having to make decisions quickly at the end. "Are you able to see any perimeter guns?" I asked.

"Yes. Uploading to tactical plan now."

Three new red dots were superimposed on my heads-up display. A moment later, a fourth centered between the first three. I used my hand to zoom in on the center object. The resolution was good enough to be precise, but I was looking at a building, or maybe even a group of buildings.

Approaching estimated sensor range. Arc-jet systems should not be used for the next three minutes. If the pirate base had a sensor net running, our AI would calculate the maximum effective range. Our arc-jets could be picked up by a particularly sensitive detector. If that occurred, we would be easy picking for even the most rudimentary defensive system.

Marny and I floated quietly for the next three minutes. I zoomed in and was able to make out the surface of the asteroid we were approaching. There was a large central structure with clustered habitation domes on the right, left, and back sides. I counted twelve domes in all. The habitation domes were easy to recognize since I had been living in one for most of my life. Full of just sleeping bunks, they could house fifty people altogether. That would leave the occupants no real living space. I estimated that fifteen was a more realistic number.

One side of the large building was free of other structures. I decided to think of that as the front. There weren't any ships on the surface and the larger structure didn't seem big enough to hold a ship of any real size. I had hoped the freighter used in the Colony 40 theft would be sitting there waiting for us to take it back and return my family's wealth.

"Any thoughts on how many people we might run into?" I wanted to get Marny's thoughts.

"Hard to tell," she answered. "I count room for a couple dozen in the habitats. I doubt they are full. All of the ships are out, staff would be minimal. If I were in charge, I would have at least six. That way I could run four-hour shifts with three-man teams. Two would patrol and one would be stationary at whatever command center they might have. Not sure how pirates do it."

"Let's hope they take shortcuts," I said. Two on six were terrible odds. "What's our entry point?" I had given tactical control of our incursion to Marny since I had absolutely no combat training and she was a decorated veteran.

"Need to take the control room. It's probably in that main building."

"So you want to take the big building first?" I thought I was following.

"No. That's the main target, but it's also likely to have the highest concentration of bogies. We'll have to see what we run into. Put these zip ties into a pocket." She pulled a roll out of the bag she was carrying.

We had been reducing our speed the entire approach to the asteroid, but we were still going too fast for a safe landing. I removed the cable that joined us and stowed it. It was no longer safe for us to be tethered together.

I displayed my relative fall speed into the asteroid and used my arc-jets to slow down as much as I could. If I got out of here alive, I would definitely be sending this video off to Tabby.

"We will set charges on the left side." A blinking circle outlined the building in my HUD. "If someone is on that side without a suit, they will get locked down or worse. We enter from the right. If it's locked, we reverse and set charges at the door too and enter backside. Explosives need to be a last resort. We don't know what we might run into. There could be civvies. That said, I'll punch the charges in a second if I think we need the tactical advantage."

"Civvies?" I didn't understand what she meant.

"Civilians. Noncombatants. You know girlfriends, boy-toys, whores, slaves. You never know out here."

I gently landed two hundred meters away from the complex. I was used to approaching the zero gravity of most asteroids. The asteroid was small enough that there was no gravity and this was old hat for me. Marny landed a little roughly, another twenty meters away from where I was. I heard an involuntary gasp of pain from her and suspected her med pain-patch wasn't 100%. I jetted toward her using my arc-jets sparingly, concerned that the blue flashes could attract unwanted attention.

Marny was all business. "We settle in for five minutes and see if we have any visitors. Unclip your pistol. You won't have time if you need it." I had my Ruger laser pistol in a holster, strapped across my chest. I unsnapped the strap that kept it from falling out. Friction would easily hold it in place. All I had to do was bring up my hand and it would fall right on the butt of the pistol.

I pulled the blaster rifle off my back and nudged a small toggle, causing my heads up display to superimpose what I would shoot if I were to pull the trigger. I released my grip on the stock and the heads-up display disappeared.

"Ninety minutes before Nick returns. Are you sure we have five to spare?" I asked with concern.

"Aye Cap. We get caught outside, it'll go bad for us."

I nodded and looked Marny over. She had any number of items in different pockets all over her armor and I wondered how many of those items would be used in the next twenty minutes. She bobbed around on the surface of the asteroid, obviously not very comfortable in zero gravity. I placed my hand on her arm and steadied her.

After a minute or two of staring at the complex, Marny appeared to be satisfied that we had no unwanted attention. She didn't look at me when she spoke next.

"When we get in there you need to listen to me. If I say get down, you get down. If I say get back in a room, then do it. No heroics. I know the score, and we both have to get out of here. If I have to worry about you, then I will be less effective. I am uploading a program to your suit. It will work with these flash bang discs." Marny placed a small disc on the chest of my suit right next to my hand blaster's holster.

"Flash bang discs?" I asked.

"FBDs," she answered. "Not real effective against military, but if the pirates aren't pros, these little babies will disable them."

"How's that?"

"They project incredibly bright flashes of light and an extremely loud sound. The genius of it is that our suits will black out in sequence with the flashes and create a canceling sound wave in your helmet. You will barely know it's happening. Your AI will project the last image you saw while in blackout. It will feel like people are doing everything in a jerky manner. The discs are both slaved to my tactical command so you don't need to do anything."

"Uh, okay." I was starting to get a little overwhelmed.

"Walk in the park, Cap. Just listen to my commands and pay attention to your HUD. I will upload route information as we go. When we get into a firefight, take a knee or crouch and I will fire high. Put your blaster rifle on three shot. Okay. Let's move out. Stay on my six and to my right. If we get into a firefight, get up tight on me. I want to feel your left hand on my right shoulder. Ready?"

I put my left hand on her right shoulder. It was a lot to take in. "Ready."

We swung wide of the far left habitation pods. Once we got closer, we ran into a significant amount of debris floating in the low gravity. It created a nice visual block. I pushed a small box out of the way, causing Marny to turn and give me a dirty look.

"Stay clear of the junk. They leave it out here as a poor man's warning system. The junk needs to stay put. There are three heavy turrets that can pick us off like fleas from a dog." She sounded irritated. I suspected she was.

We were using very small blasts of our arc-jets. The habitation domes had small windows built into them and we didn't want to be seen. We floated up over the domes and moved toward the end of the line of habitation pods next to the larger building.

Marny removed two rectangular devices the size of her hand and placed one at each side of the small hallway joining the left group of domes to the large central building. We jetted up and around the back of the large building, ending up on the other side. We kept moving, floating over the four right side domes. Marny placed two more rectangular devices over the airlock. The devices pulsed green twice and then nothing more.

We figured out where the command center was when we saw a big bundle of cables. If we just wanted to cause problems we could blow those cables, but that wasn't the plan.

We were almost to the back set of habitation domes when Marny exclaimed, "Take cover behind the complex. We have contact."

I let go of her shoulder and lit up my jets. Adrenaline hit so hard that everything became clear in an instant. I remembered the feeling from fighting the pirates on top of P-Zero. Laser blasts erupted just above the left-side domes and tracked my movement. I was thrilled I had avoided getting hit.

Marny was sprawled on top of one of the nearby domes. I popped up, only to be warned by my HUD that I was being targeted, so I ducked back down. They weren't firing at Marny and she wasn't moving.

"Cover the right side. We stay put a minute. They have you dialed in. Don't show your face. Also, watch any airlock back there."

Geez, anything else?

I swiveled between watching the airlock and the right side of the complex. Nothing was moving. To be honest, I hadn't seen anything when Marny started yelling commands. I had rabbited before I understood what she was saying. I felt shame that my first instinct was to run.

"Well, they know we're here," she said. "Remember when I said use explosives in an emergency?"

I saw a puff of atmosphere erupt from the left side of the main building.

"Did you blow that?" I asked.

"Aye, and don't shoot me. Incoming!" A large form jetted toward me and I raised my gun. I finally parsed what she had said and pulled my finger away from the trigger of my blaster rifle.

"What about civilians?" I worried.

"Not now. Cover me. I'm going to blow this airlock. If those turrets lock on us, we're smoke." Marny pulled out two more small bricks and placed them on the airlock. "Get tight on me, but keep your rifle out."

I closed in on her right side as she moved behind the corner of the habitation pod. She scanned the horizon for pirates and ignited the charges.

"Stay tight and remember, stay low."

We made it through the ruined airlock and entered an empty bunk room. I was relieved that we didn't find any dying people in the mess.

"I'm running out of charges so we cycle the next lock." Marny kept to the side of the room and threw a small puck into the next open room. "Clear." She quickly moved around the doorway to the side of the room and I stuck to her like glue.

She touched the airlock and it showed familiar green bars draining to orange. "This is gonna get crazy if they lock this down with us in it."

I could have gone all day without thinking about that possibility. Before I could object, she entered the lock and I followed. She already had the lock recycling. I was pleased that the orange bars were filling up with green.

"Get as low as you can and dive right when we exit." We were in .4 gravity in this room. I could lift with my AGBs if necessary.

JAMIE McFARLANE

"Roger that," I replied.

The door opened and blaster fire hit the back of the airlock. Marny dove left and I dove right. She knew what she was doing. If we'd remained standing, we would have taken considerable fire. We each landed behind tall shelving units loaded with crates. An aisle separated us.

Marny reached an arm around and threw a puck down the aisle. Immediately, the tactical display in my HUD showed four glowing figures in the larger room. Two were at the far right, up five meters, and one was standing in the aisle that ran the length of what was obviously a warehouse. The fourth was working his way down the left side.

Before I could process it, Marny dove across the aisle and fired her blaster rifle on full auto down its length. The figure standing there crumpled in my HUD.

"We gotta move," she said calmly.

"On your six." I tried to emulate her calm, but failed.

"Left side is going to try to flush us into a kill box for the two above. We take him."

I lost the ability to see the glowing figures in my HUD.

"Took 'em long enough." Marny said, mostly to herself.

Instead of heading to the right like I had expected, Marny crouched and moved across the aisle. I scurried behind her. We approached the end of the shelving unit in the corner. I imagined we would reach it at the same time the pirate did.

Through some instinct or just plain dumb luck, I turned around in time to catch a pirate burst through the shelving unit behind me. My rifle was knocked out of my hands and he was holding a blaster pistol. Purely on instinct, I grappled with him and fired off my arc-jet so we would fly upward. The figure was my same mass and I must have surprised him with my move. Just before we hit the ceiling I twisted, using one glove's jet, and slammed the pirate into a girder. Using the available gravity, I blasted my jets against the ceiling and back to the floor, twisting him under me. It knocked the air out of me, but I certainly knocked the fight out of ... oh, her.

I looked through her face shield and saw a young woman's face. She had a gaunt, poorly-fed look to her. She was definitely a spacer and I could imagine she had lived hard.

"Use your ties and bind her knees, ankles, and wrists behind her back. Make it tight. Stay focused." Marny sounded almost angry.

While I bound the pirate, Marny scanned back and forth. Once I was finished, Marny inspected my work and pulled the ties a little tighter. I winced, knowing it had to be painful. Then she did something unexpected and pulled a small black knife out of a previously unseen sheath. She grabbed the back of the pirates suit where the primary power pack was installed and tore it free, cutting it away in the process.

"If we hit vacuum, she's done," I said automatically.

"Give her something other than us to think about," she grumbled back. "Okay. Two down, we know of at least two more and we need to move. On my six."

Marny turned around again and made her way back to the aisle that went down the center of the warehouse. "Frakking cluster back here."

"Use your flash bang?" I offered.

"No good. If they have military suits they only need two minutes to sync. Don't want to use them unless we are right on top of them." She took a deep breath. "Okay. I want you to fly up to that top shelf and push a crate off. I'll make my way around the end, but you get right back on me after you push it off. Got it?"

I didn't answer, but jetted up and gave a medium sized crate a good push. It fell and landed noisily on the ground. Marny had made it around the corner by this time, so I jetted to where she had been. I turned the corner and to my horror, two figures were standing there. One was holding a pistol aimed at Marny's head and the other was ten paces off with a blast rifle pointed at her.

I heard the pirate with the rifle aimed at Marny say, "Toss the rifles over here and give me those pistols, too."

Marny pulled her pistol out carefully with a thumb and forefinger on the butt. She tossed it on the floor in front of the pirate who had spoken.

"Crap. I can't believe we got taken out by the last two guys in the building," she said.

"Don't feel bad princess. I think we can make it up to you. I always wanted to ride me an Earther. You're a big one too." His intent was clear and his tone mocking.

I threw my rifle to the side and Marny started to pull off her rifle strap. The pirate who had his pistol aimed at her head momentarily broke contact with her so she could pull the strap over her head and toss the gun to his partner.

In mid-throw he seemed to freeze in place and the gun also froze in midair only to jump forward half a second later like everything was happening in stop motion.

"Take cover and shoot 'em." Marny demanded and she crashed into the nearest pirate. In her hands a long black tube a meter and a half long appeared. I finally caught up. The jerky motion was caused by the flash bang discs. It was weird. I couldn't hear any sound nor see any flashing lights, but the effect on the pirates was immediate. Laser blasts fired wildly.

I felt like Marny's orders were contradictory. I couldn't both take cover and shoot someone so I did what I felt made the most sense. I dropped to a knee and tried to take aim at the closest pirate. Of course I couldn't do that because Marny was jumping around on him like a crazy broken vid with half of its frames missing. I swung to the other pirate and started shooting. It was impossible to hit someone who was moving like this but I got my point across and rifle fire started coming my way. His aim was almost as ridiculous as my own. The FBDs must have been devastating.

Marny put an end to it, dropping her tube down on her adversary's neck and then back up under his chin causing him to flip over backward. I hadn't even seen her move and was shocked at how easily I could have shot her. I looked back to where the first pirate had been holding a gun on her and discovered he was lying on the ground.

Reasonable motion returned to the universe and I couldn't

have been happier. My stomach had threatened to revolt and I wasn't at all interested in losing anything in my suit.

"Tie these guys up and make it tight this time. I'll cover you." Marny picked up her rifle and crouched down behind a tall shelf full of crates.

I tied up both of the pirates and pulled a lot harder on the ties. By the time I finished, one was already coming around. Marny checked, but didn't see fit to pull the ties any tighter. I left them to lie on their stomachs.

"Easier to tie 'em down once they've shot at you 'eh?" she asked and for the first time in a while she sounded more like the Marny we had met in Wuzzies.

She continued. "We need to clear the rest of the structure. Only thirty-five minutes before we have to be ready for Mr. James."

Thirty-five? Where had the time gone? It felt like it had only been ten minutes since we touched down on this asteroid. It took us twenty minutes to clear the warehouse and the remaining functional living spaces. Marny's explosives opened up an entire section of the habitation domes to space. Fortunately, we didn't find any bodies in there.

A metal staircase led to a small, windowed room on the second level of the warehouse. Inside the room was a control center. The room was sparse, boasting only a few metal chairs and a bank of vid screens. I sat down at the screens while Marny took a guard position at the door. She'd retrieved one of the room scanning pucks she had been tossing out to warn us of movement and placed it strategically in the warehouse below.

We had fifteen minutes before Nick would try to land. He would, hopefully, have put some distance between himself and the pursuing enemy ship. This was our gambit. We would use their defensive systems against them. Nothing else in this entire sector of space could provide us with enough protection against the pirates that were converging on us. I sat down at the console to reprogram the defensive systems to not fire at Sterra's Gift. I wanted to draw the other cutter in before opening fire on it. I panicked as I discovered that I was locked out of the system.

"Marny! We have a problem."

"What? Frak!! Hang on."

Marny returned in a minute with one of the pirates. She sat him down hard on the floor, legs outstretched in front of him. She ripped his helmet off and if I hadn't been sitting down I would have likely fallen over. There sat Sheriff Blaen Xid, the bastard who coordinated the attack on Colony 40 and stole my Dad's biggest payday ever. I rose up with murder in mind.

"Not yet." Marny commanded. Her fierceness was startling and stopped me. She looked over to Sheriff Xid, "Command override now or Hoffen here cycles you through the airlock."

"Yeah right. Frakking pansy-ass kid."

I stood up and held my hand out to Marny. "Knife. Go get the other one. This one isn't going to last," I said.

Marny extracted her black knife from her sheath, handed it to me and simply walked out of the room.

"You took my foot, shithead. You won't be missed." I jammed the knife into his chest, then pulled out my laser blaster and fired twice.

Marny ran back into the room with the female who had attacked us first.

"Crap. You killed him?" She was genuinely alarmed.

"He ruined my family. I swore I would end him if I ever saw him again."

"I, I don't know, Liam. That's pretty twisted. He was tied up." Marny was shaken. I could almost understand.

"You'll get paid and we can part ways. Let's get through this first. I reached over to Xid's prone body and pulled the knife out. It was dripping with blood."

I leaned over the body of the woman we had tied up earlier. "Okay. So we have one more pirate after you. Then I have to start making decisions. We could easily just shut down the power and wait for our friend, Nick. He had plenty of missiles and will have taken out your buddies' ship by now. There is no help coming for you." I looked at the now terrified woman. "Do you have the codes or not? I have five minutes before I have to figure this out."

I crouched in front of her and showed her the bloody knife.

"Houzi 498," she said, cowering.

I jumped to the console and typed in the code she gave me. I was in. I ran a quick scan of local space and didn't see *Sterra's Gift* yet. Oh man, I hoped Nick was okay.

"Marny, get something on Xid's chest or he's gonna bleed out," I said over my shoulder.

Marny's head swiveled to me and understanding slowly crossed her face. "You rat crap little spacer trash bastard!"

"You need to work on your cussing. Or are Earth Marines not quite as badass as their Mars brethren?"

"Don't push it," she said.

I figured I'd better leave that alone for now. I heard Marny working on Xid. I'd purposefully tried to miss his important parts with the knife, even though I would have been fine with things going another way. The laser blasts were completely for show. Then I hit him as hard as I could in the head with my gloved fist. That was purely personal. He probably had a concussion. Even if he were damaged for life, we still wouldn't be even.

I punched *Sterra's Gift's* signature into the defensive system and locked out all other ships. The pirates had programmed in more than one hundred ships that this computer would recognize and treat as friendlies. Great, I had made some powerful enemies.

I downloaded as much information from the defensive system as I could for Mar's Protectorate. With great relief, I finally saw *Sterra's Gift* show up on the far scan. Nick was decelerating hard and I couldn't yet detect any pursuit craft.

Nick was running the play. He had put significant distance between himself and the other cutter. I hoped it had been enough to stay safe, but not enough to discourage the pursuit. Nick's deceleration vector was such that he would blow right past the asteroid, but he would be well inside the range of the hideout's heavy turrets. He had too much faith in me. It made me proud and scared all at the same time.

After applying a med-patch to Xid, Marny dragged the last pirate into the room, dropping him on the ground.

"What about the first guy?" I asked.

"He's dead. I got him chilling," she responded.

"What are you going to do with us?" I heard a small voice from behind me.

"Quiet," Marny replied. "Do you see Nicholas yet?"

"Yes. Here." I pulled up a display showing *Sterra's Gift* decelerating. We couldn't see much, but it looked like she had taken some damage. We wouldn't be able to penetrate the hard burn with our transmissions until he passed us by.

I saw the other cutter enter the range of our sensor net, showing yellow on my screen. I didn't want the guns to shoot at it yet. The trap would be sprung soon enough. I needed them to land that ship.

Fire a pattern of warning shots around Sterra's Gift. Do not hit the ship under any circumstance.

All three turrets showed targeting solutions and fired a couple of shots.

Continue to fire warning shots for ten seconds.

The guns barked to life and sprayed laser bolts on a near-miss course. It was an impressive display and I was glad it was AI controlled. I would have surely hit the ship if I had been aiming. Nick would overshoot us enough that it would take him five minutes to get back. He had changed our plan a bit but it made sense. He would gain safety behind the asteroid and likely sail back around the bottom side, forcing the pirate cutter to stay in range of our weapons for the longest period of time.

Sterra's Gift finally passed the station, still decelerating. We could open communication with Nick.

Hail Sterra's Gift. Secure channel.

"Nick report! No casualties on station. I repeat. No casualties."

"This is *Sterra's Gift*. We are flying without pressure in main hallway. I am not sure, but I think the airlock door got blown off. I am unable to raise the brig. Engines are showing stress and we are running at 60% ammo."

It was a good report. Nick was alive. That was the only thing I cared about. To hell with the rest. I breathed a sigh of relief and felt Marny's large hand on my shoulder. I thought I might cry in relief, but of course I didn't do that sort of thing.

"You made some tough calls, Cap. Welcome to command. You did good, now don't get cocky."

"Nick, I got an idea. Give me a second."

"Hey. You want your freedom?" I asked the young woman.

"Like you would give it to me," she said.

"You got any better offers? Besides if we lose, you can say we had a gun to your head."

"What do you want?" I understood her suspicion.

"Tell them that Xid and the other guy got hit by fire from my buddy's ship. You're here all by yourself. Tell them that the defense systems disabled the ship and forced it to land."

"What do I get out of it?"

"We will drop you at Terrence."

"They'll kill me."

"Red Houzi? What if you had money? How about Terrence with a platinum brick worth twenty thousand and anything from here that you can stuff in a bag?" I wanted this to work.

"Okay?" I could hear in her voice that she didn't trust me. That's fine. I didn't need much from her.

Marny stepped toward her menacingly. "You cross us and I will kill you on the spot."

The woman glared back. "Don't think you can hurt me."

I worried Marny might take it further so I stepped in. "Look, we have no interest in hurting you. If you guys had left us alone, we wouldn't even be here."

"They can't allow Mie-su to be captured by the Protectorate," she said almost involuntarily.

Hail Sterra's Gift. "Nick, come around and set down way off to the side. Make it look like a forced landing."

"Shouldn't be too hard." Nick wasn't one for a lot of words. I watched happily as he landed *Sterra's Gift* in front of the main building. Marny was outside the airlock when he landed.

Nick and Marny cycled through the airlock as the enemy cutter hailed the station.

"Xid. What's going on down there? What's that ship doing on the ground?"

The young woman nodded at me and I knew it was go time.

"You do this right and I will live up to my promise. You say anything wrong and your life is forfeit." I helped her to the chair and cut her hands free.

I could hear Marny running up the stairs with Nick behind her.

"Alexander. They're all dead."

"Who is this? Dontal? Who's dead? What do you mean? Spit it out, you stupid bitch."

"Xid, Peng. We have a lot of damage here. They were firing on us. I think they are still on the ship. The turrets knocked them down. I haven't seen anyone come out. I didn't want to fire at them, Mie-su was supposed to be on board. I told them I have the turrets on them. Been waiting for you."

"Sounds fishy. What are you up to? Gonna come down there and cut you if you are frakking with me."

I cut communication at that point. It sounded like they mostly believed her. Nick and Marny were in the room. I stood up and walked over to embrace Nick. I hoped we wouldn't ever need to split up like that again.

"Sounds promising," Marny said, "How many on that ship?"

"Three," she replied. "Gunner, pilot, engineer."

"You will understand that I have to bind you again. Not that you're not trustworthy and all." Marny was trying to keep it light, but under the circumstances I could also understand why she didn't get a great response.

"Just like every other man," the young woman retorted.

It was eerie watching the cutter land. It looked so much like *Sterra's Gift* – although it was in much rougher shape. Our next action depended entirely on what the pirates did next. Two figures disembarked from the enemy cutter and bounded over to our ship.

I looked over at Nick, "You locked it, right?"

"Door got blown off."

Fire turrets between Sterra's Gift and approaching men.

Laser bolt rounds fired deeply into the ground in front of the approaching men and they froze in place.

Hail cutter not identified as Sterra's Gift. "This is Captain Liam Hoffen of the cutter *Sterra's Gift*. I am currently in control of your heavy turrets. Stand down or be destroyed."

I saw the turret of the enemy cutter swivel over to point at *Sterra's Gift*.

Fire five second burst two meters in front of enemy cutter. Laser bolts tore into the ground causing shards of the asteroid to explode in all directions around the front of the cutter.

"Next one goes through your ship turret. You won't get another warning. Tell the men outside to drop guns or I will fire on them. Disembark the ship and present yourself in the airlock unarmed. No harm will come to you."

"You killed Xid. Why would we expect any different treatment?"

Send video of Blaine Xid to enemy cutter.

"He is alive and bound. No harm will come to you if you surrender. If you resist, you will be destroyed."

"You appear to have all of the cards," the man replied.

"Place your weapons on the ground and enter the airlock."

After a few minutes of what must have been a very tense conversation they dropped their weapons on the ground and walked up to the main building with their hands up. We held our blaster rifles on them through the airlock.

"On your knees," Marny demanded. "Search 'em, Cap."

Nick had remained in the control room with the other three pirates, one of whom was still unconscious. Marny had given Nick strict instructions about keeping a gun on them while we dealt with our new friends. We only had a few hours before the two intercept ships arrived. These ships were our primary concern as they had a significant speed advantage over *Sterra's Gift*. If they caught us out in the open they would shred us.

"Your survival depends on following my instructions," I said calmly. "My partner here has informed me that spacing you all would make our lives a lot easier. You have fired upon us, so there would be no moral dilemma for me. Now, before you threaten us with Red Houzi retribution, understand we have been living with that for a while now. Not a game changer. Savvy?"

I got a confused look from one of the pirates. "Understand me? Geez can't anyone talk pirate?" I was getting tired and maybe a little goofy.

"Yeah, we got you," replied the blonde-headed one.

"First, give me the command codes for the cutter out there."

He paused and looked around. I had time to be patient, so I waited him out.

"They'll kill me," he whined.

"Not today and I will give you a good head start," I said.

"How do I know you won't kill us once I give you what you want?" he asked.

"You don't. Holy crap you're a pirate. Do we really need to do this dance? Threats, torture, removing limbs, all that? You hold on to the hope that I won't do awful things to you and you give me what I want. I already have control over the turrets. I have my own ship. This thing is done."

I stared. They were getting uncomfortable on their knees.

"Let me start again. You have something I want, albeit not of great importance. I get to decide if or how painfully you die. How about I sweeten the pot? We will drop you all at Terrence. You each get to load six crates with the best stuff you can find here. I will give you two of those crates and keep four for myself. From there you should be able to get wherever you want. Now, give me the command codes for the cutter. Otherwise, we start the dance. I win either way. You choose."

"Okay. Okay," the blonde-headed man replied.

We took the trio over to the still-functioning habitation pods and made them remove their vac-suits. They probably thought we were preparing to space them. There wasn't much they could do, what with Marny and me still in our armor vac-suits holding blaster rifles on them. We watched as they emptied the farthest pod and then we sealed them in. We depressurized the connecting habitation pod, making it a reasonable short-term brig.

REVENGE IS NEVER SWEET

Keeping captives was the last thing I'd ever expected to do. We were short-staffed and it took a lot of creative energy to figure out how best to keep us safe from them while preparing for the approaching ships. The young woman, Celina, was not a very nice person, but was also terrified of being left alone with any of the remaining men. According to her, she had been taken from Terrence by force. When I asked what she did on Terrence she was evasive. Marny suggested that she had likely been a prostitute.

We agreed she would remain tied to a chair while we prepared for the incoming ships. I felt like at least part of her story was straight, since she would rather be tied up than join the others.

We checked on Xie in *Sterra's Gift* and discovered that, while the hallway was open to space, the brig had kept its seal. She was pissed, but otherwise in good shape. We could deal with that later. I moved *Sterra's Gift* to the back side of the asteroid and waited for the arrival of the fast attack ships.

We received a hail when they finally showed up on our sensor net.

Nick and Marny stayed in the command center with Celina still tied to the chair. I was in *Sterra's Gift* ready to join the fight if it came to that. I hoped we wouldn't need to use our ship, I'd be terribly outclassed. But we couldn't afford to rely only on the heavy turrets. It was a precaution that turned out to be unnecessary.

Celina proved helpful again and provided the appropriate pass phrase. The small ships entered the space near the pirate's hideout and crossed the threshold where the turrets would have them in range. The trap was sprung.

"We need a status on the target," one of the pirate pilots requested.

"Stand down," I ordered.

"What the frak!" The pilot of one of the fast attack ships replied.

"I said stand down. You will land those ships. Any aggressive ..." I was cut off by the firing of guns from one of the two ships on the main building.

"Cease fire!" I yelled over the comm channel, but the damage was done. The attacking craft had turned and was making a run for it, but the heavy turrets stitched laser bolts into its hull and it exploded. The second craft turned to flee and met a similar fate.

We met back in the control room of the main building and Marny left to check on the prisoners. We had been going hard for the better part of twenty hours and fatigue was setting in fast. If we didn't have a load of captive pirates, I might have felt safe spending time on this rock. We were well protected as long as we had control of the hideout's heavy turrets. It had taken less than two seconds of concentrated fire to blow up each of the smaller attack craft. It might take a little longer on a cutter, but not much.

"Any thoughts on fixing the airlock on *Sterra's Gift*?" I asked.

"I should be able to get us to a station at least," Nick answered.

"Marny's med patch is going to wear off pretty soon and I don't think she's going to be moving much after that. When she gets back, I say the two of us work on that airlock. I'm beat, but if we push, we should be able to take off in three or four hours."

"What about other incoming ships?"

"There is only one that is even remotely close. We will have two ships on one."

"Are we taking the other cutter?" Nick asked surprised.

"Yes, I have a plan. Celina, do you want to help us with the door? The sooner we get outta here, the sooner you will have us out of your hair." She was still tied to the chair.

"What? You trust me now?"

"Not at all," I answered. "I have an idea for you though. Better than sitting here tied up."

"Fine," she spat.

Nick and Celina worked on the door while Marny stood guard. I sent a quick message to Belcose and explained our circumstances. He had sent an update on the ships still headed our way. The lead ship was a few hours out and the other ship had fallen back and was well behind that. Neither was a match for *Sterra's Gift* in speed, but our other cutter would easily be caught.

I worked on several different simulations based on when the pirates would discover our heading. If we could take off within two hours, we had a chance. I walked back to view the progress and saw the work was nearly finished. Celina was a quiet worker.

"Okay, I'm going to change things to improve our arrangement." I said to no one in particular.

"Gee. Couldn't have seen that coming," Celina said dryly. "Is this where I get to take a cold dark walk?"

I chuckled. "No, this is where you get a better deal than you have now. No strings attached."

"Oh, do tell." She wasn't a believer yet, but I would convert her.

"Do you trust any of those others?"

"Are you kidding? They kidnapped and used me for the last several months. They don't deserve to live." She was hot.

"Oh, I wish we'd had this conversation earlier," I said honestly. She just stared at me.

I explained my plan to her and she looked at me in shock. Marny looked surprised as well. To her credit she didn't express what she was feeling.

"Are you in?" I asked finally.

"Are you for real?"

"Both airlock doors will work for now," Nick announced.

"I want to be ready to sail in two hours," I replied.

We rounded up the pirates two at a time. I made good on my offer to allow them to pack six crates each. They were very efficient in their choices. Everything from real silk fabric and intricate artwork to a variety of Earth-grown spices and crates of weapons. I hoped that somewhere in the warehouse we could find some of the precious metals taken from Colony 40, but if any of them knew about it, they weren't letting on.

I picked two crates from each of the pirates and had them loaded into the second cutter. The remaining crates were loaded onto *Sterra's Gift*. I also found over one hundred kilos of frozen coffee beans, and another hundred kilos of cocoa powder. Those were worth a small fortune by themselves, but I couldn't imagine selling them. We loaded both ship's armories with blast rifles and ammunition. It was a thief's dilemma - trading time for loot.

We were finally ready to go. Sheriff Xid was in the brig of *Sterra's Gift* with a very sulky Xie Mie-su. Marny, Celina and I were on the other cutter with the remaining four pirates. Marny would fly the cutter and I would keep guard on the prisoners with Celina's help. I wasn't trusting enough to allow Celina to have a weapon, but I felt like our objectives were in line enough that she would help me foil any attempts at mutiny.

I made one last trip back to *Sterra's Gift* for supplies and we launched without ceremony.

Marny's med patch had completely worn off and she was mostly immobile, but I didn't want the pirates to know about her infirmity. We slaved our ship to *Sterra's Gift* so that it would fly in formation. We were a pretty beat up group, but now that we were in space we would be able to relax, at least until we met up with the first of the two remaining pirate ships.

The heavy turrets were set up to deactivate if we ever returned, but if approached without the correct security sequence, they would defend the asteroid. I didn't know if we would ever return, but I certainly didn't want the Red Houzi to set up shop again. We would also receive weekly logs from the sensor net. Nick would find that more interesting than me.

Twenty minutes into the trip I regretted not being on *Sterra's Gift*. This ship was disgusting and didn't have a coffee brewer. We headed to the small mining colony of Terrence. Terrence was smaller than Colony 40, but it was steadily growing as production increased. I knew a few people who had moved there from Colony 40, but it wouldn't matter. We weren't planning to dock.

Celina and I sat in silence for the first couple of hours. I tried talking with her, but it was fruitless. After four hours, Marny hobbled back to where I sat. She wanted to take over guard duty. I'd been up for twenty-eight hours and was fighting off sleep and didn't have it in me to argue. I made it back to the bridge and slumped in the chair. I sure hoped we wouldn't have an emergency anytime soon. I set an alarm for four hours. We had a minimum of five hours before any possible contact with the first ship and I needed to be a little sharper before that happened.

Four hours came almost as soon as I laid back. I didn't feel at all refreshed.

Hail Sterra's Gift. "Nick, you there?

"Yup." His voice sounded groggy. I hoped he had gotten a decent amount of sleep.

"Anything new?"

"Nope."

"Did you check for anything new from Belcose?"

"Yup, nothing."

"Roger that. Changing shift with Marny."

I escorted our prisoners one at a time to the head and got them each a meal bar. We had been accelerating since leaving the pirate hideout. If the approaching pirates hadn't discovered our new course, they wouldn't be able to adjust quickly enough to intercept. Only time would tell.

Marny and I continued flip-flopping shifts. After twenty-four hours, I started to feel considerably more rested. It was almost a letdown when Marny informed me that Nick had received a message from Belcose and the two pirate ships had changed course and broken off their pursuit. We were out of danger.

Terrence was ten days out on the most aggressive burn plan I could come up with that also left us enough fuel to get to our final destination. I was willing to use our fuel inefficiently if it meant getting rid of our passengers sooner.

Celina started to warm up ever so slightly by the fifth or sixth day. We weren't going to be buddies, but she was able speak to me without glowering. She had stopped referring to Marny as a man. I hated to think about what kind of experiences could make a person so hard.

On the ninth day, both ships cut power from our deceleration into Terrence. We were only a day out and were getting close enough that it was time to part ways with Celina and our three prisoners.

"You understand? *Sterra's Gift* has missiles locked on?" I was looking directly at Celina. "You will be locked out of the helm until we have cleared a full five minutes of hard burn. After that we will release the bridge and the armory to you. It is your responsibility to release the other pirates. Do you understand?"

She looked at me with her eyes full of distrust, "Forgive me if I still don't believe you." Her voice was softer than I had ever heard. She wanted to believe. I imagined there had been a time in her life where she had believed in something or someone good. I didn't think it had turned out well for her.

"We will burn for five minutes and then turn it off. I will contact you by comm. Good luck Captain Celina Dontal. You are now in charge." I pulled the five hundred gram bar of platinum out of my pocket and handed to her. It was our deal, after all.

Marny had already cycled through the airlock and was on board *Sterra's Gift*, manning the turret.

I turned away and cycled the airlock. When the outside lock opened, I waved at Celina through the window, then turned and jetted toward the welcoming door of *Sterra's Gift*. I almost felt guilt leaving Celina on the badly damaged ship. I knew from experience that the repairs needed were more costly than what it was worth.

I reminded myself what she did have, however, was the one thing she most desired: freedom. Something I had taken for granted.

When I walked onto the bridge, Nick announced, "Captain on the bridge." My chest filled with pride. Having spent the last ten days on a poor imitation of *Sterra's Gift*, those words were ones I could really appreciate. How much like home this ship and her crew felt.

I relieved Nick on the bridge. He had been all but chained to his chair and it looked like he would appreciate stepping away.

Engage burn plan for the Protectorate Platform Valhalla. Burn at forty percent and disengage after five minutes.

I hadn't spent much time on *Sterra's Gift* since it had received its overhaul and I had spent a solid ten days on a cutter with engines that felt like they could fall off at any time. It felt great to hear the engines hum to life as they smoothly spooled up.

Five minutes passed quickly.

Hail the nearby cutter. It would have been handy if we had given the cutter a new name, but we hadn't so I had to reference it by proximity.

"Celina. Are you there?"

"Where else?" she answered. She sure had a bad disposition.

Transfer full control of cutter to Celina Dontal. Release control by crew of Sterra's Gift from the same cutter.

"That's it. Ship is yours. Happy sailing," I said, not expecting a response.

Her voice was softer and didn't hold the contempt I had come to expect. "I didn't think you would do it."

"Roger that. Celina. Look us up sometime. I bet I will be looking for sharp captains in the future. You know, once I get my business going full tilt."

"Thank you, Liam Hoffen. Someday. Maybe. Dontal out." She closed the communication channel.

I didn't immediately spool up the engines again. I wanted to see what Celina's first actions as a captain might be. I zoomed my viewscreen in on her ship expecting her to fire up and make a burn for Terrence. What I saw didn't surprise me but I can't say I was expecting it either. I probably should have, given the nature of Celina's experience.

Three suited figures were ejected from the airlock. I could tell they were still alive but apparently Celina had decided they were undesirable passengers. It was illegal to eject passengers from a working ship in space but then, these were pirates. I couldn't imagine they would be filing a complaint.

Normal burn plan for Protectorate Platform Valhalla.

It would take us fifteen days to get there.

EPILOGUE

It took a couple of days to establish our schedule. We had problems with storage. Every square meter of space on *Sterra's Gift* had been crammed with crates. There were only two beds, but with at least one person on watch at all times, it wasn't a huge deal. I had never had a sense of propriety regarding my bed, so I didn't mind that Marny used it, too.

I preferred to take the night shift. I shifted my sleeping pattern by six hours and found I could easily sleep until noon. I would have killed for this schedule at home and now Nick and Marny thought I was some kind of hero for it. I spent my days working out with Marny. She was teaching us both a new self-defense style called Krav Maga. It was an ancient martial art invented by the Israeli military sixteen or seventeen hundred years ago.

I found I liked that Marny slept on my couch. She wasn't much for perfume, but whether it was her soap or something else, my couch smelled like her. After a couple of days I was disappointed to find I had become used to the smell and no longer noticed it. That was until I was headed back to grab some coffee on the fifth night and happened to glance in our cabin. I noticed Marny wasn't on the couch. I didn't think it was that odd, she could be up checking on something.

I got my coffee and when I didn't find her in the galley, I checked the armory. No success. I grinned when the answer finally hit me. I poked my head back into the cabin and saw Marny wrapped around Nick's much smaller body. I couldn't have been happier for them. I had known Nick was smitten with Marny from the first time he had seen her. What I hadn't known was whether or not Marny would accept him. The only jealousy I felt was that I couldn't spend the same time with Tabby.

We were still three days away from Platform Valhalla when we were approached by the first Naval Destroyer either Nick or I had ever seen. The *Kuznetsov* had been 120 meters long and shaped like an arrow. This destroyer was shaped like the end of a sledge hammer and was 180 meters long and five times as wide and tall as the *Kuznetsov*. The ship's mass had to exceed that of the *Kuznetsov* by at least thirty times. There was nothing sleek or subtle about it.

Two ships never meet in space by accident. You might pass within a couple hundred thousand kilometers of another ship, but you would certainly be heading on radically different headings at radically different speeds. This destroyer slipped into space five kilometers off our port side before we had recognized they were even close. They even matched our current speed.

"*Sterra's Gift* this is the Destroyer *Walter Sydney Adams*. Do you read?" My heart jumped into my throat.

"Nick, Marny, could you come to the bridge? We have company."

Hail *Walter Sydney Adams*. "Roger that *Walter Sydney Adams*. This is Captain Liam Hoffen, *Sterra's Gift*. We read you."

Marny and Nick piled into the bridge and looked through the armor-glass. I pointed in the direction where the *Walter Adams* sat.

I switched the video comm onto the heads up display of the bridge so Nick and Marny could also participate. "Greetings Captain Hoffen. Commander Joe Alto here. We have been asked to escort you to Platform Valhalla." The video showed an officer in a uniform vac-suit. He was older, with graying sideburns, a close cut haircut, receding hairline and bright gray eyes. He epitomized my idea of what a hawk might look like.

I responded. "Fair enough."

"With your permission we will synchronize navigation and put your weapons systems into passive mode." His message must have contained a command request as it popped up on my vid screen. I didn't think we had any real option. I accepted the request.

"Thank you," the commander responded. "Are you in any need of assistance?"

"Nothing some downtime wouldn't solve," I replied glibly.

"Roger that. *Walter Sydney Adams* out." I guess he wasn't much for chatter.

The approach to Platform Valhalla was an exercise in outrageous. A cross section of the platform was a shallow triangle. The top was half a kilometer wide with the two sloped sides of the triangle meeting in a point underneath at the mid-section. The platform was twelve kilometers wide and ships of all different sizes were docked beneath it. From our vantage point it looked as if it was only 10% occupied. I wondered if the entire Mars Navy could dock at the same time. That is, until I saw the battleship.

You never forget the first time you see a battleship underway in space. At almost three times the length and girth of the destroyer, I had difficulty imagining what could ever stand up to the amount of firepower on display.

I also counted two cruisers, half a dozen destroyers, and at least ten different corvettes in addition to the battleship. Hundreds of smaller craft were flying back and forth between the different vessels. I had never seen so many ships in one place.

Commander Alto provided the location of a docking bay on the platform. We were to await further instructions once we landed.

The approach was straightforward enough but the landing instructions didn't make sense to me. The final destination showed we would be thirty meters below the deck surface. When we arrived it made more sense, there was an open hole in the deck of the platform. I lowered *Sterra's Gift* through it and with help from the ship's AI, I landed on the sub-deck.

A small group of marines in full armor, awaited our arrival.

"Captain Hoffen, do you read?" It was a familiar voice.

"Roger that. Lieutenant Belcose?" I responded.

"Yes. Request permission to board. I would like to send a squad of Marines in to secure the prisoner. Will you comply?" Geez, the guy always sounded like he had a stick up ...

"Good to hear your voice. Permission granted. Let me open the door. It isn't in that great of shape. Oh and we have a bonus prisoner for you," I added.

"Repeat last?"

"We have two prisoners. We ran into Sheriff Xid and decided we would bring him along. I was hoping you would take him off our hands."

"Wait one," he replied. It took more than five minutes for him to get back to me. I suspected he was looking for permission. "Okay. We will take possession of both prisoners."

The Marines were a professional group. With a minimum of fuss, they extracted both Xid and Mie-su from the brig. After babysitting them for the last twenty days, if I never saw them again it would be too soon. Xid was a disgusting slob and Xie had a mouth on her. I felt a little sorry for their new jailors.

I watched the Marines remove Xid and Mie-su from the door of the bridge. When they were gone, Belcose remained and approached me.

"Nice job, Captain. Commander Sterra would like to extend hospitality to your crew. Would you be available at 2200 for a shared meal?"

"We would be delighted," I answered without hesitation.

"Oh, and there is the matter of the offline storage device you are in possession of?"

I pulled the black marble out of the pouch in my suit and handed it to him.

"We will get this analyzed. Looking forward to dinner." He nodded and exited. It took me a minute to realize he hadn't been wearing a vac-suit.

"Is this bay pressurized?" I asked.

Marny answered. "Sure is, Cap. We dropped through a pressure barrier."

"Didn't know such a thing existed."

"Takes a crazy amount of power, but these platforms have energy to burn," she answered.

"There is more than one of these platforms?" It was hard to imagine the Protectorate had one, much less several of them.

"Last I knew, Mars Protectorate had five. They are spread out at different elliptical orbits around the Sun. There are probably more that we don't know about." I wondered what other surprises I was in for.

We met Gregor Belcose and Commander Sterra on board the *Kuznetsov*. It seemed like it had been years since the last time we had been there. In reality, it had been forty-five days. Nick and I chose to wear our new civvies, as Marny called them. She was wearing a normal vac-suit.

Steward Gellar once again provided an amazing meal. It was far superior to any of the restaurant food we had eaten. She put out a spread of what she called fried chicken, mashed potatoes and cream gravy. In addition, there was a fresh salad and a vegetable called asparagus. We ate until I didn't think I could eat anything more. At the end however, I smelled the now familiar scent of fresh coffee. I wondered if we would get to have her chocolate cake again and drooled at the thought. Her dessert course wasn't cake, but a pie made with fresh peaches and vanilla ice cream. I thought I'd died and gone to heaven.

"Commander Sterra? Is it possible to request Steward Gellar's company for a moment?"

"Certainly, Liam." She spoke quietly into the collar of her suit.

The smiling face I had come to associate with the steward appeared at the Commander's left side.

"Ms. Gellar, thank you for a most excellent dinner."

We all clinked our silverware against the crystal glasses. I had learned this gesture of appreciation last time we had eaten on the *Kuznetsov*.

"Just as your dinner was appreciated, my crew wants to also thank you for supplying us with coffee for our last trip." More clinking from Nick and Marny. "To show our appreciation we would like to present you with a small token."

I pulled out two small boxes I had wrapped in bright floral silk scarves. Loot from the pirate hideaway.

"Oh, pretty," she responded.

"I am not sure what you will do with its contents, but if anyone would know how to use it I imagine it would be you. The boxes contain five hundred milligrams of both saffron and cocoa. I understand they are both very desirable ingredients used for cooking."

She pulled her hand up to cover her mouth and looked at me in shock. She then looked at Commander Sterra for permission.

Commander Sterra nodded and responded, "Normally we can't accept gifts, but it would appear this is simply a trade of supplies and I see nothing inappropriate." She winked at the steward.

The hug I received for my 'trade' was a bit uncomfortable, mostly due to the excessive overeating I'd just done.

Commander Sterra continued, "I believe you have business to discuss with Lieutenant Belcose and I have a trial to prepare for. On behalf of Mars Protectorate, I can't thank you enough for putting your ship and crew at risk. The intelligence we gather from the prisoners should put quite a dent in the Red Houzi's operation for some time, and our experts have already extracted a considerable amount of information from that storage device. You should rest easy knowing you have brought to justice the pirates responsible for the attack on Colony 40."

We all stood as Commander Sterra exited.

Belcose started the conversation, "Have you given any further thought to payment?"

"I have. The Protectorate stood behind us when we needed it the most. Without that open account and intelligence, we wouldn't have been able to escape Baru Manush. Would you consider providing repairs of the combat damage to our ship, removal of the temporary brig and a load of fuel and oxy?"

"We could probably do better than that."

As much as I wanted a big payday, I needed Commander Sterra and Lieutenant Belcose to know they had made a good decision in granting us the Letter of Marque. I wanted to send the message that we were not only mercenaries, but that we were also team players.

"Okay. How about you throw in a combat bonus to Ms. Bertrand. Without her, we most certainly wouldn't have made it."

I looked at her and winked, she looked back slack-jawed.

"Do you have a number in mind?"

"Thirty thousand," I shot back.

"Done. I will have an engineering crew contact you in the morning to see about repairs. It has been a pleasure, Mr. Hoffen."

You couldn't have found a giddier threesome as we made our way back to *Sterra's Gift*.

Just before we entered the airlock I turned to Nick and Marny, who were holding hands. Nick looked a little uncomfortable. We hadn't talked about it yet.

"I was just thinking," I said. "Maybe we should convert BR-2 into the captain's quarters. I'm really not comfortable on that couch anymore.

ABOUT THE AUTHOR

Jamie McFarlane has been writing short stories and telling tall tales for several decades. With a focus that only a bill collector could inspire, Jamie has finally relented to recording some of his most of requested stories.

During the day Jamie can be found at his home, writing in front of a neglected fire, with his two cats both conveniently named Dragon. When not writing, Jamie can be found at the local pub sharing his stories with any who will listen.

Thank you for reading Rookie Privateer, I'm so glad you enjoyed it. Please consider using one or more of the following links to learn about additional books in the Privateer Tales series or just to stay in contact with Jamie.

Blog and Website: fickledragon.com

Email: jamie@fickledragon.com

Facebook: facebook.com/jamiemcfarlaneauthor

Twitter: twitter.com/privateertales

Made in the USA
San Bernardino, CA
12 November 2017